Drums Without Warriors

OTHER SAGEBRUSH LARGE PRINT WESTERNS BY
FRED GROVE

Warrior Road

Drums Without Warriors

FRED GROVE

Library of Congress Cataloging-in-Publication Data

Grove, Fred.
Drums without warriors / Fred Grove
p. cm.
ISBN 1-57490-481-7 (lg. print : hardcover)
1. Large type books. I. Title.

PS3557.R7D78 2004
813'.54—dc21 2003004669

Cataloging in Publication Data is available from the British Library and the National Library of Australia.

Sagebrush Large Print Westerns are published in the United States and Canada by Thomas T. Beeler, Publisher, PO Box 659, Hampton Falls, New Hampshire 03844-0659. ISBN 1-57490-481-7

Published in the United Kingdom, Eire, and the Republic of South Africa by Isis Publishing Ltd, 7 Centremead, Osney Mead, Oxford OX2 0ES England. ISBN 0-7531-6916-9

Published in Australia and New Zealand by Bolinda Publishing Pty Ltd, 17 Mohr Street, Tullamarine, Victoria, Australia, 3043 ISBN 1-74030-923-5

Manufactured by Sheridan Books in Chelsea, Michigan.

For Jane Pattie
and
Nelson Nye

CHAPTER 1

HE REMEMBERED THE HUMPED-UP PLACE AHEAD FOR its sweeping view. His anticipation grew as he went bumping up the rocky road in second gear to the spine of the long limestone ridge, the loaded horse trailer jerking and rattling behind the Chandler touring car. At the top, he swung out of the way and braked to look.

There, as if they trembled and were alive, mysterious and indestructible, possessing some eternal secret denied to mere man, stood the rounded hills of the Osage Nation, bucking and tossing in massive swells, their lush bluestem coat now browning under the July sun's brassy eye. He felt the stir of a returning emotion, an impression of infinite space and peace in an emerald world, bound to boyhood's illusion of the perfect time, when all things were possible.

Sam Colter frowned at the deception, wondering why he had jumped at the chance to come home again, knowing it would not be the same as before. He set the emergency brake and stepped back to the trailer to look in on Slip Along. The aging gelding, one ear down, muddy-colored, rangy, yet heavy-muscled, had endured the trip up from South Texas mighty well. He seemed to slouch as Sam spoke to him, rubbing the small white star on the forehead, "You're gonna eat supper in town tonight, pardner. I want you to watch your manners."

Always Sam had talked to his horses, for long ago he had learned that horses are individuals like people, each different, with whims, some bad actors, some good-more good than bad. A good horse was company. Although Slip Along wasn't much for looks, he had a short horse's prime assets of good manners and common sense, a fast break, speed, and heart, which added up to character. In addition, he was a "using" horse. You could work cattle on him all morning, then race him that afternoon after a long trailer haul. You could even hitch him to a wagon. He was kind and easy to keep. He had dignity. He was honest.

Sam checked the trailer hitch, got in, and drove on.

Within less than an hour, he was nearing his destination. Car after car began passing him. Breathing their dust, he reflected on what the big attraction could be in Red Mound, Oklahoma, Osage County, in the middle of the week. Saturday was trade day, the big day, unless the Osages were cashing their quarterly oil royalty checks, which, never failing, came on the fifteenth of June, September, December, and March. He could picture payment day as he remembered it: the hand-rubbing flurry; the cat-smiling merchants and the bankers like circling vultures; the bootleggers boldly in evidence, parked on the side streets, waiting, or rushing back to their corn whiskey caches in the country.

This was "the Osage," so called since the oil boom began, spoken in the same gusto as men had "the Comstock" in Nevada.

Red Mound, population one thousand, more or less, when Sam had lived west of town and ridden horseback to school, crouched on the flat where, old-timers said, the Big Hill band of Osages had camped in the early 1870s after their removal from the Kansas lands. An encampment that became a trading post with the proximity of wood and water and grass, then a little town growing on Indian trade, booming when oil was discovered in the county. Red Mound's main pulse was the Santa Fe Railway. Twice a day, the northbound chuffing up from central Oklahoma in the morning, the southbound shuttling down from Kansas each afternoon; trains paused briefly, and the town took on an air of transitory importance.

Bouncing across the flat, Sam stared in surprise at Red Mound's growth. Since his last time here, the summer of 1917, it had spread well out on the plain; that far in eight years. Now, entering the town, and seeing the new houses and neat lawns and the shiny cars parked in the concrete drives, he understood Scotty Hinton's report on Red Mound's booming affluence.

Sam drove on, into thickening traffic, forced to slow down as he approached the crowded, three-block business section. A banner hanging across Main Street, from the Osage Mercantile to the Bailey Hardware Company, took his eye. It read: WELCOME HOME, HANK. A hero's welcome, whoever this Hank was.

Sam began looking for a livery stable, remembering that there used to be three. But where the Osage Livery and the Pioneer Livery used to stand, he saw brightly painted filling stations. He pulled on toward the north end of Main, noticing that a crowd was beginning to gather at the depot, and suddenly hit the brakes when from a side street a young Indian behind the wheel of a purple Cadillac roadster shot across in front of him.

Sam grinned reminiscently. That was one thing that hadn't changed, the way Indian boys drove. And neither, he saw in warm relief, had the Star Livery. There it was in the last block. The old metal weather vane in the form of a prancing horse still rode the peak of the barn's high front, seeming a last symbol of defiance against the onrushing auto age. He hoped Fargo Young was still kicking. The place looked deserted, as silent as the depot crowd was noisy. No one loafed out front as they used to, and the once-bright red face of the barn was peeling and graying. However, as Sam continued on, he saw that the runway door was open. Good. He would circle Main once, in hopes Scotty Hinton spotted him, then put Slip Along up for the night.

Sam made a U turn and crawled along in the line of cars. At the south end of the street, he turned again and headed for the barn. It struck him that he hadn't sighted one familiar face on the street; maybe that was best. Parking just beyond the entrance of the barn's runway, he turned off the ignition and walked back.

An angular, dark-skinned man, wearing a floppy hat, left the office. Sam recognized Fargo Young, somewhat stooped by now, his ox-bow mustache showing gray, and his step less lively; but his horseman's eyes were already trying to judge the gelding in the trailer.

"I'd like to board my horse a few days," Sam said, shaking hands. "I'm Sam Colter. Used to live around here."

"Colter? Colter?" Fargo Young, blinking and squinting at Sam, appeared to roll the name around in his mind. He snapped Sam a penetrating look. "Wouldn't be kin to Matt Colter, would you?"

"His son."

"Well, now. How's your father?"

"Passed away three years ago."

"Sure hate to hear that. He'd come by here and we'd talk horses by the hour. I used to start a heap of races around Red Mound."

"I remember."

"Don't get asked much these days, the way times have changed, an' all. Could be because I like to see both horses get an even start."

"That's not always easy."

"Nope—but a man can try. Well, I didn't mean to get off on that . . . Let's see. Matt moved to South Texas in the fall of 1918. I remember that stud he had—Old Baldy. Boy, howdy, he knew where the wire was. Wasn't Old Baldy by Peter McCue?"

"You bet he was. And this horse is by Old Baldy out of a half-Thoroughbred Louisiana mare named Wendy. He's past seven, but still gets down the track." Now wasn't the time, Sam thought, to hot air about his horse, or to tell Fargo Young that Matt, favoring chunky conformation in his short horses, had made a rare mistake in judgment and gelded an ugly, stringy-looking colt that turned out to be a hard-knocking money runner in Texas. In fact, Slip Along's conception was a mistake in the eyes of Matt Colter, who believed that breeding to a Thoroughbred was "breeding down," as he termed it. Why? Because, Matt reasoned, Thoroughbred blood took something off the quick break, which was so essential in short races. Slip Along appeared to refute that theory. He had lost a shade of his flash as a three- and four-year-old, but he was a fast breaker and as sound as the day he was foaled, and yet a real running horse up to seven furlongs, that extra distance acquired from his unjustly maligned mammy. Word would get around soon enough after Slip Along had won a few, though many things were more certain than winning horse races. At the moment, Sam saw time as his principal need, time for listening and observing and mixing and getting the "feel" of the Osage after his lengthy absence. He needed time before he raced his horse. Later, he would be counting on Slip Along to open some doors otherwise closed to him, a stranger among the swarms of newcomers drawn by the oil boom and the honey of easy Indian money.

But this was the time for Sam to drop word why he was ostensibly here. "Fact is," he confided, "I'll be looking for some match races before long. Be a little while yet. Slip Along, here, needs rest after that long haul. He's not in top running condition."

"First thing," Fargo Young said critically, "is get him outa that damn hen-coop trailer. He'll be stove up, stiff as a board."

Sam unlatched the trailer gate, dropped it, untied Slip Along's halter, backed the veteran campaigner out, and led him clattering inside the barn and out to a cool-looking stone watering trough in the corral. While Slip Along filled himself, the old man eyeballed the brownish horse back and forth, up and down, and moved slowly around him. "He's got one gotch ear. How'd that happen?"

"On a barbed-wire fence when he was a colt."

"Too bad."

"Can't say it slows him any," Sam replied defensively.

"The Lord sure didn't paint him pretty, either. Like He stood back and throwed mud pies at him. However, I learned a long time ago never to judge man or animal by looks alone. So he won't win any beauty prizes—that why Matt cut him?"

Sam nodded and saw a knowing I-told-you-so expression enter the lively black eyes. The old man circled the horse once again, more slowly, more intently. Of a sudden he slapped his leg. "You know, it's just his manner, I reckon, and that floppy ear and his color. And he's tall-fifteen hands or better. Makes him look a bit rangy for a short horse. Reckon that's that Thoroughbred blood. How's he on the break?"

"Gets off right well," Sam said, feeling conservative. "I like to start him a little sideways as he comes up to the line. That lets him push off, sort of. It's quicker than a flat-footed break."

"Hmmnnn." Fargo Young kept looking and jogging his head approvingly. "You know, this horse has good conformation. Stout hindquarters, like Old Baldy. Long underline. Strong back. Big shoulders. Deep barrel. Straight legs. Stands square on all four feet. Matt's idy, I recall, was to breed fast blood to fast blood, but stick to your own breed."

"That's right," Sam agreed. "Only sometimes he didn't get the conformation he wanted. Then he was critical. This horse's mammy wouldn't take any beauty prizes, either, but she could bust the breeze."

"What's conformation without performance?" Fargo Young opined, looking wise, gesturing as if to an audience. He bit off a chew from a wedge of black tobacco and wallowed it around before continuing. "Some of the prettiest show horses in the world can't run fast enough to scatter dust, or cut quick enough to turn an old milk cow. Couldn't fetch you to the store and back in time for supper."

"Dad said you could always sell a fast horse, in good times or bad. Trouble was, he hated to sell a fast horse, even when he was hard up, which was most times."

Afterward, the old man made a show of leading Slip Along to a stall and throwing down fresh hay and dumping oats in the wooden feedbox. Sam noted only one other horse in the barn, and none loose in the corral. His father's old friend was barely hanging on here, fighting a losing battle against change.

On the way back to the office, Sam said, "Mr. Young, you happen to know a little place not far from town a man might rent for a few months? Say through the fall, maybe into winter?"

"Name's Fargo," came the gruff reply. "You call me 'Mr. Young,' folks won't know who you're talkin' about." Fargo thought a moment, head lowered as he walked. He halted suddenly, his craggy face lighting up. "My old place five miles east of town might do for a good short-horse man. Fella I had out there took a job in the oil fields last spring. Too far out for me to make it back and forth every day, so I live in town. Maybe I'll hole up out there when the livery game plays out, and that's not far off, looks like . . . Too many folks joyridin' around in too many blamed cars." He spat his disdain. "Why, just the other day a fella come in here, said he saw six cars between Red Mound an' Hominy. All goin' like a bat outa hell, dust so thick he had to squint to see the fences. Him in a white shirt, too. Said he liked to run off the road three times." He shook his head, deploring the state of things. "Anyway, you can look the old place over tomorrow, if you want to. Good pasture. Barn. Corral. Plenty water."

"Sounds good, Fargo. I'm much obliged to you. I'd like to get settled soon as I can."

"You can park out back tonight. Feed bill's on the house, for old times' sake."

"Whoa now. Want you to stay in business. What's the rate?"

"Oh, dollar a day."

"That's what it was years ago."

"That's what it still is—an' that's what it's worth," Fargo insisted stubbornly.

Sam laid a five-dollar bill on Fargo's dusty, rolltop desk, strayed to the door, and looked out at the busy street. "Who's the big welcome for? Who's this Hank?"

"Hank Vail, world's champion steer roper. Cleaned up at Cheyenne on the Fourth of July. He's due in on the three-twenty. Be a big blowout in town tonight, you betcha." Fargo, however, did not appear impressed.

"I remember him," Sam recalled. "Married to an Osage woman."

"*Was.* Leonora Eagle Dance. She died about eight years ago."

"I remember they had a ranch north of town."

"*She* did. You wouldn't know it now. The Forked Lightning Ranch. Big show place. Big house. Fences painted white. All registered Herefords. Horses fast and fancy. Vail runs a big breeding operation, too. Even built him a track and put up some stands. Has races out there ever' Sunday or so. Rodeos, too. Imagine you could match up something thereabouts." Fargo paused, his jaws grinding with deliberate reflection. "If you do, I'd kinda be on the lookout as to who does the startin'."

"Meaning?"

"Just what I said. Be on the lookout. Fella can lose his shirt out there an' still have the best horse."

"I'll remember that. I can see Red Mound has changed. Was wondering if some of my old friends are still around. Charlie Small Bull? Ted Iron Shirt?"

Fargo shook his head. "Both dead. Charlie was killed in a car wreck south of Pawhuska. Drinkin' . . . went to sleep . . . hit a culvert. Ted drank himself to death. Took the Keeley Cure time after time in Kansas City." He shook his head again. "I remember when those boys used to come to town on their paint ponies. Always laughin'. Never worried about tomorrow."

Sam felt a stabbing sense of loss. Dreading to, he asked further, "What about Carl Strikes Fire? Homer Big Wolf?"

"Gone," said Fargo. "Like the rest. One thing or another. And Antwine Cloud-Walker. Know you remember him. Antwine was shot and killed northwest of town three months ago. Found in his car. Been shot behind the left ear. Old John Cloud-Walker has put up a five-thousand-dollar reward . . . You know, everybody had high hopes for Antwine. Him helpin' corral Kaiser Bill, the way he did. Gettin' that medal. His picture in all the big papers back East; Tulsa and Oklahoma City, too . . . came home from the war. Went to A&M College one year. Even made the honor roll. Then he started drinkin'."

"Any suspects?"

"Woods are full of 'em. No charges filed yet. Likely won't be any."

"Why not?"

"Ever hear of a white man charged in Osage County with killin' an Indian?"

Sam had no answer to that, thinking to himself that murder was uncommon when he was growing up.

"We had more regulatin' when the country was first opened up," Fargo stated. For emphasis, he launched a stream of tobacco juice toward a coffee can streaked with brown stains. There was a distinct ping. "As a matter of fact, the main suspect is right here in Red Mound right now—on Main Street. Works here." Rather abruptly, he compressed his lips, and Sam sensed that the old man had finished his say, indeed, as if he had said too much.

"Must have been an investigation," Sam reminded him, drifting back into the room.

Fargo almost sneered. "Oh, the county sent some deputies over. They bumbled around and asked questions. Even came in here. I told 'em what I thought, all right. They hung around town a day or so, drinkin' coffee at Jimmy the Greek's."

"What about the man on Main Street?"

"Oh, they questioned him, all right. Upshot was they said there wasn't enough evidence to charge him. Said they couldn't link 'im to the crime. I figure runnin' around with Antwine's full-blood wife, Nora, was link enough. Married her, too." Fargo pushed to his feet and stepped to the doorway and gazed toward the depot. "Well, everybody's crowdin' up over there to see their hero come in." He drew a thick pocket watch and squinted and scowled at it, inching it farther and farther from his eyes. "About twenty minutes yet. Only two things ever on time in Red Mound: the southbound and Osage payments."

"Believe I'll go over for the show," Sam said. He drove around and parked behind the corral and brought in his suitcase, which he left in Fargo's office. His black .45-caliber semi-automatic pistol was in the suitcase, which Scotty Hinton would say was dangerous laxity; instead, that its place was on you.

At three-ten Sam was part of the milling, talkative crowd, not yet seeing one man he had known by name. Now and then a sunburned, older face or a roundish, full-fleshed Osage face tugged dimly at his memory. Neither did he see Hinton. He leaned his back against the depot wall and resumed his idle watching, feeling more like a stranger every minute. A realization he resisted went through him: He recognized no Osages near his own age because those he had I known well in Red Mound's small high school were all dead. Sam had carried a Springfield rifle in France with Charlie Small Bull and Ted Iron Shirt and Antwine Cloud-Walker. They were buddies with Ira Pipestone, Russ Donovan, and Gig Tanner. Russ and Gig were white boys. Like Ira, they didn't make it back home. Chatillon Ridge was as far as they got.

For the most part, Sam judged, this was a young crowd. He saw squawmen, expensively dressed and overweight, displaying their newly acquired status of well-being; these men were the loudest, and their dark-eyed women the quietest. He saw a scattering of brawny oil field workers and, flashing silk shirts and big hats and handmade boots, a more numerous representation of rodeo performers and hero-worshiping young bucks from area ranches; and less noticeable, but undeniably in force, the hardcases riding the fringes of the Osage oil boom, ready to hamstring any individual dropping behind the herd. These men ran to types, and Sam knew types. A hijacker in Texas fit the same mold in Osage County. They were all here, like camp followers, part of the Wild frenzy that the newspapers said was sweeping not only the fabulous Osage, but also the nation itself, and that the papers often referred to as the Roaring Twenties.

There sounded the distant toot of a train whistle; at that signal, the hum of voices ceased, and every face looked uptrack. In moments the southbound materialized, a short black snake chuffing furious importance. It disappeared behind a low hill, its voice muffled, to emerge within seconds. It emitted a clanging as it passed the water tower and slackened speed, brakes shrieking, trailing clouds of cinders and steam. The crowd milled toward the tracks. Expectant voices strained upward. As the train lurched to a hissing stop, the crowd pressed closer, hushed for the first time.

Nothing happened. The crowd was riveted by an interval of tense anticipation. Finally, figures moved behind the murky windows of the first passenger car. An elderly conductor appeared in the vestibule. With casual agility, he dropped to the platform and set a footstool at the bottom of the steps and stood aside, unmoved by the gaping throng.

A lean, handsome man came next. He took one downward step and paused, his timed entrance that of a trained performer greeting a vast arena of admirers. He was a spectacular-looking man in wide-brimmed hat, its dove-gray crown peaked high, and purple silk shirt and tailored whipcord trousers of light tan tucked inside glistening black cowboy boots decorated with white steer heads across the tops. He wore a yellow scarf, knotted at the throat, and he was clean shaven, which accented the dark, strong features: his high-bridged nose, his cool, confident eyes, his firm mouth. Even though Hank Vail had to be in his early forties, Sam decided, he looked ten years younger.

Suddenly, Vail flashed a smile and waved, and still waving descended the steps to the platform, his movements as balanced and poised as those of a professional boxer. At the same time the crowd found its many worshiping voices and lapped around him like a wave.

"Hank! Hank! . . . Welcome home, Hank! . . . Hey, champ!" Everyone was clapping and shouting or talking. Men crowded forward to pump Vail's hand and slap him on the back and utter extravagant greetings:

"Where's that hot rope?"

"Forget your horse in Cheyenne?"

"Reckon you showed 'em how it's done in Osage County, huh, Hank?"

"Mighty proud of you, Hank!"

"You sure put Red Mound on the map, old friend!"

A good-looking young white girl pushed through and kissed Vail on the mouth, leaving a smear of lipstick. Everyone roared and gawked, straining to see. Vail wiped with the back of his hand, and with a gallant bow swept off his hat and bussed her back The crowd roared again. Hank Vail laughed with them.

The sound of a speeding car pierced the babble. Sam, who had held back near the rear of the platform when the crowd surged around Vail, heard the driver pull in behind him and stop. A car door slammed. Light footsteps fled over the cindered parking and onto the platform. A woman, a white woman, perky blue-and-white hat pulled slanting over her dark hair, rushed past Sam into the thick of the crowd and made her way to Vail.

"There's Fay Vail," Sam heard a woman say. "Bad time to be late."

Now the woman in the blue-and-white hat grasped Vail's arm and hugged and kissed him. Vail, momentarily, seemed to ignore her. When he did look at her, a kind of rebuke lay behind his eyes for a moment. He smiled at her, then, and said something, but he did not kiss her. Instead, he turned away as more greeters swarmed about him to shake hands and clap him on the shoulders and back.

However, the woman did not leave. She slipped a hand under Vail's left arm and clung there, a wife's public gesture of possession. Sam continued to stare at her, doubting his own eyes. Of all the possible complications that he had tried to foresee before coming back, she had not been among them. Of course, he had thought of Fay Marcum, now Vail, because you didn't forget a woman like her; but he hadn't expected to see her again. And not in Red Mound. Long ago, he supposed, she had gone to a big city and married.

Now he was startled and even angered at himself that the sight of her could yet quicken his pulse.

He started to leave. When he did, the train engine suddenly snorted steam, moving off, and the crowd broke up. Without warning, the Vails were making a beeline for their car, heading in Sam's direction. To turn away would be ridiculous; besides, they would go by several feet from him and she could hardly recognize him in the confusion and her concentration to hold onto Vail's arm.

Such would have been the case had not someone behind Sam chosen that moment to yell at Vail and wave. Vail didn't notice. The admirer, a white man who could whoop like an Osage, gave voice and waved again.

Vail heard and turned, waving, and his wife turned likewise, and Sam's eyes met hers.

Her attention was fixed beyond Sam at first, on the whooping greeter. And then, as her eyes drew in, and as if against her will, he saw the wide-eyed face frown. Next he saw recognition of him shock her eyes even wider. As for himself, he knew a controlled numbness and again his self-annoyance. By that time she and Vail were past, striding out to a light blue Cadillac touring car.

While Sam joined the town crowd gravitating across the tracks up Main Street, a thoughtfulness fell upon him. Eight years ago to this summer, self-conscious and alternately dead serious and joking, he had lined up on the depot platform back there with the other volunteers, while the Red Mound High School band played ragged renditions of patriotic tunes, and townspeople and ranchers and Indians looked on solemnly, and some women wept. Bib-bearded Grandpa Price tottered among the dignitaries on the speakers' stand in his Union blue—Grandpa Price, as brave as any man could be, who three times had the flag shot out of his hands in charges against the Confederate breastworks at Vicksburg.

Toward the end Mayor Chubby Sparks, who had made it up San Juan Hill, flung out a hot speech about "mopping up on the dirty Huns" and "making the world safe for democracy," delivered with such vehemence that his face grew beet red and he got a "catch" in his side and had to sit down. And Old Roman Lost Elk told the boys to be brave and "get in close," to fight the enemy "white mans" hand-to-hand so they could bring back many war honors. That, he stressed, was more honorable than killing at long range. It was touching the enemy that counted, he said, ending his speech with a whoop.

Afterward, while the band played "Over There" and the women wept again, and as the volunteers shuffled toward the train taking them to Oklahoma City for physicals and hoped-for induction, Fay Marcum, her dark head shining, tears streaking her flawless face, ran up and embraced Sam, and they kissed good-by.

"I'll wait for you," she promised.

That was the last time he had seen her until today.

Sam looked up, annoyed to see that he had come half a block, unaware of where he was or of the persons about him. He crushed the scene from his mind and began looking for Hinton on the crowded sidewalk. An unbroken line of cars, their tooting a constant din, crept along the street. Sam idled on to the Osage Hotel, its plain sandstone face unchanged since its birth shortly before statehood, 1907. There Sam cut through the traffic to the other side of the street and on back to the Star Livery. Fargo wasn't in, so Sam took his suitcase and went out.

He was climbing the steps of the Osage Hotel when he saw the light blue Cadillac touring car. Vail was driving and constantly waving and flashing the broad smile as admirers tooted at him. Fay sat beside him, yet somehow apart from the celebration.

Sam, not pausing, entered and registered and climbed the stairs to his room on the second floor, washed up for supper, shaved, and still leaving the .45 in his suitcase, he locked the door and came down to the lobby. A poster, prominently placed on a stand near the clerk's desk announced:

HONOR HANK VAIL TONIGHT!
DANCE AT THE LEGION HUT!
FROM 9 UNTIL—
$1.00 PER COUPLE
TULSA RHYTHM KINGS

Sam, seeing that, wondered at his concentration. He had missed the poster when he entered. Boot heels clicking on the tile floor, he crossed the lobby window and looked out on the street, forcing calm into his movements against his now-familiar irritation that he should still retain vestiges of old feelings that he thought had run their course long ago. He had damn well better take himself in hand, because there was work to do.

After supper in the modest dining room of the hotel, he bought a cigar from the desk clerk and stood on the hotel's steps in the growing dusk. Some minutes later he turned down the street, now run dry of traffic except at the south end of Main, where a few early-bird couples were arriving at the Legion Hut. Already the dance hall blazed with lights. While he looked, a bus drew up and disgorged the band, one by one, attired in white trousers and striped coats. Over by the parked cars somebody whooped.

Sam walked the three blocks of the business district on the west side, past the First State Bank on the corner, the open Rexall Drug, and Jimmy the Greek's City Cafe, which was enjoying a late run of customers. Scanning the faces going and coming, Sam was reminded once again that he saw none he remembered from his time, not one. And he reflected grimly that after what had happened in the county, starting with the fevered oil boom, and the violence still continuing unchecked, you could say that almost an entire generation of young Osages, trusting and unprepared for sudden oil riches, was vanishing by one cause or another. On second thought, "rubbed out" was the more accurate way to put it, he decided.

He crossed to the east side of the street and loitered before the Osage Mercantile, apparently viewing a display of men's hats.

A man moved along the street from the south, his walk unhurried. Although Sam didn't glance that way, he knew. Without stopping, the man said, "Nine o'clock in my office over the bank," and stepped on.

Sam turned in the other direction. Strolling to the hotel, he felt a wind, cool and clean, rising out of the dark-humped hills west of town. For a briefness he actually smelled grass; in the next moment he knew it was only his imagination, an extension of his desire to come home again, his feeling for this empire of grassy hills where his life had begun.

Inside, he bought a copy of the *Tulsa World* at the desk, took the stairs to his room and locked the door, cleaned and oiled the .45, then settled down to kill time reading . . . A record lease sale of oil and gas tracts was predicted at the Osage Agency in Pawhuska. Oil production was up . . . Bank robbed at Barnsdall, eastern Osage County. Two masked men made their escape driving a Hudson Super-six . . . An Osage rancher robbed at his home north of Hominy. Five thousand in diamonds taken . . . An Osage grave dynamited in Red Mound Cemetery. Investigating officers said the ghouls, whose blast failed to open the steel vault, were believed looking for jewelry buried with the deceased . . .

And so, he thought, laying the paper aside, the frenzy goes on.

Just before nine o'clock, the .45 tucked in a holster inside the waistband of his trousers, Sam Colter climbed the wooden stairs leading over the bank. The sallow eye of a single bulb cast a dim glow down the hallway. A light also burned in the office at the end of the hall, its door ajar.

Sam considered it a moment, then walked ahead. On the frost panes of the other offices, he noted lettering after lettering that read the same: ATTORNEY AT LAW. He paused before the open door, and was scanning the lettering there, HINTON INSURANCE, below that, PROTECT YOUR FAMILY, when the mildest of voices spoke within, "Could I interest you in a policy?"

Breaking into a grin, Sam pushed the door open wider and entered.

Behind his desk, the ghost of a smile playing across his accommodating face, Scotty Hinton looked the small-town Texas businessman and accountant he had been and the church deacon he was not: steel-rimmed glasses resting on the sharp prow of a nose; conservative blue serge suit and white shirt and dark maroon tie; thin, sandy hair parted on the side—a smallish man, yet wiry, whom a larger adversary might underestimate. His fatherly expression was a composite of trust and cheerful patience and efficiency learned over forty-odd years. It was the eyes that told about the inner man, however: light blue and a glint therein.

He shook hands, saying, "Sit down and leave the door open. I'll make it brief, Sam. As you probably noticed, there are lawyers on both sides down the hall. They seldom work at night. No need to when you're guardian for Osages who don't have their competency certificates. Nice racket, practiced in every town in the county. But not our concern." He scratched one side of his neck and leaned back, half smiling again. "Saw you drive in this afternoon. You and your horse. *That* a racehorse?"

"He'll do," Sam said, grinning back. "And Fargo Young's offered to rent me his place east of town."

"Already? Good, Sam. Gives you a base right off the bat. Gene Poole and Blue Sublette are here. Drifted in several days ago, one at a time. You understand how you're all to operate?"

Sam nodded, thinking they were like blind men, stumbling around in the dark, groping for leads.

"Tomorrow night we'll meet at the loading pens on the spur line east of town. That's 3½ miles past Fargo's place."

"I know where it is. What time?"

"Say between ten and eleven. I need to bring you fellows up to date. There's a good deal to go over." An amused irony replaced his seriousness. "Hard to believe

. . . but I'm selling life insurance policies like crazy. Busier than a bootlegger on Saturday night. After so many funerals around here, including some for white people, I might add, seems folks are beginning to consider the uncertainty of life in the Osage. Been here just four months and I'm leading my district in sales. Arrived just in time to get my name in the phone book. Guess that's it for tonight. Just wanted you to know I saw you come in, and where we rendezvous."

As Sam stood, Hinton cautioned, "Another thing. Don't mail *anything* of an official nature from the local post office. Don't make any phone calls from here to Blue or Gene. This town has a thousand eyes and ears. If something comes up you can't funnel through me to Oklahoma City, mail it at Pawnee, Ponca City, Hominy, Pawhuska, Wynona. Anywhere but Red Mound." Hinton raised a further detaining hand, and his voice dropped even lower. His face was a mask of grim competence. "You understand you're on your own, Sam. We all are. If you get in a tight, the Bureau can't go to bat for you in the open. That would blow the whole operation. Even the governor of Oklahoma doesn't know we're in here. Nor the Osage County attorney. Neither does the Osage Tribal Council, which made the plea for help through Senator Curtis of Kansas, himself part Kaw Indian, who placed the matter before the U. S. Attorney General."

Sam saw the mobile face switch back, once again that of affable Scotty Hinton, Red Mound's leading insurance salesman. "Good night and good luck, Sam. Guess I'd better get this raft of policy applications ready to send off to the home office."

Sam descended the creaky stairs to the darkening street, thinking of the steadfast, considerate man he had just left. Scotty Hinton was trained to control his emotions. He would fool a lot of people. Underneath, when the occasion demanded, he could be as hard as flint, his mind like a metal file.

Night was clamping down. The wind, strengthening, flung a spatter of dust off the street against the sandstone flank of the bank. More cars were jamming around the Legion Hut, for the dance had started. The band was playing a fast number, featuring racehorse piano and wildcat fiddle. More couples trooped inside. Somebody raised a high, drawn-out "aww-haaa," which prompted rippling laughter.

Passing the closed drugstore and the emptying City Cafe, he could not but discern a certain mockery in his situation, as if time had stopped for Sam Colter, for him alone, while the Indian friends of his time had mysteriously vanished, their rightful places pre-empted by intruders, leaving him a stranger prowling old haunts.

It was ironic that Charlie and Ted and Antwine, after surviving one of the greatest and most costly American military victories, had returned home to their beloved hills only to die by dissipation and violence, their lives wasted—Antwine murdered. The brutal horror of the war had marked them all, himself as well. Sam Colter despised war. He hated guns. Had his Indian buddies drunk so much just because they didn't give a damn? Because they had seen too many visions of life and death? Whatever, that or victims of too much sudden wealth flowing through prodigal hands, they had lost the wonderful innocence of their youth on Old Europe's senseless battlefields. Maybe that was it. Maybe they had left too much of themselves "over there."

Sam was conscious of a fierce loyalty for these

doughboy friends, who had gone off singing to the bloodiest of wars, for he had never known the real meaning of love until he had fought alongside them *("I'm hit, Sam—I'm hit!)* and, powerless, wrenched, raging, had seen their still young faces.

His hotel room was stuffy. Opening the window high, he could hear the music blaring stronger down the street; now and then a dancer whooped. His mind too full yet for sleep, he laid the .45 on the night table by the bed, made a restless turn of the room, picked up the newspaper, and sat down to read.

Perhaps an hour or more had passed when a tentative *rap-rap* on the door startled him and he realized he had been dozing. He called, low, "Who is it?" and left the chair, feeling no alarm, no more than curiosity. It had to be Scotty, who had thought of something else.

"It's me . . . Sam. It's me."

A woman's voice, rich and melodic.

An absolute knowing struck him, and the self-anger that he had felt earlier, and that he awaited now, was lacking. He hardly hesitated. He unlocked the door and opened it.

Fay Marcum Vail stood there. She was looking up at him and smiling.

CHAPTER 2

"DO I GET TO COME IN?"

Sam stepped back.

She came in as if today were eight years ago and nothing had gone wrong and you, just turned twenty-one, were marching off to war so that liberty would not perish from the earth, knowing that when you returned in glory, your girl would be waiting for you, and the two of you would live happily the rest of your days.

He closed the door behind her, catching the heady scent of her trailing perfume. When she turned to face him, she was smiling the evasive, compelling smile that he so remembered. Obviously, she was glad to see him.

He looked at her without speaking, through the revealing light of maturity—at the rouged, wide-eyed face and its bold contours, at the full lips, which sometimes had expressed the pouting of a child, at the fine gray-green eyes, which mascara made look even larger. She had bobbed her lustrous dark hair, which shone in the light. She had acquired a different look, the detached insulation that money brings, a confident air that seemed a bit unsure when he spoke no greeting. She wore a low-cut blue dress of some glossy-looking material he didn't know. Blue, he remembered, was her best color. In all, he saw, she had grown from a very pretty girl into a mighty good-looking woman.

"Sam," she said, "don't you know me?"

He started to reply something absurdly gallant or bitter, but changed his mind. "It's just been a long time, is all. You surprised me."

He saw her draw forward a step and tilt her dark head a trifle, an almost imperceptible movement that he knew said that she expected him to embrace her, at least. When he did not respond, she said, "You look so good, Sam. So lean and brown. Your eyes were always so blue . . . I saw you at the depot. Later, coming into the hotel. So I put two and two together."

"Why?"

She seemed to search for a suitable reply. "Hank took me to the dance. I'm married to him, you know. Hank Vail."

Sam said no word, feeling no more than an immobilizing numbness, a sense of unreality.

"Hank," she said, "had time only for his public—the whole town must be tight tonight—and I was tired of drunk cowboys pawing me. So I decided to look you up—that's all." When he kept silent, she assumed a near pouting. "You could ask me to sit down."

"Sure." He gestured toward the one chair near the night stand. Looking at him all the while, she sat and crossed her slim, silk-clad legs. She wore her sheer hose rolled just below her pretty knees, and her short skirt, flapper style, could not hide the ivory smoothness of her thighs.

"Frankly," she said, speaking faster, her voice uncertain, "I wanted to see you to explain." For the first time she wasn't smiling.

Sam was silent. Why rake up the past? Why tell her that her bombshell letter couldn't have reached him at a worse time? just when they were getting ready to move into the lines at the Meuse-Argonne. *(A gloomy day at best as you stared off through the rainstreaked sky of late September at the forbidding woods and hills, and tangled thickets and savage ravines where the Heinie bastards waited, dug in, with everything they had. After what the outfit had been through at St.-Mihiel, every man had long since resigned himself to the certainty of dying. Right now, this broken thing between a boy and girl didn't matter one goddamn. Yet how stricken he knew he looked to Antwine and the others!)* And he found himself saying:

"That was a long time ago. We were both young. You were just nineteen." That last had slipped out of him, because he hadn't intended to apologize for her, or to defend her. Neither did he intend to accuse her. But he had no desire to hear any explanations.

"I wanted to see you after the war," she persisted. "But you never came home, and I didn't know where to write you."

"Dad had moved his horses to South Texas. I went there."

"I guess what I'm trying to say, Sam . . . after all these many years . . . is that I hope you'll forgive me." She crossed her long legs and pulled in vain at her short skirt.

"There's nothing to forgive. It's long past, water down the creek."

"You keep saying that," she said, self-condemning. "I wish I could feel better about what happened. I never have."

"We can't change the past." As yet he could not bring himself to speak her name; to do so might encourage her further along this backward journey into the past he did not wish to travel.

"But you were hurt, Sam. I know I hurt you."

"I got over it." He wouldn't tell her how long that had taken, for when you're young you bleed easier and you keep on bleeding. How, in Texas, working with horses, finally he had found himself again. And he wished she'd quit saying his name that way, which both irritated and affected him somehow, despite his self-control.

"My mother didn't help," she went on apologetically, contritely. "I wonder sometimes if I got half your letters, Sam. For a long time I didn't get any. She watched the mailbox like a hawk. She didn't want me to write you. She wanted to break us up."

Sam could believe that . . . up to a certain point. Fay could twist things to get her way. Nonetheless, the Marcums had not approved of Sam Colter, the son of a horse-and-mule trader and short-horse man. The Colters were socially unacceptable for another and more prohibitive reason: Matt Colter raced horses at the Osage County Fair, and sometimes matched races with other horsemen, and of course racing was associated with gambling and other immoral pastimes. What the Marcums didn't understand was that Matt Colter raised and raced horses mainly because he loved them, and because racing developed the qualities for which they were created—beauty, speed, courage—besides the pleasure of owning and riding them.

Betting at the races? You bet, pardner. Sam had seen men literally bet their shirts and boots, which explained why people like the Marcums referred to short horses as "gamblers' horses." Down in Texas, where Matt Colter hailed from, you heard them called "Steel Dusts" —after the legendary size of that name—or "Billys," after Old Billy—or "Tigers" and "Whips" and "Cold Decks" and "Rondos"—or "Big Jaws," because of their bulging jaws. To young Sam Colter those broad jaws indicated strength and tenacity of will to win.

("Your father is a horse trader, is he not?" Mrs. Harrington Marcum twitched her nose squeamishly, as though she smelled something.

"He sells horses and mules, ma'am, but mainly he breeds good short horses."

"He also races them, does he not?"

"Yes, ma'am, he matches a race now and then. Sometimes I ride for him, though I'm getting too big."

"In other words, your father gambles on horses?"

"It's a gamble anytime you race, ma'am. But it's a great feeling to ride a fast horse."

"I dare say you make it perfectly clear what your father does," Mrs. Marcum concluded archly.)

Trouble with the Marcums, who had spoiled their pretty daughter, they nursed ambitions beyond their prospects. They were painfully pretentious in a small town where affectation stood forth like a drunk on Main Street as church was letting out. Mrs. Marcum often sang lengthily at local church functions and funerals, including Red Mound High School assemblies. Sam could yet hear her stilted voice: "Appreciation of the higher arts must be instilled in the young, if Oklahoma is to advance beyond its primitive state." He could picture the plump, powdered face beneath the flapping wings of the enormous white hat, and the exaggerated operatic gestures, as she strained toward the higher tonal range of her limited contralto. Meanwhile, Harrington Marcum, his bored eyes suffering his surroundings, scratched out a modest living as bookkeeper at the Prairie View Lumberyard, which nowise diminished his self-importance. When he walked the dusty streets of Red Mound, he had the lordly air of a visiting dignitary whose mind was fixed on distant worlds more appreciative of his spurned superiority.

Fay Vail was saying, ". . . and that's why I came here tonight," and he discovered that, while pieces of the vivid past swarmed through his mind, he had been only half listening to her.

"I had to set things straight," she went on.

He let that pass without comment, aware of his growing strain. "Now you can tell me what brings you to Red Mound," she said, her change of tone suggesting that everything was well between them once more, and he thought of a relenting child who assumed that her smile of penitence made all wrongs right.

"Brought a horse in. Aim to do a little match racing."

"You'll have to come out to the ranch," she said,

showing an immediate interest. "We have roping and bull riding and match races almost every Sunday. We are this Sunday afternoon. Things start around one o'clock or so. Hank's horses have won so many times, it's hard for him to find any takers. But somebody will match a race."

"Maybe I can make it."

"How long you plan on being here?"

"Depends."

She reflected on his vagueness and she seemed somewhat puzzled, regretfully so. When Sam did not elaborate, she rose to leave. As she paused uncertainly, her attention caught the .45 on the night stand. "That go with horse racing?" she asked, smiling through her surprise.

It was a relief for him to grin. "That's for hijackers. I understand there's one behind every bush in Osage County." He shrugged off any dark implications. "I've carried one ever since the war."

"You're very casual about it."

"Habit, I guess. No more than that."

"You haven't told me about yourself, Sam."

"Not much to tell. Worked on ranches mostly. Kept a few short horses. Nothing important. Just that."

She became more intent. Her expressive eyes had not left his face since she had entered the room. "I can't believe just that, Sam," she said, her voice searching. "You were meant for big things."

Something in the way she said his name jerked again at his senses, and, unaccountably, he perceived that she was waiting for him to kiss her. He could take her in his arms if he wished. And beneath the made-up surface of the well-formed face, he saw betrayed her dim but deep-running need, leaving her vulnerable and appallingly open. Fay

Vail was a lonely woman, dissatisfied with life.

That touched Sam, but he did nothing.

She sighed after a moment. Her shoulders rose and fell. "You're married?"

"Nope."

She was smiling once more. "Still holding out?"

"Hasn't been hard," he said with a grin.

Again she started to go. "The rodeo events will be first. Afterward, a party at the ranch for close friends. I'm inviting you, Sam. Especially you. Will you come?"

It occurred to him that he was permitting old emotions, rather the ghost of emotions that longer existed, to distract him from his real purpose for being here. By going out there he could mingle and listen, get acquainted again; possibly set a match race in motion. He overcame the impulse to refuse.

"I'll be there," he said. "Thank you."

She smiled. Her teeth glittered. Her long-lashed eyes deepened. Suddenly she reached up and kissed him fully on the lips, a kiss that was deliberate, yet also tender and hungry, and that sent feeling racing over him. She went to the door and opened it. Looking back at him, she smiled again and said, "See you Sunday, Sam," and pulled the door closed behind her.

He stood still, listening to her fading steps down the hall, the drift of her perfume lingering about him. He touched his mouth. Wheeling, he saw the .45 and was displeased with himself. He should have had the presence of mind to place the handgun out of sight before she came in, and he knew that the sound of her voice had caught him off guard. Why, he had rushed to open the door like a smitten schoolboy.

He lay awake for a long while, listening to the whooping dancers and the pulsing music.

CHAPTER 3

FARGO YOUNG'S MODEST SPREAD EAST OF RED MOUND consisted of a four-room frame house sorely in need of painting, a rock-lined well of sweet water, a weathered relic of a barn, an old-timey pole corral, and a sizable pasture of uncropped bluestem standing knee high. Fargo, showing Sam around, apologizing for the rundown condition of things, balked at first when Sam paid an advance on the rent money.

"Ought to be the other way around. I ought to pay you for stayin' out here. That last fella *just lived* here. Worked in town at whatever he could find. Didn't know a fence post from a cuckleburr. Don't know where he was brought up that ignorant. Didn't even keep a cow—him with three little youngins. I felt sorry for his wife, a thin woman. He left owin' me, but I was glad to get shed of him."

"Better take it now," Sam said. "I might lose my shirt to these Osage track burners." Noticing the sagging gates and the loose wires of the pasture fence, he made a mental note to do some fixing up.

"I'll sure pass the word you want some match races," Fargo said.

"A jockey, too. Only I'm mighty particular who rides my horse."

"Who'll ride till then?"

"I will."

When Fargo left, Sam cinched a stock saddle on Slip Along and rode out into the pasture. After those stiffening days on the road in the trailer, his horse was eager to move out. Sam let him go as he pleased. A wooded creek flanked the pasture on the west. When Sam pulled rein at the edge of the thick woods, the gelding went to grazing at once. "Pardner," Sam said, "you're gonna like the Osage hills. You've never filled up on grass like this."

Sam drank his fill of the woody scent of the blackjacks. Along the creek bottom would be stately sycamores, elms, cottonwoods, and walnuts. A breeze purred about his face. He thought of a sailor smelling land after months at sea. These hills and the creatures and people of these hills had shaped him long ago, had influenced his thinking and, unknown to him, pointed him in a certain direction; their stamp was in his drawling voice, in his reverence for life.

When asked whether or not he was a Southerner, he would reply that he was from the Southwest; there was a difference, for he had not felt the fetters of strict social boundaries, the Marcums excepted. In his view, besides the Indians, the Osage was a genial mixture of Texans, men like his father who savvied horses and mules and cattle, and families out of Tennessee, Virginia, Mississippi, and a lesser portion of Kansans, all drawn by the promise of better times in a new land. Likewise, the county's early oil fields had attracted industrious Pennsylvanians, men who knew how and where to drill holes in the lucrative Osage earth. The hills had molded them also.

Somewhere he had read: *The desert waits*. Well, my unknown friend, these hills also wait, aloof from the impermanence of man. While he mused, the realization occurred to him that he would not have admitted earlier today or the days before: Sam Colter was homesick; that was one reason why he had come back, besides knowing that the freedom he had enjoyed here growing up was now threatened.

Riding the fence line for breaks, he found a level stretch of several hundred yards; some careful rock-picking would make it suitable for working out his horse. The fence would hold a gentle horse until Sam could administer some wire-tightening and patch it here and there.

At the house Sam watered and unsaddled and turned the gelding loose in the pasture. "Enjoy yourself," Sam told him. "You look a mite gaunt" Searching the saddle shed next to the bam, he found hammer, wire cutter, nails, staples, and a coil of wire, and set about fixing the corral gate and the one opening into the pasture. As he worked, he glanced off and on toward the pasture. It gave him a good feeling to see his horse taking to the grass.

After supper, Sam sat on the back steps and smoked while evening settled down and the whippoorwills called in the timber. Occasionally a car whined by on the road. Deeper dusk drew a purple veil over the hills. Contentment swam through him, something he had not known for a long, long time. He decided there was one drawback to renting Fargo's old place. It brought upon him what he had missed these eight years. It led him to considering what Fargo might take, if Sam could raise the money. Further, he reflected, if a man leased more pasture, he could stock whitefaces.

He checked himself abruptly. He was dreaming, and there was no place for foolish dreams anymore. His life had narrowed. You couldn't come back and expect conditions to be the same as before, when you were much younger. Even though the land hadn't changed, the people had, and the frenzy was everywhere.

Before ten o'clock Sam drove away from the house

and turned east. Moonlight washed the silent road like day, which careful Scotty Hinton wouldn't like.

Coming to the road turning off to John Cloud-Walker's ranch house half a mile on, he expected to see darkness there; much to his surprise an eerie cordon of lights wreathed the house. Sam drove ahead with the thought fastening in his mind: So it's come to that. A few miles and the road twisted sharply to the right, and he rumbled over a loose-boarded wooden bridge that spanned the deep cut that let the spur railroad through a line of stubborn hills. A short distance on he slowed down, sighting for car lights behind and in front of him. Seeing none, he snapped off his headlights and turned across a cattle guard of clanking oil-field pipe and entered a broad pasture. A whiteface cow resting in the center of the dim tracks humped up and lumbered off. About three hundred yards and Sam saw the spread-out clutter of the cattle loading pens. He drove around to the other side and cut the motor and stepped out, about him a chorus of insects. The grass smelled sweet and faintly damp. He was the first man. Scotty had chosen a rendezvous too far from town for the convenience of young lovers. Early in the fall, however, the pens and the big pasture would become a seething mass of bawling, milling cattle and dusty, yowling riders and strings of slatted railway cars when ranchers gathered their stock here at shipping time.

After about ten minutes, Sam heard the low roar of a car traveling slowly. He moved to the pens and waited. The driver rounded the pens and stopped, keeping the motor at idle. That had to be Scotty, making certain he knew the driver of the parked car before he showed himself.

Sam left the shadows of the pens and walked across.

"Hi, Scotty."

Hinton silenced the coupe's motor, turned, and opened the door.

"For a second there I almost took you for a bootlegger visiting his cache. Get settled at Fargo's?"

"This morning."

"Fast work." Hinton lit a cigarette and carefully snapped the dead match in two before tossing it in the grass. "Guess you saw the lights when you came by John Cloud-Walker's place?"

"Couldn't miss 'em. Lit up like a Christmas tree."

" 'Fraid lights—the Osages call 'em. Nobody can name a thing like an Indian. Literal. Fits to a T. John had the lights strung up after Antwine was murdered. A good many Osages are doing that . . . buying mean dogs . . . even hiring bodyguards."

"Used to, folks never locked a door."

"The Osage is a lot like the old frontier was, Sam. What little law and order there is often comes under the influence of politics and the leverage one powerful individual can apply. A man can get by with just about what he's big enough to pull off."

"Meaning anybody in particular?"

"Meaning a heap of people. For instance, the way an Indian is fleeced. On the surface it's legitimate, and it's going on in every town in the county. Some stores have their *Osage add-on,* which runs 20 per cent in addition to the cost of the merchandise. Excuse is, they claim some Indians are hard to collect from. It's a way of operating. The agency's complained, but it still goes on. And there's the guardian racket I told you about. New lawyer or businessman comes to town, first thing he does is see about being guardian for some Osage without competency papers."

"My father made some early-day cattle drives to the northern pastures. He used to say the frontier brought out the best or the worst in a man."

"He was right. And mix in an oil boom with plenty of loose Indian money, hijackers, bootleggers, car thieves, and bank robbers, and you have a situation that makes Dodge City look like a tea party. I don't care what Wyatt Earp would say."

They fell silent as the hum of a motor droned across the prairie. Bouncing and rattling, a sedan drew up. A big man got out, looming ever bigger in the moonlit night.

"Join the chin session, Blue," Hinton said.

"Howdy, Scotty. Howdy, Sam," Blue Sublette greeted them and thrust out his hand. "Sure is a pretty night. Reminds me of along the border. Makes a man think of when he was a danged sight younger and had to fight the girls off with a club, maybe one in each hand."

Hinton made a clucking sound. "Sure it wasn't the other way around? You don't strike me as being bashful."

Blue Sublette stood an erect 6 feet 3, topped 220 pounds, and was about 38 years old. Sam's knowledge of him was limited to the somewhat hurried initial meeting in Houston: a rancher and deputy sheriff before coming to the Bureau prior to the war. Of coppery coloring, he could pass for an Indian with his high Roman nose and prominent cheekbones. His wide-brimmed hat made him appear a foot taller. A black-eyed, hearty man, he radiated strength and confidence and laughed a good deal, Sam liked him.

"Seen Gene?" Hinton asked Sublette.

"Not yet."

"He knows we're meeting."

The three conversed in low tones, visiting mostly. Sam guessed that Hinton was holding back until Poole arrived. Soon afterward a car hummed in the distance and, shortly, a roadster appeared. A stocky man left it, walking fast. Gene Poole shook hands and said apologetically, "Got hung up at Burbank."

"Business, already?" Hinton asked.

"A girl . . . works in this little cafe. Believe me, she knows what's going on. I took her home. She insisted I meet her folks. Her mother insisted I stay for ice cream and cake."

"Find out anything?"

"Plenty. Mama's swingin' a big loop to get daughter hitched, and daughter's got the same fever."

"And you?"

"Figure I'll have to find me another place to eat."

"What you get for posing as a rich cattle buyer from Texas," Sublette said, laughing. "You'll have to cut down on the old Lone Star charm."

"That might be harder than you think, Blue, since it comes natural."

Hearing Poole's good-humored voice, Sam felt a rush of warm memories. Poole, who had come to Houston after Sublette and Sam had gone, hadn't changed much since Ranger days right after the war, when he was considered "a fine mixer" and entertaining raconteur. There was a closed chapter in his life that Sam knew about vaguely. Gene had lost a frail wife and infant son. Sam used to wonder whether his friend's jesting wasn't forced at times, a self-defense to cover up that terrible gap. Now in his midthirties, he impressed Sam as the same Gene Poole who, in a moment, could switch from funning to deadly seriousness with a .45.

"Well, boys," Hinton began, "let's get at this. See

where we stand. Any leads, Blue?"

"Found out one thing: You don't get acquainted right off with Osages. Takes time. I've been over to Hominy and up to Wynona and Pawhuska and around. Looked up the names you gave me. Only nobody's asked me to make any medicine yet."

"What's in that stuff?" Poole jibed him.

"Little sugar and water."

"Ever cured anybody?"

"I'll put it this way: It's never hurt anybody. It's all in a man's mind. If he thinks it helps, it helps him."

Hinton broke in. "Idea is that by posing as an Indian medicine man from New Mexico, you can get into places a white man can't."

"Don't forget, I'm also looking for lost Indian relatives," Sublette said, as if he needed to review his role. Sam remembered that the elder Osage men, themselves large of physique and quite straight, liked the sight of a large, powerful man. Probably they would like Blue Sublette.

"What tribe?" Poole bantered.

"Ute. One of my French trapper ancestors took him a Ute woman. Guess I'm kind of an oddity. The Osages I've met never saw a part Ute, let alone a full-blood Ute."

"I'm convinced some Osages, particularly the full-bloods, have information about these murders they haven't told county and state officers," Hinton said.

"They're afraid to talk," Sublette said. "I know that much. I would be, too."

Hinton turned to Sam. "Reminds me. You said in Houston that you and Antwine Cloud-Walker served together in France. That should give you access to his father, John."

"I'll drop by there tomorrow."

"Sam's got his horse at Fargo Young's place east of Red Mound," Hinton explained to the others. He seemed to pause to organize his thoughts. Poole squatted on his heels and built a cigarette, while Sublette sat on the running board of Hinton's coupe. Sam leaned against the fender and folded his arms.

Hinton said, "There's more loose ends to these murders than a busted gunny sack. Hard to tell where to start."

"Can you see Antwine's murder tying in with the Bear Claw killings?" Sam asked him.

"Don't see how, yet. Antwine's headright went to his widow, Nora, a full-blood, and now she's married to Billy Gault."

"Which makes Gault a suspect," Poole added. "Nora, too."

"Does, sure," Hinton agreed. "Plenty of motivation. However, Gault is keeping his head high. Goes to work every day in the men's department at the Osage Mercantile. Smartest thing he did was not run. The county boys questioned him pretty hard. Gault said he was with Nora that Sunday. She backed him up."

"Wouldn't she?" Poole inquired cynically.

"For the time being Gault's story has checked out. No charges filed. Of course, he could have hired him a killer." Hinton rubbed his forehead. "Let's go back over the old tracks of what happened to the Bear Claw family . . . Julia Bear Claw, mother of the girls, also a ward of the U. S. Government, died unexpectedly in April 1920, at her home south of Red Mound. Found dead in bed. True, she was getting on in years—yet she was considered in excellent health for her age. Still active. Her headright and her deceased husband's went to the girls—Elsie, Grace, and Maggie. If Julia Bear Claw was murdered, it occurred on land belonging to a restricted Indian, which would throw the case into federal court, away from local influence."

"By the way, Scotty, what's a headright worth?" Poole asked.

"About twelve thousand dollars a year per capita. The Osages are said to be the richest people in the world individually. When an Osage dies, his headright goes on to his heirs. You can see the motivation for murder."

Poole gave a low whistle. "How'd all this come about? It's plumb new to me."

"Somebody was smart when the Osages were moved here from Kansas in the early days. The tribe retained all mineral rights in community on the reservation, so even if an Indian sold his allotted land, the oil underneath still belonged to the tribe communally. Every person on the tribal rolls, full-blood or mixed-blood, received a headright . . . They closed the rolls in 1907 . . . These oil royalties are distributed quarterly on a per capita basis. There again you see the fortunes in both money and land."

Scotty, Sam thought, was talking like an accountant now, drawing on that encyclopedic mind of his.

"Next," Hinton said, "comes Elsie Bear Claw. She married a white man named Warner. . . divorced him after six months or so. She was unmarried in June 1922, when she was found shot to death in a ravine northeast of Red Mound. Her estate passed on to sisters Grace and Maggie. She and her mother each had some of the finest grazing land in Osage County."

"Guess nobody went on trial for Elsie's murder?" Sublette asked.

"Nobody. She drank a lot. Ran with a rough crowd.

Hard-drinking Indians and deadbeat whites. There's another word for whites who hang around the Indians and live off them. The Osages call 'em *potlickers.*" Hinton lit a cigarette and with care snapped the dead match and dropped it. His voice hardened. "Brings up the case of Grace Bear Claw Jordan and her white husband, Ben, and their teen-aged housekeeper, pretty Holly Abbott. Absolutely the most brutal crime ever committed in Osage County. Somebody got paid plenty for blowing up that house. Red Mound won't be forgetting the date, ever—three o'clock in the morning, March 7, 1923. A wonder it didn't kill twenty or thirty people . . . Fortunately, the house next door was empty, and the Jordan house sat on a corner on a hill. Whoever did it planted the stuff in the basement garage, right under the bedrooms—then slipped up the hill and set it off. The wires were there next morning. That eight-room house went up like matchsticks. The whole town shook. Everybody was paralyzed with fear. Men ran out in the streets and fired rifles and shotguns . . . One man told me he thought a giant bomb had gone off. Another told me he found himself rigidly erect beside his bed, not knowing why he stood there, until the dying sound of the blast registered on him."

Hinton paused and took a pull on his cigarette. "I want to make something clear. Most people in Red Mound are law-abiding. They want these murders solved and the killers brought to justice as much as we do. Blowing up the Jordan house has hurt Red Mound—set it back for a long time. Decent citizens shy away from settling there . . . Because Grace Bear Claw Jordan had her competency papers, was not a ward of the government, and therefore was not murdered on land belonging to a restricted Indian, the Jordan case and that of poor Holly Abbott falls within state jurisdiction. Our job will be to beef up the prosecution . . . help county and state authorities as much as possible."

A dull anger caught at Sam. Not until the undercover agents, hand-picked on the basis of background and experience, were called to Houston had he known in detail what was happening in the Osage. And tonight Scotty was getting down to particulars not covered in that first general briefing.

"One thing puzzles me," Sam said. "Every small town has dogs. Red Mound seemed to have more than usual, I remember. Especially hunting dogs. How could a killer prowl around at night like that, go in and out of the Jordans' garage, string that wire, and not get barked at?"

Sam couldn't see Hinton's face, shadowed by the brim of his hat, but he could imagine its grimness as Hinton replied, his voice clipped, "For a week before the blowup, the dogs within a block of the Jordan house had been dying—poisoned. All the killer had to do was slip down the hill and into the garage. Until that night nobody in Red Mound thought of locking a garage or house. Believe me, they do now?"

"You figure nitro was used?" Poole asked.

"That's the theory in town. Nitro's easy to come by this close to the oil fields."

"It's also a damned sight more dangerous to handle than dynamite," Poole observed. "Takes a cool nerve. A man used to handling it. Just one little jar—and boom!—you're gone."

"Now," Sublette remarked, voice a mock cheerfulness, "all we have to do is check out every nitro shooter in Osage County."

Sam spoke up. "Didn't Ben Jordan live a little while

after the blowup?"

"About two days," Hinton said. "In such pain his talk didn't make sense. Out of his head. I know what you're getting at. No, he didn't name any suspects, though the night before the blowup, he confided to a neighbor that he and Grace had moved to town from their country home because they were afraid. Especially Grace. Ben Jordan said some strange things happened out there . . . People slipping around the house at night—out by the barn and around the sheds . . . Scary voices off in the woods by the river. The Jordans got to where they couldn't sleep . . . I've been out there. I've seen the house. It's built on a flat—just one story, built before the Osages started getting big money. One thing struck me: It was easier to blow up the house in town. It was made to order. Maybe the idea was to drive the Jordans into town."

Hinton went on matter-of-factly. "Grace and Ben had no children. They were mighty fond of Holly Abbott. A poor girl. Her daddy was a tenant farmer. They took her in. Bought her nice clothes. Paid her a good wage. Grace's estate—which was considerable, plus her share of her mothers and father's and Elsie's—passed on to Maggie Bear Claw Burk. Maggie's husband is Tate Burk, a white man. So that leaves all the Bear Claw headrights and three more ranches, in addition to Maggie's, concentrated in Maggie's name. She's one very wealthy Indian."

"Which makes one Tate Burk a red-hot suspect," Sublette snapped.

"Maybe not as hot as he seems," Hinton cautioned. "He and Hank Vail, the big rodeo star and rancher, were attending the Fort Worth Fat Stock Show the night of the explosion. I checked that out. He was with Vail. A perfect alibi."

"That gets back to handling nitro," Poole reasoned. "It had to be a hired job."

"Yet," Hinton replied tonelessly, "Tate Burk posted a five-thousand-dollar reward in the Jordan case."

"Could be a coverup. What's this Tate Burk like?"

"Typical squawman in some ways. Spends a good deal of time playing pool at the Sportsman's Billiards and driving around in Maggie's cars . . . Round-faced fellow. Dresses like a dandy. Not averse to chasing waitresses at Jimmy the Greek's City Cafe. Not a heavy drinker, though. And I understand he takes pretty good care of Maggie's money. Not a lavish spender. Never been in trouble with the law. Is soft-spoken and quiet."

"So is the devil," Poole snorted.

Hinton rested his chin reflectively in the palm of his left hand. "There's another suspect. Name's Rex Enright, a reckless young rancher who owed Ben Jordan six thousand dollars on a cattle deal, so the story goes. They say Enright gambles a lot. Some people figure that's where the six thousand went. Ben Jordan pressed him for payment shortly before the triple murder. They had words on Main Street. . . exchanged some blows. Tate Burk broke it up."

Sam's thoughts were reaching out. "If Maggie died, Tate Burk would get the whole pot."

"There are two children—May, six; Richard, seven. They would figure in the will, of course. Not in a big way until they became of age; meanwhile, the agency would hold their shares of the estate in trust. Regardless, Burk would likely get one third of all the Bear Claw estates and control considerable money and land." Hinton smacked his hands together. "We'll have to follow up every lead, turn over every damned rock in

Osage County and see what's under it—that's what it's gonna take. You fellows know there have been some twenty-odd Osage homicides in the past four years? I tell you this is rough country." His tone changed. "Wasn't time to go into everything at Houston—but the Bureau's on the spot. This is not the first time undercover agents have come into the Osage. Two men came in to help state authorities. Good men—but they didn't know the Southwest well. Something leaked. All of a sudden their informants seemed to develop lockjaw. Everybody and his dog knew our men were federal agents. Entire investigation came to a standstill, and the Bureau pulled the agents out."

"When was that?" Sam asked.

"After the Jordan house was blown up." Hinton began a back-and-forth pacing. "We're operating differently this time. No county or state or even tribal official knows who we are. All the Osage Tribal Council knows is that an investigation has been promised. As I reminded Sam last night, we're strictly on our own. Our orders are clear: Stay until we break this wave of terror."

When no one spoke, Hinton said, "We'd better not rendezvous the same place two times running. Two weeks from tonight we'll meet at the Indian cemetery east of here. How far is it, Sam?"

"About three miles."

"Meanwhile, might be a good idea to take in Hank Vail's Sunday rodeos and horse races. I've seen enough hardcases out there to fill Leavenworth." Hinton went briskly to his car, started the engine, and drove off.

Blue Sublette said, "I'm headin' back for Hominy," and left next.

Sam dallied, wishing to talk, and sensed the same in

Gene Poole.

"Glad to see you again, Gene."

"Same here, ol' podner."

"Been almost three years since we had a good visit. How you been, *hombre?"*

"First-rate. And you?"

"Fine."

"I've bought a little ranch in the Texas hill country," Poole said, his voice taking on a wistfulness. "Before long I aim to quit chasin' badmen and go back to diggin' postholes."

"I'm all for you."

"In fact, I've decided to do that as soon as we wind up here in the Osage. Never figured I could pick up the pieces and start over again. Met a mighty nice girl, Sam. I've been a lone wolf too long. Time I settled down and got to livin' again."

Sam put his hand on Poole's shoulder. "Sure glad to hear it. Good luck to you, Gene."

Poole turned toward his car. "Just wanted you to know. Remember we used to have some good times together." He opened the door and slid in. "See you in two weeks, podner, if not sooner at Vail's. Reckon it's all right to meet at a cemetery as long as we're all on our feet."

CHAPTER 4

THE NEXT MORNING SAM SPENT TWO HOURS SEARCHING over the long, level stretch in the pasture for troublesome rocks, then loosened up his horse, walk, trot, gallop. The morning was typically Osage County for July, hot and dry, although the wind out of the southwest was not unkind, and the sky was a dome of clearest blue. He pulled Slip Along up for a rest. A car passed westward on the dusty road to Red Mound. A red-tailed hawk soared over the woods, suddenly diving, its exulting scream faint and high. To the north he could see miniatures of cattle fattening on bluestem, and the mirrors of stock ponds. The hawk had missed its prey and was high-circling again. Taking in all this, Sam could not but think of last night without unreality and dread of the days ahead. The meeting seemed remote now, unrelated to the immense silence and peace of land and sky.

Toward middle afternoon he drove off the main road, crossed a noisy cattle guard, and followed narrow tracks winding up to John Cloud-Walker's ranch house. It was symbolic of affluent Osages, almost a type: red brick; two stories; the usual cool, broad porch across the front. Although it wasn't visible, Sam would bet there was a summer house in the rear, an open structure covered with boughs; maybe some drying racks for beef. A large American flag hung from the porch. That was not unusual, for the Osages were patriotic people.

At once he noticed departures from the past. A high, stout, hog-tight wire fence enclosed the yard, and the front gate was padlocked. A string of electric lights ringed the porch and ran on around the house.

As Sam shut off the motor, a handsome German shepherd, gray as a timber wolf and much larger, rushed from the porch and out to the gate, barking furiously. Antwine Cloud-Walker, contrary to orders, of course, had smuggled a male and female puppy aboard the homebound transport. This snarling, teeth-baring guard dog with the broad head of a full-grown male must be from that pair.

Sam, unhurriedly, strolled to the gate and spoke in low tones to the dog. Sam was getting nowhere, the dog continuing to bark, when a sturdy Indian man near Sam's age appeared on the porch. He had on a gunbelt.

"Who are you?" he called. "What you want?"

"My name is Sam Colter. I've come to pay my respects to Mr. Cloud-Walker."

"Colter, you say? Sam Colter?"

"That's right."

"You some Pawhuska lawyer or bill collector from the Osage Mercantile? Mr. Cloud-Walker don't owe nobody."

"No, no." Sam felt a stab of impatience. "I said I want to pay my respects." And before he could get out that he had been a friend of Antwine's, the Indian shouted:

"Where you live?"

"Used to live around Red Mound. In Texas now—"

The Indian turned into the house. A minute or so passed. The dog's voice settled to a menacing growl. The Indian came back out. "You said you used to live around Red Mound? Where?"

"West of town. My father was Matt Colter. He raised horses. I was going to tell you that Antwine and I served together in the war." The Indian became motionless. "What division?"

"The 42nd. Rainbow Division."

The Indian listened without changing expression, neither impressed nor unimpressed. He went inside again. A longer wait, and he stood again on the porch, his stolidness informing Sam that he wasn't yet convinced. "What brigade?" he called.

"The 84th."

"What regiment?"

"The 166th Infantry." And expecting more, Sam called, "2nd Battalion, Company C. We were at St.-Mihiel, the Meuse-Argonne—and some other places I could tell you about."

Once more the Indian disappeared. Sam thought he heard voices near the door, though he could see no faces; the interior of the house through the doorway looked dark. About then the Indian reappeared and called sharply, "Bruno—come here—" and the big dog ceased growling, though reluctantly, and padded wolflike to the porch. The Indian pointed downward, a staying command, and the dog rumped down. Striding down the steps and out to the gate, a revolver wobbling on his right hip, the Indian unlocked the gate and swung it open.

"Mr. Cloud-Walker will see you . . . come in," and as Sam entered, the Indian barked, "Wait!" and expertly shook Sam down.

He wouldn't trust me if he knew my .45 was on the floorboard under the seat, Sam thought, *and I wouldn't blame him.*

"Go ahead," the Indian said, and followed Sam closely to the house.

An elderly Indian opened the screen door and waited on the porch, dressed in the old-time Osage way, beaded moccasins, leggings, and loose-fitting, flowered shirt.

He offered his hand, placing relaxed fingers lightly in Sam's palm, a ceremonious handshake, brief, courteous, without pressure. His thin, ash-colored hair hung in two braids. A tall man, heavy, straight, dignified. Sadness grooved the fleshy folds of the bronze face.

"I left Red Mound in 1917," Sam said. "I've just come back. Brought in a short horse. I heard about Antwine. I'm very sorry."

John Cloud-Walker's dark eyes seemed to expand, to reflect new depths. He inclined his head courteously. He spoke, his voice low, yet distinct and heavy. "I remember your father. I bought a sorrel saddle horse from him. It was a good horse. I told him I wanted a gentle horse. He said all his saddle horses were gentle. It was a gentle horse, too . . . We can talk here on the porch. Sit down."

After Sam was seated, Cloud-Walker sat across from him, and the dog rose and lay down at the elder Osage's feet. Cloud-Walker gave the dog an especial smile of understanding. The Indian bodyguard took a chair at Cloud-Walker's right, facing Sam.

"Evil has come to us since you and Antwine and the other young men fought across the great waters," Cloud-Walker said formally. "We live like coyotes hiding in caves, slinking through the brush, afraid to show ourselves, afraid to turn our faces even to Grandfather Sun. We keep brave dogs in our houses. We hire bodyguards. We string lights around our houses so bad white mans cannot sneak in at night and murder us in our beds."

"You have to protect yourself," Sam said gravely.

"It is bad, this thing. The whites call it civilization, I believe. We Osages know it is the white man's bad road. There are many white man's roads leading to what white man wants. The white man is like spider, I believe," and the old man, his fingers closing and his arm retracting, made a luring motion. "If there is good white man's road, I have not seen it. Down this bad road I can see what will happen. Someday there will be no Osages following this bad road. All Osages will be dead because of white man that is bootlegger and sells poison whiskey, and white man lawyer that is guardian and cheats restricted Indian *[Eendin,* he pronounced it, which seemed to soften the word and lend it a musical intonation, the way Sam remembered the full-blood boys saying it], and white man that runs big store and has one price for white man, one price for Indian, and white man that is doctor and sells dope to Indian."

Cloud-Walker paused, in thought, in pain. He said, "I cry for my son, my only son. My heart is on the ground, too heavy to lift. It was not like this when the Osages did not have much money. This evil thing had not come among us. Now Osages have too much money. The Otoes and Pawnees do not have enough. They are poor. But this evil does not surround them. The bad white mans let them alone because they have nothing the white mans want, unless it is land. That young man there is Otoe. He is brave. He fought across great waters like you and Antwine."

"Your son fought in close," Sam said, his tone reminiscent. "Many times he did. Hand-to-hand, with the bayonet. You can be proud of Antwine, Mr. Cloud-Walker. He was brave."

The elder's seamed face softened perceptibly. He rose and entered the house, the dog at his moccasined heels. In a very short time he emerged, bearing in his ritualistic hands, like an offering, it seemed to Sam, a small, heart-shaped pillow of rich blue velvet, pinned thereon a Distinguished Service Cross.

Sam caught his breath.

Cloud-Walker said, “It would have been great honor if my son was killed across great waters. Not murdered here. Sometimes now I think about that.”

The old man extended the pillow, and Sam gazed at the bronze cross and its superimposed spread eagle hanging from the red-and-white-bordered blue ribbon, and the oak-leaf cluster resting there. *For Valor,* it read below the wings of the eagle. Nodding, Sam said, “I know when Antwine got this,” and heard the old voice go on:

“I was proud when my son showed me this honor. Later he asked me to keep it for him. I was proud again. I was not proud when he followed white man’s bad road. When he drank white man’s whiskey and took dope and went to hospital in Red Mound. When he had bad dreams and sweat ran down his body that used to be strong and brave and he was not like my son because of this bad thing inside him.”

Sam was touched, feeling a tremendous respect and sympathy for John Cloud-Walker, who bravely followed the old, straight road of the Osages through the killing frenzy. Sam groped for something comforting he could express, and found himself wordless. He’d never been a fluent speaker. He was better with his hands, he guessed. Uncomfortable in the midst of another’s pain, he considered taking his leave. The thought dominated for a moment. He suppressed it roughly. Hell, he was letting his emotions deter him from his main purpose again, such as when Fay had invited him to the ranch.

The ritual was over. The elder Osage took his treasure back into the house, returned, and sat again, his heavy body creaking the chair, a remembering filling his dark eyes.

Sam put it as considerately as he could. "Mr. Cloud-Walker, do you have any idea who killed your son?," and uncertainly awaited the old man's response. Maybe more naked hurt, maybe the tight silence of fear that Blue Sublette had discovered among the full-bloods.

"If I knew," came the immediate and surprising reply, "I would avenge my son myself. I do not know."

"Did Antwine associate with any particular people?" Sam reproved himself almost as be finished. Damned if he didn't sound as if he were interrogating a prisoner. "Who were his friends?" he amended.

"Anybody who had whiskey," Cloud-Walker replied, pained. He shut his eyes.

"Can you think of any person who had reason to take Antwine's life?" Sam asked, recalling the suspect, Billy Gault. "Anyone who stood to profit?"

"I do not believe that white man in Red Mound who works at Osage Mercantile and who was running around with my son's wife killed my son."

"Why do you believe that?" Sam asked gently, hating to punish the old man further.

Cloud-Walker straightened, his head high. "My son wore two big diamond rings. The diamonds were missing when they found him. He was killed for his diamonds—not for his woman." The old man's eyes glowed, a proud expression that said Antwine as an Indian could not have lost his Indian wife to a mere white man.

"It seems to me," Sam began and faltered. "I mean . . . I wonder why the Osages haven't organized an Indian police unit? It could work under the agency officer. County officials shouldn't mind. They haven't solved anything."

"We are too scattered. We no longer live in bands. We are helpless. That was first thing white mans wanted: Break up the bands. Break our power. Allot our land. We are helpless."

"Not as helpless as you think," Sam insisted, his indignation coming through.

But the old man shook his head. "The drum beats, but there are no warriors. They are rubbed out, like my son. Old men, like me, can only hide."

Sam held his silence, sensing that the elder would continue after a while. The guardian dog stirred and rested its fine head between broad paws, its ears flicking now and then. A grass-scented breeze rose. The American flag trembled like a leaf. Presently, Cloud-Walker spoke:

"When Osages moved to this place, White Father promised to protect us in our new homes. He promised white mans would not cheat-us or kill us. He promised white mans would not be allowed on our reservation. His tongue was not straight. Many white mans came. White mans blew up that house in Red Mound . . . killed ever'body, even two whites." His right hand described a chopping motion. "Why these bad things? My friend, it is because Osages have something mean white mans want. Always it is like that. That is why my son was killed. That is why other Osages have been killed. My heart is heavy and cold. Hate is evil, I believe, but my heart is full of hate. White Father has lied to us, his Osage friends. Osages never went to war against White Father. We never fought pony soldiers long time ago. We have gone to Washin'ton and asked White Father for help, and he said he would send us help, but still these mean white mans rob us and kill us."

"It could be the federal government has men here

now," Sam encouraged him. "They would have to gather evidence to try these bad white men in court. They would have to work in secret to get that evidence. That would take time."

The deep, dark eyes glinted. "If White Father has sent men here, why was my son killed few months ago? Why are Osages still robbed? Why does Washin'ton let white man lawyer that is guardian still cheat Indian?"

"I understand how you feel. It is bad. At the same time, if an Osage knows who the killers are, or has any evidence, he ought to tell White Father."

"Some white man would kill that Indian."

"Not if the Indian told the right people."

"Ah, you did not say have talk with county or state white mans officers."

Cloud-Walker's eyes were so piercing that Sam questioned whether he was letting go too much. He framed his reply carefully. "The thing to do would be to drive to Oklahoma City. There's an FBI office there in the Federal Building. Some Indian who knows who blew up the house could go there to talk to the FBI."

"That Indian would be killed somehow."

"Not if he didn't tell anybody he was going to Oklahoma City."

"I do not know about this thing, this house."

Sam saw it then for the first time, in the farthest reaches of the dark eyes, the flare of fear, momentary but nevertheless real. Sam left the subject, hoping that Cloud-Walker might talk around the edges of the Jordan case. Talk from the suspicions of an Indian. Why anyone would want the Jordans and young Holly Abbott dead.

Instead, the elder Osage was silent so long that Sam feared he had offended him. After a while, Cloud-

Walker seemed to call his thoughts from far away, seemed to struggle within himself, seemed to come face to face with something he desperately wished, yet also dreaded, because he would relive his grief. A near-pathetic wistfulness removed all confusion from his intent face.

"Tell me," he said, "about my son when he was a warrior."

Sam sat motionless, deeply moved to understanding. Antwine's war record was the one phase of his only son's tragic life that his father could look back on with pride and honor; it helped sustain him.

And so, while his listener hung on every word (never interrupting, for an Indian of the courteous old ways did not break in when another was speaking), Sam began talking. He reached for what he thought a father would want to hear about his son, and need to hear. Not the getting drunk they all did on French wine, the infrequent times they could find any, not the French whorehouses they found, especially the one called Fifi's Palace of Love, and when a C Company platoon wrecked the place one night. And as Sam talked he realized that he was pushing aside and leaving out the real horror of the war: the ever-present smell of death; the cries of the men you couldn't reach; the broken bodies of doughboys strewing the tan wheat fields and shattered woods; German and American dead in the same machine-gun nests; the German gas barrages and the deadly vapors hanging low over the pocked earth, a victim turning ghastly green, frothing at the mouth, and passing out; the bone-chilling rain, the sea of mud, and the awful fear that balled up your guts.

No—not that. He preferred to tell about funny incidents and, for the sake of a grieving old man, about the bravery he had witnessed many times, and the songs the doughboys sang marching up to the front, songs like "Smile, Smile, Smile," and "Mademoiselle from Armentières," and "K-K-K-Katy." And outwitting MP's and stealing chickens, and about the cooties that could walk off with a sweater, and how damned good a cigarette always tasted, and what a letter from home meant.

In spirit he took full-blood John Cloud-Walker overseas with Rainbow replacements in March of 1918, and serving with French units, and into the Baccarat sector. French names, not spoken for years, rolled readily off Sam's tongue: Souain, Camp de Chalons, Experance, Epieds . . . "The French would be amused when Antwine and the other Indian boys talked Osage. The Frogs thought they were putting on . . . One time the Osage boys used a big tin can for a drum and did a war dance for the French. Threw in a lot of extra whoops and yelps and stomps. I remember Antwine told a French major who spoke English that there was considerable French blood in the Osage tribe. Antwine told him the French blood made the Osages wild. That major smiled. I think he was flattered. After four years of war, the French didn't have much to smile about."

Sam said the 42nd Division saw action near Suippes in July, when the Germans tried to widen the Marne salient, and near the Ourcq River, after the Yanks crossed the Marne and the enemy pulled back.

He described St.-Mihiel. How the salient, seized by the Germans in the first weeks of the war, was like a giant thumb jammed into the side of France. How the Americans, eager to prove further they were first-class fighting men, wanted a Luger pistol or a pair of Zeiss binoculars. How early one morning in the black of a furious rainstorm the Osage County boys heard the St.-Mihiel bombardment commence.

"At daylight we went over the top. I was too scared to yell. Our division was on the south side—between the 1st and the 89th . . . There weren't many Germans left in the first-line trenches. We walked over or cut the barbed wire. But resistance was stiffer in the second and third lines."

Sam told how the Rainbows took four villages. How squads and platoons of Germans surrendered. "Their morale was low. They'd been told the U-boats would sink all ships carrying American troops to France. We got pretty cocky after that. What we didn't know was that the St.-Mihiel was just a warm-up for the Meuse-Argonne offensive in late September."

Sam had never talked so much about the war. Bits and pieces of experiences spilled out of him; some he had forgotten until now. Cloud-Walker's face was as engrossed as a small boy's. The Otoe drew his chair closer and nodded now and again. He said he was with the 36th, the Lone Star Division.

Going on, Sam told how gloomy and forbidding the tangled woods looked, and the rough hills veined with ravines. Machine-gun nests everywhere. Belts of barbed wire. He told about networks of trenches, dugouts, concrete bunkers, and about taking them yard by yard. And about the deadly German artillery, which seemed to have every road and gully plotted. About just before an attack some boys opened khaki-backed Bibles and turned to the Ninety-first Psalm, especially the seventh verse, which Sam recited: " 'A thousand shall fall at thy side, and ten thousand at thy right hand; but it shall not come nigh thee.' "

He paused, then continued, seeing Cloud-Walker's

heightened expectation. "None of us expected to come out of the Meuse-Argonne alive. All through there the Heinies had their heavy machine guns echeloned . . . By echeloned, I mean they had the traverse pins of each gun set so the gunner could swivel about and cover his neighbor. Our guys would overrun a nest, bayonet the last surviving gunner, only to get killed in turn by another Spandau. Those Spandaus lead a wicked chatter I'll never forget.

"Most of us Red Mound boys were in the second platoon, I remember. And I remember when Antwine got his DSC. It was around a place they called the Musarde farm. M-u-s-a-r-d-e-Musarde—you never hear of it now; but for a few days that was the only and most important place we knew, because we had to take it. We did, and it cost a lot of boys.

"As usual, Heinie machine gunners were holding up our advance. A squad in charge of an acting corporal was ordered to outflank five Spandaus. They crawled around through the underbrush"—Sam drew a half circle with his right hand—"but before they could work around close, the Heinies spotted 'em, pinned 'em down-every man wounded but Antwine and the acting corporal. They didn't dare move, so every man played dead. Now and then the nearest Spandau gunner fired a burst that way.

"About an hour passed. Maybe the Spandau crew figured all the Yanks were dead, because the Spandau was firing the other way now. I mean toward our front. When Antwine and the acting corporal saw that, they jumped up and charged. The acting corporal took a stray bullet in the leg and went down. Antwine shot and bayoneted the gun crew, grabbed the spade handles of the Spandau, and turned it on the other machine-gun positions. Every time a Heinie gunner tried to swing his gun around, Antwine would fire a burst. Pretty soon the Heinies started surrendering . . . Antwine brought back all the wounded and twenty-some prisoners. There was a big ceremony later. A general pinned the cross on Antwine, and he was made sergeant . . . Ted Iron Shirt and Charlie Small Bull used to laugh. Said they put on such convincing acts, playing dead, they deserved medals, too."

Sam sighed and sat upright, surprised at his eloquence, surprised to see that the afternoon had worn away. The scene still burned before him, the figures like live images. His eyes were wet, his throat dry. He felt depressed.

Cloud-Walker sat gripped in his own personal silence for a long while; his mind likewise seemed far away. But somehow his broad face looked relieved, Sam thought, and not so sad. Now Cloud-Walker's heavy-lidded eyes brightened. He was proud. He looked inquiringly at Sam and asked:

"This man who took stray bullet in leg, this acting corporal man? Was he Red Mound boy, too?"

Sam nodded. "Was he Osage?"

"No, Sir. He was white."

"Who was this man?"

"Me—I saw it all. That's why I can tell you what Antwine did that day. I had a front-row seat."

Cloud-Walker's intense eyes played an even stronger interest on Sam, and after a moment or two Sam heard him say, "You will eat with us." Rising, trailed by the great dog, John Cloud-Walker shuffled softly into the silent house, his heart at ease.

Early darkness screened the conical hills when the elder Osage and the faithful dog accompanied Sam to his car. "My friend," the old man said, "your talk has made my heart glad again. My son did not tell me this thing." Ceremoniously, he presented Sam a blanket. "You were all brave," he said, and turned back through the gate. Sam heard the padlock snap.

Driving to the main road, Sam stopped. Some sense prompted him to look behind him. Already the lights blinked eerily, ringing the house. He swore under his breath, incensed that an old man, grieving and broken, had to live in fear.

CHAPTER 5

EARLY SUNDAY AFTERNOON, LEAVING HIS HORSE behind, Sam Colter drove to Red Mound and took the north road into the bulging hills toward Hank Vail's ranch. Every aspect of the case pointed to a drawn-out investigation. Likely he would have all the time in the world to match some races.

He reflected on Fay Vail's invitation. Why should he be nervous? He was, just a little, and that irritated him, as well as his pulling back, his shying away from seeing her again, when by accepting he couldn't ask for a more opportune chance to sniff the wind of the frenzy in the vicinity of Red Mound.

All at once a car whipped by him, and he was eating dust. From there until he came to the turnoff to Vail's, he drove in a brown fog. Turning in, he saw on the archway over the cattle guard: HANK VAIL'S FORKED LIGHTNING RANCH. He crossed the cattle guard and followed a graveled road across continuous bluestem pasture dotted with fat whitefaces.

He drove to the brow of a rounded hill and looked

across and felt an intake of surprise. He had expected a large spread, but hardly such impressive improvements. Where the frame ranch house that he remembered used to stand, a fortress of brown sandstone dominated the far slope. On the broad flat below the house clustered a maze of rodeo pens and chutes and a fenced arena, including an open wooden grandstand that could seat several hundred persons; farther on, a straightaway track extended six hundred yards or more, flanked by a smaller wooden grandstand. Directly below the great house spread Vail's horse-breeding operations that Fargo Young had mentioned—a massive tin-roofed hay barn and satellite smaller barns and corrals; beyond them lush pastures holding brood mares and foals and other horses. Buildings and fences a glittering white. Like Kentucky, Sam thought, noting the proud stallions pacing their private paddocks, alert to the passage of cars and horse trailers. Down the slope next to the road, where incoming visitors could not miss them, grazed a scattering of buffalo.

Sam parked behind the rodeo stands, hearing in the distance the shouts of riders driving up calves for the roping, and strayed on to the track, drawn there irresistibly, curiously, impressed. No brush track, this. Here the grass was trimmed as short as a mowing machine could cut. There was evidence of careful grading where the land dipped slightly. The two hard-beaten lanes looked fast.

Sam moseyed back to the rodeo stands and waited for the roping to start, sitting in the hub of an audience of good-humored ranch families, Indians, squawmen, cowboys, and the inevitable sprinkling of oil field workers off from wresting black gold from the Osage fields. An old white man was busy selling red soda pop to Indian kids out of an iced washtub. Parked cars filled the open side and end of the arena.

Listening, observing, Sam had the frustration again of stumbling through deep shadows, of reaching out blindly. And he thought: Probably somewhere in this crowd is the man or men who murdered Elsie Bear Claw in the canyon, and the ones who blew up the Jordan house, and the killer of Antwine.

He noticed Fay Vail speaking to a heavy full-blood woman and knew that, unconsciously, he had been looking for Fay. His attention lingered on her. She was constantly turning her head as someone spoke to her or waved. She seemed to know almost everyone.

He looked away when the announcer bellowed through a megaphone at the timers' stand near the chutes, "Good afternoon, folks. Welcome to the Hank Vail Ranch. Hank says EN-JOY YOURSELVES!" Applause rippled across the stands. A cowboy stood up near Sam, clapping vigorously. At that impetus others began standing. As if pulled on a string, the entire crowd was soon up and applauding.

Sam stood with them, thinking how people were like sheep, quick to follow the leader. When the applause ebbed, the announcer bellowed, "Remember, folks, you're welcome to stroll over to the barns and take a gander at some of the finest horseflesh in the whole country. The mighty Tomahawk is over there—still unbeaten. Be some match races after the rodeo events . . . We're gonna rope 49 calves and ride some sure-'nough mean bulls . . . Catchin' the time is Mr. Tate Burk and Mr. Scotty Hinton of Red Mound."

Sam felt himself grinning. Scotty was about as close to the action as he could get without swinging a rope.

"First roper up," the anticipatory voice boomed, "is

Rex Enright . . . from out west of Red Mound. Get ready, Rex!"

Sam tensed. Enright was the top suspect so far in the three-murder Jordan case. Maybe so. But he wasn't hiding his face. Sam looked toward the chutes.

The crowd hushed. Enright waited behind the barrier string on a blocky buckskin. Hatless, black hair swept straight back, he looked competent and reckless. He clamped the pigging string between his teeth and built a small loop with his rope and held it high, close to his right ear. He slouched in the saddle, sure of himself and his horse. He nodded to the gateman that he was ready.

As the gate swung open, a whiteface calf broke for the open arena. The flagman's hand dropped when the calf crossed the line, and Enright spurred his horse, which bounded like a short horse, breaking the barrier.

Sam followed the race, automatically watching the flying buckskin. It was taking Enright up fast. Suddenly the daylight between calf and horse shortened. But as the rider started to cast his loop, the nimble calf cut sharply to the right. The horse seemed to sense the move and closed in. Now was the moment.

Enright threw his loop. It dropped over the calf's head and down its neck. Enright jerked the rope, and the buckskin dug in, hindquarters low. The calf hit the end of the rope, bawling and struggling. By this time Enright was out of the saddle and running down the rope to the calf. Grabbing a foreleg and flank, he flopped the calf on its side and tore the pigging string from his mouth and slipped its loop over the front leg. Bringing the hind legs across, he wrapped and tied and leaped to his feet, hands high. It was done.

Fast, Sam knew. Enright should be in the money, at least. That cut the calf made had cost him a second or two, but his horse had done all a good horse could do.

Enright loafed back to his horse, which had held the rope taut from the moment the rider had run toward the calf. Enright stepped lightly into the low-cantle saddle and sat there, slouched, waiting for an arena helper to untie the calf. When that was done, he turned for the chutes, past the crowd, slowly gathering in his rope, while the still-eager buckskin tossed its head and danced.

"Here's the time, folks," boomed the announcer. "Thirteen seconds flat for Rex Enright!" Car horns hooted approval, and the crowd applauded.

As the afternoon drew on and there came a lull, Sam left to mingle with the crowd milling between the stands and the chutes. Gene Poole and a cowman were chinning, around them a little circle of listeners. Sam saw Poole raise his eyes and rest them on him for a moment, not pausing in the story he was telling:

"I heard tell this happened out in New Mexico. Seems a fussy, overdressed eastern dude was at the bar. Been in there some time, complainin' about this and that. Kept sayin' he wanted a clean glass . . . Just then four young punchers, in town to whoop it up, rode their horses right into the saloon. One of the horses happened to bump the dude, who turned to the barkeep and complained again. 'Bartender,' he said in outrage, 'evict these ruffians.'

"Now, what the dude didn't know was that the barkeep was an old-time cowpuncher, too stove up to ride for an outfit anymore. Besides, the barkeep had all he could take from a finicky outsider. He glared at the dude and growled, 'What the hell you doin' in here afoot anyhow?' "

The cowman exploded with laughter and whacked

Poole across the shoulders, and the other listeners guffawed. Sam, walking on, decided Gene Poole was making fast headway.

Sam's mind kept wandering to Fay Vail while he watched the bull riders and a ubiquitous rodeo clown, his long face painted mournful dabbings of red and white. When a bull turned on its pitched-off rider, the clown would dash in and wave his floppy hat and make faces at the bull and throw out his chest and snap his suspenders, and, when the bull invariably gave brief chase, streak nimbly for the fence while the crowd ooohed.

"That's the last event of the afternoon, folks," sounded the announcer. "There's time to pay Tomahawk a visit before the match races start."

Sam set off for the horse barns. Passing a red Buick sedan drawn up to the arena fence, and hearing hearty, familiar laughter, he glanced that way and saw Blue Sublette and an Indian family. So Blue had made ground since the meeting.

Onlookers were lining Tomahawk's white-painted paddock when Sam arrived. Tomahawk's name was written in gold letters on his private barn. Sam stepped to the fence.

A handler was leading a handsome chestnut sorrel stallion around the paddock.

"Nothin' like a free rodeo to build up the fee business," drawled a crotchety voice in Sam's ear. "Take your choice—speed, saddle, or ropin' studs, at your service."

Sam met Fargo Young's friendly eyes. "Good-looking stud," Sam said.

"That he is—an' strung as tight as a fiddler's string."

"He's young."

"Just little past four."

"The announcer said he's unbeaten."

"Around here he is," Fargo said, jaws working, loosing a stream of amber at a milk weed.

"Meaning—?"

Fargo glanced left and right before he answered, his voice lowered. "Vail's mighty choosy what he matches. Mostly local horses. He guards that record like an old hen watches her nest."

"Any outside matches against top horses?"

"A few."

"Can the horse run?"

"Oh, yes. And I don't mind some brags—long as they're accurate. For instance, Vail claims his horse has run the quarter in twenty-three flat. Well, I timed the race that day myself. Had a pretty fair Tulsa stud in here. I caught Tomahawk in twenty-four and three fifths. That ain't twenty-three flat. One of Vail's ranch hands was holdin' the other watch."

"Either time is flyin' from a flat-footed start," Sam said. "Some fellows prefer three watches, taking the slowest time." He grinned knowingly. "If it's not your horse, which has just run like a bat out of Carlsbad." He regarded Tomahawk intently, admiring his conformation. "Wonder what his breeding is?"

"Vail claims he's by an English stud in Virginia—sort of imported," Fargo sniffed, showing a pained face. "Makes a horse sound more mysterious, more valuable. You know how people are. If something's from a long ways off, it's always better—they think." Fargo doused another milk weed. "One of Vail's hands spilled the milk one day, though. Tomahawk's imported, all right. Right out of Illinois. His daddy was Ridge Runner."

"That won't hurt him. Ridge Runner's a boss hoss."

"Then why don't Vail say so? But he ain't *imported*—that's the point. Who gives a damn so long as a horse can run?"

Sam cocked an eye at Fargo. "I take it you're not extra high on Mr. Vail."

Fargo squinched his mouth.

"Didn't you tell me you used to start races out here?" Sam asked him.

More onlookers crowded up to the fence, and Fargo, his voice an undertone, said, "Let's go down to the track." Free of the crowd, he said, "Now I can talk. Sure, I started for Vail till I got the bugle call, loud and clear, that I was expected to give Vail's horses the edge . . . Never saw a man that hated to get beat like Hank Vail. He takes it as a personal insult . . . He's got a couple of other sprinters he runs besides Tomahawk—Plunger and Osage Chief. Plunger's a good horse, but he can't quite cut the mustard against Tomahawk. There's Thoroughbred blood in all three horses. That's why Vail likes to go for distance."

By the time they had walked to the stands, two horses were being readied for the first race. "That bay yonder is Miss Whizzbang, Art Cook's three-year-old," Fargo explained. "She's comin' along. By Bullet, a Flint Hills stud, out of a Mexican mare. Don't know about that palomino gelding. I told Art you got a good horse. He might want to run you."

"Why are most short-horse men prejudiced against golden palominos? Even my father was."

Perceptibly pleased to be asked his opinion, Fargo bit off a sizable chew and rotated it reflectively. "They think a palomino is just a show horse. A picture-book horse. They favor the old colors—the solid bays, the sorrels, the browns, the blacks—because that's what they're used to. Color don't make a horse slow or give him less heart, no more than it makes him fast or gives him courage. It's the bloodline that counts, and conformation. Now, my favorite color is a bright-red bay with a star on his forehead. That's the best," he said, winking. "Wouldn't have any other horse."

Slowly, the handlers led the horses past the stands to the starting line. There was a flurry of excitement as the last of the straggling crowd from the barns scrambled for seats. The announcer raised his megaphone:

"First match of the afternoon features Miss Whizzbang, owned by Mr. Art Cook of Burbank, and Gold Dust, owned by Mr. Bill Willis of Ponca City . . . They'll go 220 yards . . . Ready to catch the time at the finish line? We're gonna let 'em go in just a jiffy."

The starter gave instructions to the jockeys, who rode back a short way and reined about, walking their horses toward the starting line. If they reached it together, lapped, the starter would drop his hand and shout "Go!" But Miss Whizzbang, eager to be away, lunged ahead too soon, and the starter waved them back. Next time Gold Dust acted up.

They approached the line again.

Suddenly, the starter dropped his hand. Gold Dust jumped into the lead, breaking fast. He owned a length of daylight at 100 yards, then drifted left.

Miss Whizzbang, coming straight on, closed the length and opened daylight of her own. Gold Dust's jockey had him straightened out by now, but the filly was flying.

It was over in the blink of an eye. Miss Whizzbang by a length. Fargo shook his head. "That palomino's a fast breaker. If he'd run straight, he'd won. Wonder what made him drift out?"

"Thought I saw the jock hit him right-handed. Maybe that made him bear out. When a horse is out front like that, going straight, I say let him do it on his own. Then, again, maybe he needs a tap to hold it. You can't go by the book."

The timer, holding his stopwatch, hustled up to the announcer, who called through the megaphone to the crowd, "Miss Whizzbang's the winner in 14 $^{2}/_{5}$."

"That's traveling," Sam remarked. He and Fargo watched two more short races, which completed the afternoon's program. The crowd was breaking up, some making for the house on the hill, when Fargo said, "I see Art Cook's still down there. Still showin' off his pretty filly. Like to meet him?"

"You bet!"

Cook, a grinning, buck-toothed man of stringbean proportions, was yet flushed from Miss Whiizzbang's victory. He had a cooling blanket on his speedy three-year-old, and he held her halter rope and rubbed her white nose, while he shot the breeze.

"I figure she can do a lot better than she showed today," he said. "She got off slow. Gonna have to work on the break. No reason why she can't chop the time down to thirteen or under." Someone whistled at that, which would be around record time, Sam recalled, but Cook went on talking, unabashed. "She's run seven times this year. Taken six firsts and one second. Run second over to Newkirk on a muddy track, when she got bumped at the break. I calculate she can hold her own with just about anything around here."

"Aim to match her against Tomahawk one of these days?" a man asked, his tone sly.

"Hell's fire," Cook retorted, "she's ready right now—at 220. That's her best distance. Only Vail likes to go longer, and somehow he always seems to have just a little more foldin' money to put up than an ol' brush racer like myself." He rubbed Miss Whizzbang's nose again.

That evoked grins. Sam could understand. Cook wasn't about to race Tomahawk, secure in the knowledge that he could brag about his horse against less swift competition at the shorter distance, besides guarding his pocketbook.

When the horse talk wore down and the little group faded away, Fargo introduced Sam. "This is the fella I'se tellin' you about, Art."

"Glad to make your acquaintance," Cook said, interested, as he shook hands. "So you got a runnin' horse?"

"Seven-year-old gelding. Brought him up from Texas."

"You fetched him that far, he must have a lot of run left in him."

"He's consistent."

"Think maybe he can outrun this little lady?"

"Maybe."

Eagerness, tempered with caution, whetted Cook's eyes. "About how much you figure on bettin'?"

"Not much. I'll run you 350 yards for 25 dollars."

"Hell, I wouldn't sling a saddle on my horse for that."

"How much would you saddle up for?"

"All depends. Want to see your horse first."

"Sure. Come by Fargo's place east of Red Mound."

"Tuesday morning all right? Say around nine o'clock or so?"

"Fine with me."

"I'll be there. Glad to make your acquaintance."

CHAPTER 6

CLIMBING THE STEPS TO THE GREAT SANDSTONE HOUSE, Sam had the distinct incongruity of ascending a citadel on guard over the broad flat and its plethora of land and animals. He noted a Spanish effect to the structure, the flat roof and heavy beams projecting at the corners; yet the windows were mere slits, more like the loopholes of a frontier post, and there was no courtyard entrance. His initial impression returned: a fortress. Built by a man hungry for wealth and power, and, having obtained such, determined not only to hold what he possessed, but also to expand his holdings.

The front door was open. Through it rolled the chatter of goodtime voices and a fiddler's lively cowboy tune.

Sam entered a long hallway, which led to an inner courtyard. There he saw the guests gathered. He took off his hat, and as he paused, looking for a face he knew, a figure left the nearest group and crossed to him.

Fay Vail, being the attentive hostess. Fay, dressed in a cowgirl outfit: tight-fitting light blue blouse and darker blue skirt that hugged her slim hips. Beautiful tan boots. Rings glittered on her left hand. Her careful makeup accented the bold contours of her wellshaped face and the gray-green of her eyes. She showed surprise and open pleasure.

"Sam," she exclaimed, taking his arm, "I was afraid you wouldn't come."

"Wild horses couldn't keep me away."

"What do you think of the place . . . of everything?" She seemed to await his approval.

"Quite a little spread," he said, smiling behind his understatement

"See the rodeo?"

"I took in the works. Saw all the races. Nice track."

He became aware that she was looking steadily into his eye, deeply so not glancing away. A look that made him uncomfortable Then she took his hat and hung it on an elkhorn rack at the end of the hallway and canted her head. "The bar's over there. Corn whiskey, beer, even red soda pop. But first I want you to meet Hank. He's here somewhere. You can tell him about your horse."

"From what I've seen this afternoon, especially of Tomahawk, maybe I'd better keep still."

Her face underwent one of those subtle and unexpected changes of mood that he remembered, an arresting expression that held his attention. She seemed to shut out the noise of the crowd and the music, to segregate the two of them. Her eyes seemed to grow large and more intent. "Still staying in Red Mound, Sam?"

He didn't want to tell her where, but he saw that he had to. He shook his head. "Found a place where I bunk and keep my horse."

She pursed her lips, an attitude of guessing, which was altogether attractive, and he saw that she did not intend to let him escape s easily. "Let's see. . ."

"It's Fargo Young's place east of town," he said, caught.

"Isn't that this side of John Cloud-Walker's ranch? On the south side of the road? There's a winding creek and woods?"

"That's it."

A rising animation pinked her face, and it flashed back to him even before she said, "We went on a school picnic there once. You took me. I remember how scarlet and gold the leaves had turned What a good time everyone had. Funny that I'd remember that."

Sam shrugged. "I always say remember the good times. Try to forget the bad ones." He was looking across the courtyard, and he discovered Scotty Hinton chinning with a cowboy who was feeling no pain, weaving a little as he talked. The fiddle player stopped and wiped his brow and received an uproarious hand. Somebody hustled him a drink from the bar.

"There's Hank now."

Sam saw Vail come to the edge of the courtyard and pause, arms folded, head high like a stag, much the same as he had descended from the train that afternoon in Red Mound, his high-bridged nose adding a tilt to his tanned, strong-featured face, his deep-set eyes restless. A flamboyantly dressed man—rainbow-colored shirt, tailored twill riding pants tucked inside the glossy, steer-head boots, purple silk scarf at his throat. The perfect picture of the movie cowboy, Sam acknowledged, with one distinctive difference: This man performed to perfection all the feats of the working cowboy. An athlete on horseback. Hank Vail was no cardboard figure parading behind a colorful getup. His flamboyance became him. He was what he was. You had to admire the man.

A cowboy weaved up to Vail and muttered something and offered his hand. Vail took it, tolerating the man, and said loudly, "Take it easy, Tug," and frowned when the cowboy headed for the bar, where a young white man in rodeo garb served the guests. A townsman came over to Vail and spoke, and kept nodding as Vail talked. Sam discerned the same element in these greetings. Each man deferred excessively to the host. Hank Vail was king.

Sam moved beside Fay across the courtyard, and as

she introduced them, Sam read some of the same deference in her. "Sam and I went to school together. He's just brought a short horse up from Texas. But I'll let him tell you how fast he is," she said, leaving them.

"Howdy, cowboy," Vail greeted him, shaking hands. His grip was strong.

"Saw your horse Tomahawk today," Sam said, "and I doubt if my old gelding can run with him. Aim to match him in a few weeks. Talked to Art Cook. He's interested."

Vail nodded approval. "Art's got a good little filly at the shorter distances. So you saw Tomahawk?"

"Had to elbow my way in to get a look."

Vail smiled. "What do you think of him?"

"Perfect conformation."

"I see your eye is true. Furthermore, Tomahawk has the capacity and ability to pass on his looks and speed. I'm seeing that now in his first crop of foals. I've bred him a little early but lightly, only to topline mares." Vail shifted his arms, head up in that characteristic poise. He struck Sam as a man totally in charge of himself. Vail said, "There's not a horse in Oklahoma that Tomahawk can't outrun. He's run the quarter in twenty-three flat."

"That's splittin' the breeze right smartly," Sam agreed, Fargo's story about the time coming to mind, and thinking that was also pretty strong gas about having the fastest horse in Oklahoma. Still, you couldn't criticize a man for puffing up his horse when he had a good one, for that was part of the enjoyment of racing, the give-and-take talk. Old Baldy, in Sam's boyish pride, had been *the* fastest and greatest horse in the whole country. Over the entrance of the stallion's quarters, which was no more than a shed, Sam had painted: OLD BALDY CHALLENGES THE WORLD—BAR

NONE.

"Some of the boys complain about my breeding fees," Vail went on. "I won't come down. This operation won't run on brush-track change. You have to pay for quality."

"I'm with you there," Sam said, and wondered if he didn't sound too agreeable.

A ranch hand walked over questioningly to Vail, who told Sam, "Make yourself at home, cowboy." Sam thanked him and made his way to the bar. His bottle of beer turned out to be home brew, thick and malt-flavored. Not bad.

The fiddler struck up a fast tune. A cowboy whooped and cut a quick jig, the heels of his boots beating a staccato. Scotty Hinton was conversing with the townsman who had spoken to Vail. Not far away raconteur Gene Poole was telling another story, throwing in gestures and grimaces. Fay Vail hurried to the hallway to greet more guests, her hip-swinging, slim-legged walk across the courtyard drawing the cowboys' eyes. By far, Sam saw, the best-looking woman here.

He heard her greet a couple and introduce them around as "Billy and Nora Gault." Sam shifted for a clear view as the crowd continued to grow and the fiddler played faster and everybody seemed to be talking at once.

Billy and Nora Gault, drinks in hand, sat apart to themselves, trying not to appear ill at ease. Gault looked about twenty-five, his wife four or five years older, close to Antwine's age. A full-blood woman, not yet too heavy. A woman of unusual, natural beauty, a somewhat oval face, a proud face, made striking by her bronze Osage coloring, her full, sensuous mouth and charcoal eyes, her crow-black hair drawn back and massed high on the back of her head.

She's not hiding, Sam decided. They've both come here to show they're not afraid of public opinion. Trouble is, when your track record is bad and everybody knows about you in a little burg like Red Mound, you're immediately suspect when something goes wrong, such as murder.

The cowboy whom Vail had called Tug crossed between Sam and the Gaults. There was nothing extraordinary about him. He was about thirty-five and full-faced, and his sloping shoulders made him look heavier than he was. He fancied a full mustache, and his yellow hair hung low on his neck, remindful of a Wild West show rider, and his colorful dress, complete to red neck scarf, was imitative of Vail. Sam wouldn't have noticed him particularly if not for the aggressive thrust of his face and his eyes, which were pale and quarrelsome, and his manner, which was arrogant, and his strange sort of twisted grin.

Something plucked at Sam's memory, a going back. He had seen the man before. He knew he had. Where, he had no idea. He didn't fit into Sam's recollection of Red Mound people. So where? The Army? Somewhere in Texas?

Fay Vail came up to Sam at that moment. "Don't run off. I want to show you Hank's trophy room. Promise?"

"I'll be here," Sam said. How like a child she still was, eager to draw attention to some newly acquired prize.

She was off again, swishing across to greet more arriving guests. A white man and an Indian woman.

Sam let his eyes travel back to the Gaults. Gault was a sharp dresser for Red Mound. Double-breasted tan suit. White shirt and striped tie. Sensitive eyes set in a square, clean-cut, boyish face. Curly brown hair cut short.

The Gaults sat close together, their hands touching, like two outcasts banished to a faraway land, each drawing on the other for understanding and strength.

As Sam studied them, not without sympathy, he hoped they hadn't killed Antwine. He saw how young Billy could be attracted to a sensuous, lonely woman older than himself, therefore much wiser than he, and she to him because of an alcoholic husband doomed to die by drink or violence. Yet, together, they could make murder.

Sam's bottle was empty. He sat it beside his chair and worked out of the noisy throng.

"I wondered how long you intended to nurse that bottle of brew," Fay Vail said, stepping in front of him. So she had been watching him. "Here's the trophy room," she said. Unknowingly, he had gravitated toward it.

They passed other couples coming out. Sam expected to find more guests inside, but when he entered the vast room, there was no one but Fay and himself.

"Look," she said, waving a graceful hand.

He raised his eyes. The image of a great feudal hall leaped to his mind. Trophies lined the stone walls. Heads of bighorn sheep, bear, elk, buffalo, deer, antelope. And hide shields, lances, war clubs, tomahawks, feathered headdresses. Bear and buffalo skins on the polished floor. Two Winchester rifles crossed barrels above the mantle of the cavernous fireplace.

"That's a Kodiak bear there," she said impressively. "Hank is quite a hunter."

"Guns, horses, cattle, land . . ."

Her emphasis pulled his eyes toward her, but she was gazing down, saying, "This tile came from Italy. Hank even brought in Italian artisans. He likes the best."

A walnut gun cabinet attracted his attention. A regular arsenal, he saw. He walked to it, seeing handguns, shotguns, and several telescopic rifles.

Sam turned his head. Fay stood beside him. She was looking at him instead of the gun cabinet. "I'm glad you came, Sam."

"Good chance to get acquainted again. I feel like a stranger."

"You ought not."

He saw her glance swiftly toward the doorway, and was unprepared when, suddenly, she kissed him on the mouth and drew back and glanced again at the doorway.

"I had to do that," she said, coloring. "Welcome home."

"Best way I know to get a man shot." He discovered that he was angry.

"No one saw."

"I never liked to cross another man's fence line."

"Maybe you're not."

He sensed again what he had at the hotel, her discontent, her appealing need and openness, and without warning he felt his own loneliness. He said, "We can't bring back 1917. We're not the same people. We're grown up."

"You mean we never meant anything to each other?"

"We did then, I thought."

She had a rebuffed expression. "Did you come back just to race your horse?"

Sam heard voices. Relieved, he turned to leave, Fay with him. A couple entered. Fay spoke a cheery greeting.

As they left the trophy room, the cowboy called Tug pushed through the crowd and over to Fay. "Hank wants to know 'bout the barbecue." His voice was thick. His bold eyes prowled her face, her body.

"Tell him everything's ready."

The man flung Sam a cursory look and reeled away. Several steps and he wheeled and dug Sam another look, a much longer look, a stabbing scrutiny, and went on.

"Who is that?" Sam asked her.

"Tug Lay. Works for Hank. I don't like him. He's rude. He makes me feel naked."

She was being intimate again, telling him her innermost thoughts. "What does Tug Lay do?" he asked.

"Works around the ranch. A hand."

But Lay had neither the manner nor appearance of an outside "hand," it came to Sam. He was too soft. He paid too much for his gaudy clothes. Instead of a hand, he looked more like a well-kept squawman, with time and money to burn, whose prosperity was adding tallow around his middle. Tug Lay didn't dig any postholes. Sam would bet on that.

Lay's cryptic face bothered Sam, brushed at his memory. A face was one thing you didn't forget in this game. Still, he couldn't yet call it out of the crowded, often furious, past. It was, he thought, like looking at a mask. The name meant nothing. Men traveled under many names.

She said curiously, "The way you two looked at each other I thought you were acquainted."

"Never saw the man before in my life."

"I have to go now. Hank wants everything just so." She held her gaze on Sam, an unwavering appraisal.

"Will you come again, Sam?"

"Will—if Art Cook and I match a race."

He saw the candor light her purposeful eyes. She laughed, a consuming, delightful laugh, and said, "Count on it. I'll put a bug in Art's ear."

A little later Sam was standing at the rim of the talkative swarm. The house was filled. Guests stood three deep at the bar. Another fiddler had relieved the first one.

Scotty Hinton posted himself at Sam's shoulder. In an almost inaudible voice, he said, "That's Tate Burk and Maggie over there."

Sam saw the white man and Indian woman Fay had greeted earlier. A sandy-haired man, about forty; even features, heavy jaw, his face pinkly fresh. No loud western-style getup here. Rather, stylish gray suit; diamond stickpin alight in the carefully knotted yellow tie. His bored eyes those of the Osage squawman of leisure and wealth.

Taking a gold toothpick from his vest pocket, Burk probed delicately along his front teeth, up and down, and returned the toothpick to his pocket while he ran a swabbing tongue in and out. Burk drew his gold pocket watch, snapped open the case, glanced down, and shut the case, his eyes lingering on the handsome timepiece, and returned it with care. He smoothed his slicked-down hair, pulled at his tie, and adjusted the stickpin.

An image filled Sam's mind: a small-town dandy from the Osage Mercantile. Maybe that alone, that affectation, had caught the credulous eye of full-blood Maggie Bear Claw. Otherwise, Tate Burk was a nondescript man, apparently unresponsive to the whir of people and voices around him. His boredom seemed to increase. He rose, brushing at the right sleeve of his new suit; without speaking to his wife, he wandered off into the crowd, a saunter to his walk.

Now Maggie absorbed Sam's interest. He judged that she was some years younger than her husband. So keenly did he watch her that he averted his eyes when she turned her head toward him.

He looked again.

She was a heavy woman; as the years went by she would become heavier. To all appearances, despite he wealth, she was devoid of pretension—simple, purple dress, no diamonds. Her lone vanity, if any, was the bright shawl she held and constantly fingered. She wore her straight, black hair parted in the middle and combed behind her ears and tied on her neck. Her nose was large, even for her round, fleshy face, but it was a good nose, straight and strong. Her black-brown eyes were exceptionally soft, gentle in that way of persons who have suffered beyond human bearing and who still suffer. All her life she would grieve for her lost ones. Someone spoke to her. She smiled through her engraved sadness.

Sam looked away, still seeing her brooding resignation. It tore at him. This was war. War against the innocent.

Fay spoke to Maggie, one hand resting on Maggie's arm. They carried on an animated conversation. Maggie's brooding faded. She liked and trusted Fay, perhaps as she did few white people.

Fay went to the bar and brought Maggie a bottle of pop, which told Sam something more: Maggie didn't drink whiskey. She was strong.

The fiddler rested, and during that pause Sam heard an outbreak of angry voices, one accusing, by the crowded bar. Two men faced off. Tug Lay and Rex

Enright, the roper. Lay mouthed something and swung at Enright's face. He missed, and that was a mistake. The athletic calf roper knocked Lay against the bar. Glass shattered. A woman screamed. Before Enright could land another smash, men grabbed his arms.

Lay wiped blood from his mouth and staggered up, muttering words that Sam couldn't catch above the uproar. A man came muscling through the onlookers, a stocky man with eyes set deep under thick brows. A man with the thick neck of a wrestler, whose head sat like a bowling ball on the powerful bulge of his shoulders.

He reached Lay. In one grasp, he took hold of Lay as one might a quarrelsome child and marched him for the rear of the courtyard, ignoring Lay's protests.

Sam heard Fay call for music. The bartender started sweeping up the glass. In moments the party resumed. Enright pulled on his ruffled shirt front and scrubbed a hand through his black hair. His quick eyes still glittered temper. He stood alone, isolated like the suspected Gaults. Abruptly, he wheeled and walked out, past Vail, standing in the hallway. Vail appeared to speak appeasing words. Enright rushed on, in anger.

Tactfully, then, Fay Vail called her guests to the barbecue. Moving with the crowd from the courtyard and into the backyard, Sam saw the likes of bounty he hadn't since leaving the Osage—a whole steer carcass hanging redly over cherry-hued coals. Hungering smells honed the evening air. Two aproned men were expertly carving the mountain of beef and relaying it to huge platters.

Sam heaped a tin plate with meat, beans, salad, and bread, and found a seat at one of the long tables. A man slipped in beside him presently, remarking, "Nothin' barbecues like registered beef."

Gene Poole was the genial guest.

"Other man's beef always tastes better," Sam said. "Especially if the steer's been on Osage County grass."

"Why, there are old-timers in Texas who never knew how their own beef tasted."

Soon one of the fiddlers sawed into a cowboy tune, playing while torches dispelled the dusk. At times Sam caught Fay's contagious laughter. Somehow the scene lacked reality to him. The guests could be participants in a grim masquerade, relishing the delights of feasting against a background of murder. This afternoon he had confirmed what Scotty had reported at the rendezvous. More than once, while the principals passed before his eyes, like actors on a stage, he had the detachment of an observer. Very soon that must change.

Afterward, when the guests began departing and crowding around the Vails, and Sam spoke his thanks, Fay's eyes met his for only a moment, but in silent appeal. He moved outside, aware that Poole wasn't far behind him.

Sam walked on to his car behind the rodeo stands, hearing the click of the agent's boots. When car lights and voices fell away, Sam stopped. Poole caught up. He said, "Scotty's changed the meeting. It's tomorrow night. Same time. The Indian cemetery."

"What is it?"

"Don't know. See you, ol' podner."

CHAPTER 7

IT WASN'T YET TEN O'CLOCK AS SAM FOLLOWED THE road leading to the Indian cemetery, several miles cast of the loading pens. The night was faintly cool and full of the languor of hidden promises. Wind hummed off the pastures, bearing the sweet scent of native grass. A velvet-soft night, like he used to know, that whispered and caressed; tonight it brought upon him the consciousness of his solitary living. Gene Poole was right. You couldn't go on forever like a lone wolf. You needed to put down roots. You needed a family. He wondered where the wall was that he had so carefully built around his emotions.

He cleared his mind to examine the possible reason for the meeting coming so soon after the first one. In this game the unexpected was more usual than not. Sometimes Scotty Hinton reminded him of a restless bird dog, forever moving, forever sniffing.

The yellow eyes of car lights were approaching. He saw the car slow down and turn off the road, the lights bobbing as the driver crossed the bar ditch and stopped at the fence line.

Sam's outthrown lights picked up the figure of a man opening a gate. Driving by, Sam caught the blur of a white face in the front seat, the face of a young white woman, before she turned the other way.

He was but a short distance past when recognition clicked. That was Tate Burk opening the gate. Burk and a town girl, which agreed with what Scotty had said. Likely a waitress at Jimmy the Greek's. Well, that was strictly Burk's business and the girl's.

When the cemetery hill loomed out of the night, dark, conical, mysterious, Sam switched off the car lights and followed the pale lanes of the road upslope to the mass of blackjacks. Near the crest he parked under the trees, shut off the motor, and got out. He saw cars then, another and another, nearby, off the road. So he wasn't the first tonight.

He started walking up the moon-drenched road.

A fence enclosed the cemetery. He stepped gingerly over the cattle guard and saw another car. Three men waited there. Gene Poole's jesting voice floated across to Sam:

"Lives the closest, and danged if he's not the last one here."

"We're all early," Hinton said.

"I'm the farthest away of any of you," Blue Sublette said, "and I got here first. Driving a Packard tonight. Belongs to one of my Osage friends."

"This case is gonna spoil you, Blue," Poole said. "You'll never be able to go back to Texas."

"Don't think Mama would like that"

Hinton, sitting on the fender of the coupe, got up and faced them. "This will be short and sweet. I was called to Oklahoma City by the Bureau. The Osage Tribal Council has renewed its plea to the justice Department for more action. They want us to work faster."

"Don't they realize we just got here?" Sublette said, his voice taking on the edge of a field agent, speaking out when he felt that his superiors, behind far-off desks, little understand what was going on.

"I know. I know. I pointed that out. Just happens we're way behind on a case that's already a national scandal. Sam, did you see John Cloud-Walker?"

"I did. He's all forted up. Besides 'fraid lights, he's

got a bodyguard and a big German shepherd. After we got acquainted, I asked him point-blank if he had anybody in mind who might have had reason to kill Antwine. He didn't name even one."

"Same old story," Sublette echoed. "The Osages won't talk."

"I don't think he suspects anyone. He said Antwine went wherever he could get whiskey."

"Did you ask him about Billy Gault?"

"He ruled Billy out for one reason. He said whoever killed Antwine did it for his diamonds. Billy's motive would be to get Antwine's wife, and Billy already had her."

"Not married, though," Hinton pointed out. "Nora had filed for divorce when Antwine was shot. But Antwine could have contested it pretty hard on grounds of infidelity. Antwine's murder cleared the way. Now that Billy's married to her, he has access to plenty of Osage money. Sure beats working in the men's department at the Osage Mercantile."

"Only he's still there," Sam reasoned. "Most white men would take it easy, wouldn't they? Live the life of a squawman?"

"Working makes him look honest," Hinton replied cynically. "Probably the lone working squawman in the whole county."

"From what I saw at Vail's, they seemed genuinely fond of each other."

"Money can make a man mighty loving."

"Something troubles me, Scotty. That guy Tug Lay. I've seen him somewhere before, but I can't place him."

"Army, maybe?"

"Don't think so."

"I can tell you one thing about him. He bootlegs.

Drives around in a yellow Buick coupe. Good advertising. When an Indian sees that yellow car, he knows there's whiskey in it, or Lay knows where to go get it. I've seen him peddle whiskey on the side streets in Red Mound."

"Fay Vail told me he works for her husband."

"He could bootleg on the side, if Vail didn't keep him too busy."

"She said he was a hand. Only you don't have time for side jobs when you ride for an outfit. You hit the heavy. You feed cattle in the winter and ride fence. You break horses and dig postholes and cut calves. You cut and bail hay. There's always somethin' that needs fixin'. If nothin' else, the boss may put you to pullin' nails. Maybe you'd have Sunday off . . . Tug Lay is not a common hand. He's too soft-lookin'. If he works for Vail, what does he do?"

Poole gave a grunted laugh. "Maybe he's the ranch bookkeeper?"

"Or he's Vail's rodeo manager?" Sublette suggested archly.

"Hank Vail can manage himself," Sam said. "That's a cinch. He's one cool *hombre.* You fellows should see his gun collection. It's an arsenal. He hunts big game. Fay showed me his trophy room. Looks like something Teddy Roosevelt would bring back."

"You know Fay?" Hinton's voice contained a surprised key.

Sam hesitated in spite of himself. "We went to high school together. We were sweethearts. We broke up while I was overseas." He was trying to sound natural, but knew that he wasn't. And as close as he was to Gene Poole, he had never told him about Fay.

There was a hang of silence until Hinton said, "You

don't have to explain, Sam. That's your personal business."

"I don't mind. Never said anything about it before, at Houston, because there was no reason to. Didn't expect to find her still here. I figured she'd be gone. I didn't know she'd married Hank Vail till I met her in town. If I had known she was here, I wouldn't have brought it out, because there was no connection with the case." He was talking too fast and saying too much, when explanations weren't necessary.

"She's possibly a good source for leads, Sam. Like who's this Tug Lay? That's all I'm getting at. Vail's not on our list, though we ought to suspect everybody right now. I keep thinking about the toughs that hang around out there on Sunday. Men like Kirk Singer, for instance. I'd like to know a great deal more about that rough customer than what meets the eye."

"Who's Singer?" Poole asked.

"The big guy who took Lay off after the little set-to with Rex Enright. Singer quarters at Blackjack in the oil fields. Understand he runs a joint—combination speakeasy, gambling, girls—called Kirk's Place. That's all I've been able to dig up on him."

Poole shifted his feet and hooked his thumbs inside his belt. "Now, why would he be at Vail's party? A guy who runs a joint in Blackjack?"

"Maybe he was invited," Hinton said. "He seemed right at home, the way he moved about. And what was that between Lay and Enright? I wasn't close enough to hear it."

"I was," Poole said. "Lay made a remark about Enright blowing up the Jordan house. Enright got mad and let him have it. Lay was half tight . . . How do you figure Enright, Scotty? I can't see him as the kind who would blow up a house and kill three people. He's wild and reckless. He's cocky—you can see that. But murder—?"

"As far as the Bureau's concerned, everybody's a suspect till we flush the guilty ones out of the brush, Enright included. Never underestimate what a man will do for a fistful of blood money." Hinton broke off. "Anything else?"

"Time," Sublette said. "We need time."

"And that's what we don't have. One thing: Who's next? Keep that in mind. That's all tonight. Keep at it." Hinton went to his car, and the others to theirs. When Hinton pulled out of the cemetery, Sublette, then Poole followed.

Coming out on the main road, Sam drove half a mile before switching on the headlights. There was no traffic. He passed the pasture gate where he had seen Tate Burk and the girl. Moonlight silvered the pasture, creating the illusion of a shallow lake lapping the base of the distant ridge. He could make out the beginning of the little-used road leading from the gate, two pale traces that skirted a patch of blackjacks.

Sam was hungry, and the perfect night made him restless. On that impetus he drove past Fargo's spread and on into Red Mound. Seeing cars crowding the street in front of Jimmy the Greek's, Sam drove to the end of Main, made a U turn, and parked across from the cafe.

He found an empty stool at the far end of the counter near the kitchen. Jimmy the Greek, who never forgot a name or face, set a glass of water before Sam and held out his broad hand.

"Welcome back. When did you come in?"

"Few days ago."

"And you just now come to see Jimmy?" A gentle

reproof, however.

"Had to get settled. I haven't forgotten you, Jimmy."

Jimmy the Greek was thickset and balding. It was said that in the old country he had been a leading wrestler. Sweat beaded his wide forehead. Grease spotted the front of his usually impeccable white shirt. His tired smile faded as he handed Sam a dog-eared menu. "It is not the same here since the oil boom. Every night there is a fight in my cafe, and I am no longer a young man." He let go an audible sigh of weariness. "I worked hard long time in old country so I could save enough money to come to America. Always I try to be fair. Always I remember when I was a poor boy in Athens. So what happens? Tonight my other girl fails to come to work. She's out, running around. Help's hard to get. She'll show up tomorrow, with excuses." He threw up his hands. "The roast beef is good. We're out of chicken and steak."

"Roast beef, coffee, and apple pie," Sam said.

"Out of apple. But I got a piece of raisin left."

"Fine."

Shortly, the Greek brought Sam's order and plodded on to the front to take his post behind the cash register. After eating, Sam lingered over his coffee. From time to time be glanced at the loud-voiced crowd of oil field workers, cowboys, Indians, and night-owl high school kids. Whiskey smell laid a sour taint over the long room.

Sam was on his second cup when voices erupted and chairs scraped and dishes shattered as a table toppled. He jerked around. A husky oil field worker and a long-armed cowboy were slugging away. The cowboy took a swing to his face and crashed down, losing his hat, but sprang up punching.

Jimmy the Greek rushed along the counter and around its corner, yelling in Greek, then English, "Stop it! Stop it!"

The fight continued. The cowboy knocked his opponent back a step. In turn, the brawler from the oil fields knocked the cowboy back.

Just then the Greek arrived. He thrust his bulk between them, only to take a wild punch from the burly battler.

Sam glimpsed the flash of an instinctive reflex across the Greek's face as he pivoted on balanced feet, crouching. His thick hands moved swiftly, feinting. He drove his shoulder into the oil field worker's middle. The Greek grappled a moment, then hoisted the man high and spun him about two, three times, then slammed him to the floor. The impact smashed the man's wind out of him. His eyes rolled and turned glassy. He couldn't get up.

The Greek stood over him, turned to the likeness of a victor in the ring: legs braced, the cords of his neck standing out like rope, his powerful chest heaving. He made a peremptory motion.

Two men hastened over and lifted their friend to his feet and outside the cafe. When Sam looked for the cowboy, he was gone.

The Greek called for the waitress to clean up the mess. Afterward, leaning against the counter, winded and his face flushed, the Greek hacked, "This keeps up, maybe Jimmy better off back in the old country."

"I think you're needed here," Sam told him. Sam paid for his meal and left. Delaying the drive home to the dark and empty house, he paused in the glare of the cafe's light on the sidewalk. He stood there while he finished a cigarette. Some yards beyond him, standing before a darkened storefront, two men shuffled and talked and smoked.

As Sam glanced that way, the two turned toward him, and their attention held on Sam, their cigarettes winking like fireflies. The undertone of their voices cutting off all at once sent a kind of unease through him.

Shrugging off the feeling, he crossed the street to the touring car. Heading east out of town, he puttered along, viewing what distance he should dicker for when Art Cook, strong on his racing mare, drove out in the morning. Distance was no problem when Slip Along was in condition. He could go short or long. Matt Colter's dictum rose to his mind: Never match your horse at a distance longer than he can run. Judging how Miss Whizzbang had performed at Vail's, in fast time as well, Cook would prefer another one-furlong sprint. Another particular was to agree on the starter. Why not Fargo Young?

Preoccupied, Sam had let his speed drop and was driving near the center of the narrow road because there was no oncoming traffic. At almost the same instant he realized that, a powerful roaring filled his ears. It seemed to burst upon him from behind.

He stepped on the gas and pulled over, expecting the car to roar past him. Simultaneously, he heard the car pick up speed and start around.

From the edge of his eye Sam glimpsed the dark bulk of a large sedan. But to his astonishment, then anger, the driver began crowding him. Sam shouted and gave ground, though there was little to give. Still, the other continued to force Sam nearer the bar ditch.

Quite suddenly, Sam stomped the brakes, hoping the road hog would slide by.

Now the driver slowed as Sam slowed. And next Sam

saw the high ledge of the fender veering in on him. This time Sam refused to give way, and instantly he heard the clash of metal and felt the light touring car shiver. He shifted to second gear, trying to run ahead. The old car responded sluggishly, gaining a little, nosing ahead.

At once, Sam heard the roaring deepen. With ease, the sedan drew even alongside. It was coming then, he knew. Upon him the banging, the crashing grind and jolt of fenders. The feel and *thunk* of his right-side tires clawing loose gravel and dirt.

He got an abrupt jolt. His side tilted sharply, and he was in the ditch. He felt himself about to roll over, while he fought the wheel in a fury, seeing two figures as the big sedan rushed on, powdering him with dust.

Instinct warned him not to slam on the brakes. Just hang on and lean left. He felt the touring car hit a washed-out place. Something banged on the right side. Shuddering, the car leaped and fell like a stumbling runner, throwing him violently against the wheel. The touring car rocked once more, but not so much this time; it was settling. He came to a dusty, bumping stop.

He sat there a bit, still giving to his rage, before scrambling out to survey the damage. His right front tire was flat, blown when the car hit the washout. He chewed his lower lip while he stared down the road, and his car lights revealed the low outline of a culvert. Thirty more feet, he'd have met it head-on. His mind cut back. Two drunks—if they were drunks? As for the big sedan, it looked like a Lincoln.

Pulling out on the road, he set about jacking up the axle and changing the tire.

Art Cook arrived at nine o'clock sharp, herding a flivver of prewar vintage. He waved and stepped out, angular and erect, giving his buck-toothed smile.

"How about some coffee?" Sam invited.

"Mighty fine."

Across the kitchen table, they talked weather and grass and water and horses in general, a prelude to the matter at hand.

"You know," Sam said presently, hoping to steer the conversation around to the investigation, "I grew up here. First time I've been back since the war. Country's changed a good deal. Heard that one of my old friends was murdered a few months ago—Antwine Cloud-Walker."

"Too bad," Cook said, nodding.

"Did you happen to know Antwine?"

"Knew who he was, about all. He used to make the Sunday races at Vail's."

"Wonder if he had any trouble out there."

"Not that I recollect. I was always busy with my horses. Seems there's generally some drinkin' around a rodeo or racetrack." Cook blinked. He pulled on his chin. "There was that fight."

"Fight?"

"I recollect now because the commotion held up the race. Antwine jumped Billy Gault about foolin' around with his wife. They scuffled. Friends broke it up. Antwine was drinkin'."

"What else?"

"That was all. Reckon they'll never find out who shot that Indian, will they?"

"Not yet, anyway."

Cook was an open, uncomplicated man, Sam concluded. Also garrulous and opinionated and, like any horse owner, inclined to tout his horse and not averse to mixing hot air with the facts. He was probably honest, though Sam had learned early that there were two sides to a coin, and nothing was slicker than a short-horse man running the back-country tracks.

"Guess it's time I showed you my horse," Sam said.

Slip Along was loose in the corral. When they walked up, he was curiously watching the hills. Sam moved to him and slipped on his halter and led him back.

"Don't you keep him on halter?" Cook inquired. "Makes 'em easier to catch."

"Where there's barbed-wire fences, I don't. Quit that after a good young horse we had got hung up and broke his neck. I can lead him around with a piece of twine." Which sounded like hot air, but wasn't. "You can drink a cup of coffee on him and never spill a drop." That was hot air, and Cook smiled.

Slip Along appeared to slouch more than usual today, and his Botch ear looked more pronounced. Sam, seeing Cook's cagey expression, knew the other figured Miss Whizzbang had racked up another victory.

Cook crossed his arms, and looked down and up. "About how much would you like to run for?"

"I'll go up a little. Say, fifty dollars?"

Cook snorted. "That's the least I'd run my horse for. Would you consider seventy-five?"

"Might."

Cook waited, a restrained anticipation on his long-jawed face. "All right," said Sam, sounding uncertain.

Cook stepped back and ran his judging eyes over the gelding, and step by slow step, circled Slip Along, who appeared to doze. Cook halted. Fixing Sam a sizing-up speculation, he spoke right out, "Would you like to go one furlong?"

Sam assumed a thoughtful attitude. One furlong, or 220 yards, was the distance Miss Whizzbang had run while besting the palomino, Gold Dust. Her best distance, likely. He replied, sparring, "I'd like to stretch that out some. Say, 330 yards?"

Cook, unable to mask his desire, said, "I'll give a little and I'll take a little. What do you say to 300 yards even?"

Sam thought on it a moment. "Fair enough."

"Next Sunday?"

Sam, knowing his horse wasn't in peak condition, had a mind to delay a week. The impulse ebbed as Scotty Hinton's demand for action occurred to him. The race itself wasn't vital. What mattered was jumping headlong into the frenzy and becoming part of it, if necessary. And maybe, just maybe, Slip Along would be ready.

"Next Sunday's jake with me," Sam said.

"Mighty fine."

"Looks like we're all set except for the starter."

"There's Mitch Kell. He started Sunday."

"I was thinking of Fargo Young," Sam said, expecting refusal.

"Forgot about him, since he ain't been active out there for some time. Fargo's fair and square. He's all right with me. I'll drop by the livery on the way home."

They shook on it.

CHAPTER 8

FRIDAY MORNING BEFORE THE RACE, SAM CINCHED THE light racing saddle on his horse, and they headed out into the bluestem pasture. Sam chirped to him and they stepped into a warming-up jog, picking up speed gradually, working back and forth. Reaching the end of the level stretch nearest the creek a third time, Sam reined up and they turned, down to a walk, now a pause. As Sam tightened his hold and turned Slip Along a little sideways, he could feel the gelding sense what was coming. Sam started him then.

Slip Along broke with a bone-jarring leap, with such velocity that had Sam not known his horse he'd been thrown from the saddle. In two more jumps Slip Along was traveling all-out, reaching for ground, striding long, leveling off.

Sam let him go hard for three hundred yards under a light hold before easing him off, satisfied. There was still plenty of run in him, a heap more, but that was it until Sunday. This morning's workout was closer to the day of the race than Sam liked, if a man had to get finicky about his horse, except Slip Along needed the work, the sweat, the break, the loosening up, plus the distance facing him Sunday. Sam didn't believe in pampering horses. Besides, this horse enjoyed work. You could drop the bridle on him and he would run the race on his own. He knew what to do.

Sam dismounted and led the gelding to the corral and washed him down with a sponge and dried him and threw a cooling blanket over him and led him around for a while. Acting on a late thought, he examined Slip Along's feet, shod shortly before Sam had left South Texas, and brushed them clean. He made a mental reminder to tighten the shoes Sunday morning.

Sam went to bed early Saturday night. Twice during the restless hours he got up, pulled on pants and boots, and tramped to the barn to see about his horse. The last time, late, Slip Along was standing up, sleeping. Sam's experience was that a horse didn't sleep till after midnight, then only a few hours. His father had told him that when Sam was a boy; not believing, Sam had stayed up all one night and found out for himself that it was so, causing him to reflect at the time how much smarter his father seemed to get as he grew older.

Fretting awake at four o'clock, he gave up and made a pot of coffee, worrying about the handicap of his 150 pounds on Slip Along. Even so, at this early stage, it was wiser for Sam to be in the irons than same green kid likely to lose his seat at the first jolting jump of the break, and probably get hurt. Too, Sam knew his horse. He would really worry, though, if they were going three or four furlongs with that weight. But hadn't the track-burning Pan Zareta—Texasbred and some said the greatest sprinter of all—carried 146 pounds to victory over five furlongs at Juarez, Mexico? Set a world's record, too, of 57 $^{1}/_{5}$. He felt better just thinking of Pan Zareta.

At dawn he returned to the barn and fed Slip Along a light ration of oats. Standing by, he watched his horse eat breakfast and listened to him stamp and switch. When the sun brightened and warmed to his satisfaction, he currycombed Slip Along's mane and forelock and brushed him and tightened his shoes, and sponged and dried his cannons and rubbed on a nostril-prickling liniment, a concoction of his father's that smelled pungently of iodine. That done, he turned him loose in the corral.

Slip Along bucked and kicked, circling and circling.

"Quit showin' off," Sam told him, pleased. "Don't think you're gonna get pettin' every morning. You're spoiled now. Next thing I know you'll have to have an apple a day."

After watering, he trailed back to the house to eat breakfast. By damn, he was getting where he hated bunking, eating mostly the same fare day after day, living like a lone wolf.

Around noon he filled the water can at the well, loaded it and a tin bucket and the rest of Slip Along's gear in the touring car, hooked up the trailer, and waited out the sun, fretting. Reason told him not to arrive early at Vail's. That way he would miss the rodeo traffic.

One o'clock had passed when he loaded his horse and started for Red Mound, taking his time. He arrived at the ranch when the roping was still going on, drove by the stands to a clump of blackjacks south of the track, and tied Slip Along in the shade. Fretting again, he poured water into the bucket. A *few sips, pardner-that's all. Maybe once more before the race. I want you light and feisty.*

A man, his step lively, was approaching. Sam had to stare hard before he recognized an officious Fargo Young: neat, dark suit, trousers riding high water above his shoetops, white shirt and string tie, his usual stringy ox-boy mustache freshly trimmed, a gray hat replacing his flop-brimmed one.

An aroma of moth balls arrived simultaneously with Fargo. "Wondered if something was wrong, you pulled in so late," Fargo said, glancing at the horse.

"No trouble. Wanted to miss the traffic and dust."

"Art Cook's over behind the stands. Been here since ten o'clock. There's tolerable bettin'. Art's been ready with two-to-one money. Few takers, since nobody's seen your horse run. But some folks'll take two-to-one odds any ol' time."

"I'd like a little of that myself."

"It'll be a walk-up start. Like the ol' lap-and-tap of your father's day. When the horses come abreast to the line, I'll drop my hand and holler *Go*. Don't like to drop a hat or flag. Might make a horse booger. Be an even-

Stephen start, you can bet your boots."

"I'm not worried about that, Fargo. Just remember, I like to turn my horse a little sideways, so he can push off."

"I remember. You told me in town. I'll come to the track and wave you over when it's post time."

"I'll appreciate it if you'll look around for a jockey, too. Not for today. Later."

"Already got a good boy in mind. Name's Dee Oden. I'll tell him to get in touch with you." Fargo strode away, exuding an air of authority. The old man looked years younger. Walking straighter, too. Sam was thinking that when Fargo turned and called back, "Little Ned, that kid on Miss Whizzbang, is just fryin' size. Track's rough."

The red ball of the sun seemed stuck in the sky. Sam gave Slip Along another sip and drew the bucket back. The horse licked his lips for every drop, looked to Sam for more. Sam fussed over him, talking to him, eyeing him. The gelding tail-switched flies and stamped his feet now and then; otherwise, he stood quietly, eyes half shuttered. His head drooped. He could be dreaming of a sweet-water spring in Texas.

Finally, in relief, Sam heard the roar of the rodeo fade and die, which told him the bull riding was over. People began leaving the stands and their cars, parked around the arena fence, and strolling to the track.

Sam bridled his horse and checked the open reins, brushed the stout back, laid on blanket and flat saddle, and carefully cinched up. He still wore his cowboy boots. He struggled them off, pulled on light riding boots, tossed his hat in the touring car's front seat, and waited. At the last moment he remembered his handgun, under the cooling blanket in the back seat, and stuffed it beneath the front seat.

A short while later, Fargo came to the edge of the track and waved. Sam checked the cinch once more, pulled himself aboard, and rode off. He heard the announcer's voice:

"Good afternoon again, folks . . . Our feature is a match race at three hundred yards . . . It's Art Cook's Miss Whizzbang and Slip Along, owned and ridden by Mr. Sam Colter, fresh up from Texas. Little Ned Dale is up on Miss Whizzbang . . . Starting the race is Mr. Fargo Young, proprietor of the Star Livery in Red Mound . . . Holding the timer's watch is Mr. Hank Vail, himself."

By the time Sam rode to the track, Cook was parading his sprinter past the stands. Applause swelled for Miss Whizzbang. No doubt about it, Sam agreed, she was as pretty as any show horse, her brushed sorrel coat gleaming, fox ears twitching, the white blaze down her face as perfect as if painted there.

Fargo, waiting for Sam, said, "Take one sashay past the stands, then on to the starting line." His jaw fell. "Well, danged if Art's not paradin' his horse by a second time."

So he was.

Sam fell in behind Miss Whizzbang. He heard the clapping commence again, knowing it was for the favorite. Slip Along, well composed, displayed his customary indifference when slouching past a brush-track crowd. He paused to take a curious look about, and ambled on. His gotch ear drooped. He hung his head. Sam saw the grins and was not amused. They were looking at a long-striding grandson of Peter McCue, the foundation sprint sire, and didn't know it. Slip Along slackened again. Another curious look and the muddy-colored gelding meandered nonchalantly on, Sam letting him go as he liked, at his own pleasure.

Sam noticed a good many Indians, including Maggie Bear Claw Burk and John Cloud-Walker and his bodyguard. Maggie sat with her children. In the front row sat Fay Vail. As Sam discovered her, she waved at him.

Once beyond the stands, Miss Whizzbang jogged on smartly to the head of the track. There her owner hovered about her like a fluttery mother hen. He gave instructions to the young jockey. Cook tested the cinch. He pulled on the brand-new saddle blanket and smoothed it.

"You about ready, Art?" Fargo asked as Sam brought Slip Along up. Fargo's steady voice and even manner injected calmness into the always-taut start.

Cook nodded and stepped away from his horse. He darted Sam a nervous glance.

"You, Sam?" Fargo called.

"Ready."

"All right, boys. That's fine. We'll do 'er just like the ol' lap-and-tap start. When the horses walk up to the line, head to head, I'll holler *Go!* So walk your mounts back there a little way, then come ahead . . . That's it . . . On back there . . . Easy, now . . . At a walk. All together."

When Sam turned his horse to approach the starting line, Miss Whizzbang on his right, he saw that Cook had wisely taken the smoother lane. The path on Sam's side was badly cupped. Sam bit his lip. He could only blame himself for not walking over the track, then tossing Cook for the choice lane. Matt Colter wouldn't have overlooked that.

The horses were moving about right, just a few

strides from the line, when Miss Whizzbang spurted ahead. Fargo didn't move. He said soothingly, "Wup . . . That's all right. Turn 'em around and come again. Don't hurry. Got all afternoon."

A turn, and back, and turning again and forward. Sam could feel Slip Along drawing up. Very near now. Closer. Now.

Catching the downward blur of Fargo's hand and with Fargo's shouted "Go!" in his ears, Sam rushed his horse away. He took the smashing recoil of Slip Along's first jump, but felt his horse stumble and break down. Sam hung on. For yards his horse seemed to be running on his knees.

Sam got the gelding's head up, to see the filly two lengths out, going like a shot. It stayed like that, the sickening daylight the same, his horse still in trouble, unable to get unstrung.

Sam shouted into the gotch ear and Slip Along seemed to answer. Slip Along straightened a little, pulling harder. He was starting to level out at last and find himself, if it wasn't too late.

Sam began to feel it happening. A meshing. A harmony. A coordination of will and power and ground-eating stride. Slip Along was running easier, faster and faster.'

At the furlong stake Slip Along's head reached the filly's tail. His head inched past her hindquarters, past her jockey, past her withers. In a rush the horses were running neck and neck, both determined to win. The roar of the crowd drummed Sam's ears.

Miss Whizzbang's bobbing snow-white nose dropped back. The judge's box flashed by.

It was over.

Sam eased his hold and stood up in the stirrups,

letting his horse go on unchecked, for the fire was still in him. Sam could hardly believe they'd won after that terrible start. Slip Along had come ahead on heart alone, refusing to quit.

Circling back, Sam was surprised to see the crowd standing, clapping, and yelling approval. He got it, like a thunderclap. His horse was receiving an ovation. Sam felt warm all through. People streamed onto the track. An Indian touched Slip Along's nose. As the crowd grew underfoot, Sam slipped down to lead his horse. Sam heard a voice:

"That old horse can run, believe me. Stumbles, goes down, gets up, and still covers three hundred yards in a shade under eighteen." Sam craned to see. The speaker was Hank Vail, and he was holding a stopwatch. "He ran it in 17 $^2/_5$," Vail said, impressed. "You won by a neck. Quite a race. Maybe you'd like to put him up against one of my horses?"

"Maybe. Right now I'd better take a look at the front end of this horse."

"If you need anything, go up to the barns. My vet will be there. Let me know when your horse is ready again. Be a couple of weeks, anyway, before we stage another rodeo."

Sam knelt to look, scowling when he saw the skinned and bleeding knees. Sam stood up to lead him away.

Behind him a woman said, "Congratulations, Sam. You've got a mighty fast horse. And he's game to boot."

It was Fay. She held out her hand. He took it. Even here he seemed to read an invitation in her voice and eyes and feel it in her touch.

He swept the discernment aside, relieved as more people crowded around to shake hands and admire the winner. If there was one event Osage County people cottoned to, he remembered, it was a hot horse race or a knock-down fight. A couple of men said they had known Matt Colter. Their voices warmed Sam. For the first time he felt that he had come home from the war.

And Fargo, still enjoying his official role, was poking a handful of greenbacks at him and saying, "Art said to make sure you got this. He'd come himself, but he feels kinda low."

"Tell him I thank him and that he's got a fast little filly. I tell you, she ran hard all the way. Never quit. I'd like to have a foal out of her by Old Baldy."

As soon as he could, Sam left the track, for a horse crowd will stand and stand, admiring a winner, in fancy seeing qualities unnoticed until the advent of unexpected victory. He led Slip Along to the trailer, gave him water, draped the cooling blanket over him, and worriedly bathed the bruised knees, while he reconstructed what had happened.

You opened a door for us today, pardner. Now we're gonna see what's in there.

CHAPTER 9

SAM WAS UP MUCH OF THE NIGHT, SITTING ON A bucket while by lantern light he soaked Slip Along's knees in hot Epsom Salts water. It was kind of touching, the way the old horse loved to be fussed over. So far he wasn't limping, just stiff, and the joints weren't swollen.

Sam slept later than usual. Needing supplies, he started for Red Mound about ten o'clock. He was in sight of town before he saw a car coming. A red Cadillac sedan. An Indian woman driving, obviously in no hurry. Two children in the back seat. They waved as Sam passed. He waved back and recognized Maggie Bear Claw Burk.

Down the road, it came to him. He had noticed the big red sedan before on the dusty roads, it and its winged radiator ornament. Just Maggie and her kids, driving, driving. Not with Tate Burk. The one time Sam had seen her and Burk together was at the Vail ranch.

As he parked in front of the drugstore, Red Mound's Main Street appeared to slumber—to present a self-effacing mask of tranquility to the sunlit, unsuspecting world of the Osage. At the moment the Sportsman's Billiards, two doors down, had more incoming customers than the drugstore.

Coming out with his purchases, he saw that a new sedan had drawn up to the curb next to his touring car. A dark blue Lincoln. He walked past it to the driver's door of his car. As he started to get in, something kindled his attention on the sedan. He walked back and looked at the Lincoln's right front fender.

It was scraped and dented, like the left front fender of the touring car. Furthermore, the streaks of dark blue paint on his car's rumpled hide matched that of the sedan's.

Sam pursed his lips, hearing the roar again, seeing the shape of the big car looming out of the night, feeling the bump, then the solid smash, as he was forced off the road into the ditch. His anger jumped.

He backed out, drove to the end of the street, turned, came back, and parked across from the drugstore.

Close to an hour passed. The driver of the Lincoln had not appeared. Then Sam saw a man drive up and park and hurry into the Sportsman's Billiards. In moments another man, an individual of exceptional thick muscular development through the neck and shoulders, left the pool hall and went to the dark blue Lincoln.

Sam stared. It was Singer—Kirk Singer.

Sam watched him back out, go to the end of Main Street, circle, and drive north out of town, which didn't mean anything. That was the way to the Vail ranch, and also the road to Blackjack, in the oil fields, and the way to Pawhuska, which was the county seat and also the site of the Osage Agency. A man could have a dozen reasons for taking the north road out of Red Mound.

Nonetheless, Sam followed and at once was forced to push the touring car to trembling speeds to keep the Lincoln in sight on the dusty road leading into the hills.

As the turnoff to Vail's neared, Sam expected Singer to take it. Singer did not. Now, Sam figured, Singer will go on to Blackjack, where Scotty had said Singer ran a joint. Well, now was an opportune time for Sam to acquaint himself with the likes of Blackjack, born in the boom of the Burbank oil field after he had gone overseas.

North of the Vail ranch, Singer took a county road that wound deeper into timbered hills. Two miles onward Sam saw the Lincoln slow down to cross a cattle guard and enter a pasture. Sam followed. The pasture road, which from a distance looked seldom used, had the deep ruts of much passage.

Singer disappeared around a wooded hill. Another car was approaching at high speed, weaving and bouncing out of the ruts. Sam pulled out of the way. The Indian boy driving waved as he slammed by. Sam, waving back, understood: The road led to a bootlegger's.

Sam rounded the hill and, suddenly before him, huddled under the blackjacks, the place took raw shape.

One long shack, its fresh plank siding revealing its recent birth. A yellow Buick coupe and Singer's Lincoln were parked close to the door.

Sam pulled in next to the Lincoln. The door to the shack was closed. When he turned the knob and pushed the door open, a bell tinkled his arrival. Before him rose a rough wooden counter and four stools; to his right two wooden tables and chairs. He saw no one, but voices buzzed in a closed room to his left.

A stocky woman opened the door of the room and shut it behind her. Rather guardedly, she planted her ample bulk behind the counter. She wore a loose, grease-spotted gray dress. Her dyed red hair was bobbed, and her worldly eyes of rusty brown examined him suspiciously.

"Yeah?" she queried.

"Been a long, dry morning," he said, showing her a broad smile. "Good morning for a Delaware punch."

"Or something stronger."

"Always dry this time of year in the Osage," she said, her manner still guarded.

"I remember."

The voices in the room, muffled until now, sounded louder. A man said, "Get him out of here. Take him to the ranch."

The woman's voice came hurriedly, as if to cover those in the closed room. "Don't believe I've seen you around before."

"You haven't. I've been gone."

She played him a knowing smile. "Long time, eh, bud?"

"Too long."

"Like where the hours are more regular, maybe, and the boys line up for their meals, there ain't no girls, and they turn the lights out early?"

"I didn't say," Sam evaded, smiling at her description. He guessed he was in, since she had pegged him as not long out of some penitentiary.

Suddenly she relaxed. "Want a bottle or a shot?"

"A shot."

She reached under the counter, brought up a pint of murky whiskey and a shot glass, and sloshed him a drink. "That's a buck," she said. The bottle vanished underneath. Sam laid down a dollar bill.

She leaned on the counter. "Gonna serve eats when I get this place goin' good."

"Bet you're quite a cook."

"You kiddin'? I can't boil water without burnin' it." But she liked the compliment just the same.

Sam heard feet scuffling. The door of the room opened abruptly, and two men bulked there. One, unknown to Sam, supported a glazy-eyed Tug Lay, who began singing at the top of his voice, mumbling about "The Old Chisholm Trail." Kirk Singer was behind them. The pair made it to the shack's door and outside.

Singer, following, glanced back. "Thanks, Ma, for sending me word." He discovered Sam at that moment. He went out as Sam set his glass down and stood.

Sam heard a car start, back out, and roar off. Through the shack's one front window he saw the yellow coupe leaving.

"Some folks can't seem to hold their liquor," the woman said.

Sam waited for the roar of Singer's sedan. Not hearing it, he started for the door, upon him a doggedness, within it a heat that threatened to overrun his coolness as he thought of Singer ramming him off the road. Sam reached the door.

"Hey, bud, you forgot your drink." Sam kept going.

Singer was standing by the sedan, contemplating the coupe's settling dust. He opened the driver's door, and paused when Sam said, "Nice-looking car you got there."

Singer's eyebrows went up. He said nothing.

The certainty overtook Sam that he was going to force the issue. He said, "See your right fender got ruffled up."

Singer shrugged with the stiffness of a muscle-bound man.

Sam said, "So is my left fender. Somebody tried to run me off the road the other night east of Red Mound."

Singer merely narrowed his eyes.

"Happens the paint on your fender matches mine where I was hit."

Ever so slowly, Singer's eyes moved from his car to the touring car's left fender. Sam waited, keyed for violence. Singer's face was wide and big-boned. The abnormally pallid eyes, so pale they looked white against his brown skin, were recessed under brows scarred and shaggy. His expression suggested a single-minded man, unmoved by happenings around him, inflexible, unimaginative.

"That explains it," he said. "My car was stolen Monday night. Was that when it happened?"

Sam nodded.

"High school kids, I suppose," Singer said. "Found it next morning down by the depot. Guess they took a long joyride. That's how you got run off the road."

Sam caught it. "I didn't say I was 'run off the road. I said somebody tried to."

"Almost the same from the looks of your car." He got in. He faced Sam. He seemed to measure his words.

"I'm a businessman at Blackjack. I'm Kirk Singer. I run Kirk's Place. I like to see people have a good time. Don't mind saying I like to see the oil field workers spend their wages. I'm in a line of business where a man needs friends . . . If it would make you feel any better, though my car was damaged, too, go to the O.K. Garage in Red Mound. Tell 'em to fix your car. Tell 'em Kirk Singer sent you. They can call me if they have any questions."

Sam withheld a reply, thinking that throughout his experiences he had never seen a man who appeared so utterly cool and unruffled.

At the door of the shack the woman was calling fretfully. "Did you hear me, bud? I said you forgot your drink."

Sam found a car parked in the yard when he reached home. The kind a kid or young man would fancy, a stripped-down Model T flivver. And a young man was waiting on the porch. He stood up as Sam drove in, and he came across when Sam stopped.

"Mr. Cotter?"

"That's right."

"My name's Dee Oden. Hear you need a jockey? Fargo Young told me."

"I am, and I'm particular."

Sam guessed him to be in his early twenties. He was blond and slim and fine-featured, about 115 pounds, give or take, and he wore the cotton shirt and Levi's and battered hat and boots of a ranch hand.

"Come in," Sam said. "We'll talk over coffee."

"I saw that race Sunday," Oden said, when they were seated in the kitchen. "Your horse just kept a-comin'. I'd like to ride him." As if anticipating Sam's next question: "I'm not ridin' regular for anybody right now, nor workin' either. I live in town with my folks."

"Ever ride for Hank Vail?"

"Nope. He won't use but one jockey. That's Pace McKee. He's the best around here. Been up on top horses in big races in Missouri and Illinois, and down in Louisiana. Me, I just fill in. Ride now and then. Pick up odd jobs around town and what little extra work there is on ranches." There was bitterness behind the easygoing air, and the troubled blue eyes had a haunting quality that never quite left.

Sam was puzzled. "If Fargo's high on you, there ought to be steady work for you around Red Mound. If not on ranch, maybe in the oil fields."

"I'd rather be around horses and cattle, where I can see grass growin'. Fargo always tries to help me."

"You're the only jock he recommended."

"Not very many to start with," Oden said, in a tone of unimportance. He gazed down at his hands, the strong, capable hands of a rider. "I used to be known around Red Mound as a steady guy . . . was until a little over two years ago."

"Something happened?"

Still looking down, Oden squeezed his lips together. "Guess I shouldn't talk about it."

"Could be that's exactly what you need to do. Get it off your chest."

Oden looked up then. "There was a girl. My girl. She was killed—murdered—just the week before we were to get married."

Sam groaned. "I'm sorry—very sorry to bear that." He rose and filled Oden's coffee cup, feeling a sharp sympathy. He said, "I don't mind listening, if you want to tell me about it."

"You must have heard about it in town," the young man said, pain surfacing in his eyes. "Worst thing that ever happened around here." He swallowed with effort. His speech stumbled. "Her name was Holly Abbott. She was in that house they blew up."

Sam was startled, at the same time sharing the terrible hurt he saw gripping the young face. "Yes, I heard about it Who would do a terrible thing like that?"

Bitterly, Oden shook his head; bitterly, he went on. "That's why I keep on the move. Rode for outfits as far north as the Flint Hills, west to the Cheyenne-Arapaho country, on east of Pawhuska—in hopes I'd find out who did it."

Sam had to restrain his interest. "Any leads at all?"

"Not a one. I figure somebody was sore at Ben Jordan over a cattle deal."

"If so, why kill two other people?"

"Maybe they didn't care who got in the way."

"There are the Osage headrights."

"Maggie Bear Claw Burk is the closest kin. She wouldn't have her sister murdered."

"No."

"But I'll find out someday," Oden swore, smashing his right fist into his left palm, "and when I do, I'll use my bare hands." The determination hardening his face fled as quickly as it had formed, softening, as he unbuttoned his shirt pocket and drew forth a leather folder and opened it for Sam to see. "She was only seventeen," Oden said.

Sam saw the somewhat worn photograph of a plain, sweet face, pretty in an old-fashioned way. A brooch at her slim throat; her auburn hair worn long; a hidden smile playing behind the parted lips; the dark eyes rich with the hope of life to be.

Sam handed the folder back, shaking his head. "I know how I would feel."

"Nobody knows how I feel!" Oden said, buttoning the shirt pocket flap over his treasure. "And I don't want them to. Yet here I am," he let down, with apology, "burdening you."

"You're not at all." Sam let him sit in moody silence for a spell. Then: "You said *they* blew up the house. You must have somebody in mind."

"Just figure there was more than one in it," Oden answered, staring moodily at the rim of his cup.

"Dee, do you have a theory?"

"Guess you could call it that. I'm not sure. I'm not sure of anything. More like a hunch, I reckon. A feeling." He had a mannerism of dropping his chin and avoiding another's eyes that suggested a young man buffeted hard early in life, and now dreading to go the rest of the way. He looked away again.

Sam, more than ever, found himself wishing to help Dee Oden. Sam said thoughtfully, "Feelings are often true. They're like facts the naked eye can't see. In what direction does your feeling take you?"

"If I said anything—I mean, if it got out, if I named anybody—I could end up like Antwine Cloud-Walker. I won't talk about it." He became busy scattering tobacco from a string sack into a brown cigarette paper, moistening it across his lips, and sealing it and lighting it.

"I heard about Antwine, too. We were old friends. In the Army together." Sam's voice flattened. "You mean he was shot because he talked too much?"

"I don't know why he was shot. I mean the same could happen to me. I won't talk about it."

"You know, Dee, Fargo is high on you. He said I

could count on you. Best young rider in northern Oklahoma."

"He said that?" Oden asked, disbelieving.

"He believes in you. You can believe in me. If you need help, let me know."

Oden showed no response.

"Fargo told you about me, didn't he, Dee? How I grew up here?" Oden nodded glumly, and Sam said, "I come back home and what do I find? Everybody's afraid. It makes me sore as hell, and I want to know who's behind this trouble." He had spoken on honest indignation, and he saw Oden look at him, knowing that was so. Sam said no more, hoping Oden might take it from there. Oden looked away again, tight-lipped. He had said all he was going to here and now. Hell, Sam thought, he's afraid, like the Osages. Sam rose from the table.

"My horse banged up his knees Sunday. I want you to take a look at him."

Oden looked glad to go, rising at once. At the corral he led Slip Along around again and again, intently observing the gelding's movements. He stopped to examine the knees, the cannons, the fetlocks, the pasterns, feeling gently and carefully.

"Why, I think he's all right, Mr. Colter. I sure do."

"If you plan to ride for me, call me Sam."

"There's no limp. He's not tender anywhere. I was afraid he'd hurt himself below his knees. This ol' horse is as sound as a dollar." Although Sam was impressed, he did not let on. Young Oden knew something about horses; in addition, he had patience and understanding. That was a start.

"Tell me something," Oden said, and scratched his head. He was grinning, actually, like a boy venturing an uncertain question to an elder. "I've heard it said that the color of a horse has a great deal to do with the toughness of his feet. That white feet are softer and worse to split, and you have to keep a white-footed horse shod if you use him hard and steady. Anything to that?"

"Could be, though I can't quote any figures. On the other hand, I've seen bays and duns and blacks whose sidewalls were too thin to hold plates. Good horses, too. My father used to say that a white horse couldn't take heat and saddle wear like a dark one. Not in South Texas, at any rate."

"Reckon that's one reason why this horse is sound."

"Main thing, he wasn't raced too young. just a few times as a two-year-old."

"How's he bred?"

Sam gave the familiar lineage as he had heard his father recite it so many times: by Old Baldy, a son of Peter McCue, out of Wendy, a half Thoroughbred; Old Baldy's dam the sprint mare, River Belle. "Makes him a quarter Thoroughbred."

"A little more than that, since Peter McCue's dam, Nora M, traces back to Glencoe, the Thoroughbred. There's an interesting controversy about Peter McCue's sire, and you still hear it among horsemen. One story is that Peter was a son of Dan Tucker, a top short horse in Illinois back in the eighties and nineties. The other is that Peter was registered a Duke of the Highlands colt. The Duke was a Thoroughbred. But as Peter matured he looked more and more like Dan Tucker."

"Now you've got me guessing," Oden said.

"There's a reason for that, a sound one. Back there almost all racing, long or short, was restricted to registered Thoroughbreds. To get around that, if you had a cold-blooded colt you wanted to run, you would record the colt as being sired by a registered stud."

"Ever see Peter McCue?"

"Once—at Cheyenne, Oklahoma. He was a big horse. Stood sixteen hands, weighed fourteen hundred pounds. Had a twenty-sevenfoot stride. He is said to have run the quarter in twenty-one flat. He was unbeaten at that distance."

They talked horses throughout the morning. Young Oden stayed for the noon meal; later, he obligingly helped around the place, working on the sagging fences and the decrepit barn. He was lonely and drifting, Sam saw, scarred for life; time was easing some of his pain, but his deep, deep hurt would never heal completely. At Sam's invitation, Oden stayed the night, and they talked until late. Yet not once did Oden mention Holly Abbott or the Jordan house again, or Antwine.

"Come back in about a week," Sam told him next morning when Oden was ready to leave. "By then I'll know if Slip Along's all right for sure. I won't take a chance with this horse. If he's ready, I'll powwow with Hank Vail about a match race with Plunger."

"Ain't that pretty stiff competition?"

"Why not? Even Tomahawk, if Vail wants to run his main stud."

"I don't know."

Their eyes locked. Oden looked away. Sam continued to regard him with open surprise, for until now Oden was all eagerness to ride. Sam spoke roughly. "You don't *know?* You don't know what? You want to ride for me or not, Dee? Make up your mind. Maybe it is that you can't handle a real short horse?"

The bitter young eyes flashed. "Never saw one I couldn't."

"You'll have to show me, Dee. I don't let every Tom, Dick, and Harry ride my horse. Think it over."

He left it there, flung down between them.

Oden's thin face turned rigid. He looked away. He drove off without speaking.

Sam, frowning after him, hoped he would come back, but doubted that he would.

CHAPTER 10

MORE OFTEN NOW, SAM JOURNEYED INTO RED MOUND, sometimes dropping by Fargo Young's Star Livery, where generally there was a visiting chewer or whittler, or the Bailey Hardware, or the Sportsman's Billiards for a game of pool or dominoes. Men were beginning to nod to him. Some came up and gave their names and mentioned his horse; some remembered Matt Colter and Matt's horses, such as Old Baldy. Sam was getting acquainted again.

He saw Scotty Hinton on the street, outside the post office, but no word was passed, and he saw Gene Poole and a cowman swapping stories in front of the Osage Hotel. Frequently, he saw Maggie Burk's red sedan on the road. Always the kids waved, and always he waved to them; they knew him by this time, and the greetings had become a kind of game.

The going to and fro and the loafing around town were time-consuming and not without frustration. Still, how was he to find new leads unless he circulated, unless he talked and listened, and listened a damned sight more than he talked? Nothing would develop if he stayed to himself in the country, waiting for something to surface, reacting instead of acting. He had intentionally challenged Oden, hoping he knew how the young man would take it. Sam liked him and had compassion for him. Oden was wary and tight-mouthed, locked up and scared. He had strung a barbed-wire fence between himself and the world. In time it would come down, likely all at once.

This day was much like the others, unchanged, dull, unproductive, and the town; huddled in the palm of the plain under the grass-burning sun, looked deceptively peaceful. It seemed to float beneath a veil of shimmering heat. Sam thought of an old renegade resting after a series of bloody forays, and guessed that he was becoming overly cynical.

He made his rounds and started home, mulling again over young Oden's hesitation at a match race with one of the Vail horses. Why? It didn't make sense when a man said he needed work.

Fargo's place was less than a quarter mile beyond when Sam saw the car stopped in the road, and pulled off on his side. A red sedan. A red Cadillac sedan. An Indian woman behind it, struggling with a jack.

He stopped and walked forward. She looked up, and he saw Maggie Burk. At the same time two small, black-haired heads jutted out a rear window, chattering something.

"Believe you need a little help," Sam said, seeing the fiat left rear tire.

"I can't make this jack work," she said self-consciously.

He knelt down, tinkered with the jack handle, and saw that she hadn't set the catch. He went to the front, set the emergency brake, made certain the car was in gear, took a lug wrench from under the front seat, and came back. He spoke to the youngsters, who by now were standing by their mother, and removed the spare wheel and tire off the rack at the rear of the car.

He was soon sweating. Finished, he caught the thirst on the children's faces. He said, "My place is just down the road. Would you kids like some cool well water? Sorry there's no soda pop."

"That's too much trouble," Maggie Burk said.

"Oh, no. My name's Sam Colter."

As he spoke his name, her eyes were searching his face with recognition. "Your horse won the race Sunday. Your horse named Slip Along." She was smiling. "You rode that horse. He fell down, almost. But he won, that horse did. Everybody was glad. The kids got a big kick outa that . . . I'm Maggie Burk."

Sam nodded and glanced at the youngsters. "You can see Slip Along, if you want to. Think you'd like that?"

They glanced shyly at their mother, their Indian-dark eyes hopeful. She nodded, and it crossed Sam's mind that he could not recall seeing an Indian parent refuse a child.

At the house he drew a bucket of water at the well, took glasses from the kitchen, and they sat on the shady porch. The children's names were Richard and May. Tate Burk's children. The little boy the older, about seven, Sam decided. Save for their light skins, they looked like cute little full-bloods: shy, smoky-brown eyes, straight, blue-black hair, and round, cheerful faces. Would their generation be virtually destroyed, like Antwine's and Ted's and Charlie's and the others'? He brushed the thought away.

Despite the hot day, Maggie wore a maroon-colored dress of heavy material and her bright shawl. Here with her children she seemed more relaxed than at the Vail ranch that Sunday. She was shy, like her children, and said little. Even when she spoke to her children, there was a somber preoccupation underlying her fleshy, round face and her rich, dark eyes, as if her mind were fastened elsewhere.

Before him, by chance, Sam realized, was the last living member of the ill-fated Bear Claw family. Or should he say *survivor?* He withstood the impulse to leap forthwith a barrage of questions.

And so, while the children played on the porch, and he groped for a way to begin, she asked, curiously, tentatively, "Was Matt Colter your father?"

"Yes, he was," Sam replied, pleased that she remembered.

She rocked back and forth, for the moment her brooding yielding to the reminiscent past. "I remember my father bought paint pony from your father. It was for my sister Elsie. She loved that pony."

"Glad to know that," Sam said, aware that Maggie had supplied the very opening he needed.

"That pony was good pony. Very gentle. He got fat and lived long time, that pony." Her voice cut off.

When she did not resume, Sam said, "I remember Elsie in high school. She was about Fay Marcum's age. You were out of school by then, ahead of us. I remember that, too." It didn't seem that long ago, he thought. Elsie, slender, big-eyed, and rather pretty. Very quiet. The best-looking and youngest of the three Bear Claw girls. Maggie the middle one. How naive and trusting the full-bloods were! How unprepared when they came in contact with criminal types. Thus Elsie had died, shot and left in a ravine northeast of Red Mound. A whiskey bottle dropped at her side. The perfunctory investigation by county officials leading nowhere. Just thinking about it angered him.

Maggie Burk nodded and rocked as she spoke, smiling dimly, softly. "Elsie," she said, her heavy face somber once more, "would be twenty-seven now."

Maggie, who was in her middle thirties, Sam figured, had married late. About when the war started. Sam couldn't place Tate Burk back then. He must have drifted in later with the swarm of fortune hunters.

"I haven't been back long," he said. "First time since the war. I hear sad things. What happened to Elsie and Grace and Antwine Cloud-Walker, and other Osage boys."

She stopped rocking.

"This not only' makes me sad," he persisted, touching his hand over his heart, "it also makes me want to do something about it." He hesitated, watching her closely, hoping she might voice her suspicions. He waited further. She volunteered nothing. He made a determination then. She wouldn't talk unless he broke through that frozen mask to her emotions and startled her. He could hold back no longer. It had to be asked now:

"Maggie, who do you think did these awful things? Do you have any suspicions at all, and why? Elsie and Antwine and I were in the same class. Antwine and I were in the same platoon in the Rainbow Division. We were buddies. We went through hell together."

She seemed, literally, to freeze before his aggressiveness, to shrink away from him. Even so, for a fleetness, her dark eyes betrayed her, and he caught the stir of fear. She lowered her eyes to her taut, clasping hands. When she looked up, her agitation was still evident. She spoke in the dullest and emptiest of voices, "I don't know. I just don't know."

"You don't suspect anyone?"

"No."

"There must be somebody."

"No-nobody," she answered, forcible about it, and turned to her children.

They had quit playing and become bored and fidgety. Sam saw their mutual longing when the little girl, with a sidelong glance at the corral, overcame her shyness and pleaded, "Mama, we want to see Slip Along," and drew back, concerned whether she had spoken too boldly.

"You'll have to ask Mr. Colter."

"You bet," Sam broke in. "Let's go right now."

He took them to the corral, Maggie following, and bridled the gelding and threw on blanket and stock saddle and cinched up, and led him out for them to see.

They stared for a long while, speechless, their Indian eyes widening, while the horse hung his head, his attention on them one of mild inquiry.

"Want to pet him? He'd like that."

Richard edged forward, both eager and apprehensive. Sam held him up while the boy, in awe, stroked the long face'and touched the small, white star on Slip Along's forehead. After May's turn at petting, Sam asked, "Like to ride him?"

They crowded up, more confident than before. Sam lifted May to the saddle and Richard behind, and led off around the corral. Time after time, he took them around. Halting presently, he handed the reins to May. "You're a cowgirl-you ride him around. Pull the reins the way you want to go and he'll turn that way . . . It's all right," Sam assured Maggie, "He's a good kid horse. Just an old pet."

They walked the patient horse for a while, and then they jogged him a little, and then they walked him some more. They did so until Richard complained to ride in the saddle. Sam switched riders.

They were still aboard, circling and circling, lost in the discovery of their new world, when their mother said, "Have to go now. Mr. Colter can't play with you kids all day."

"No hurry," said Sam. "I happen to enjoy kids." She thanked him, calling him Mr. Colter again. "Call me Sam."

They were drifting toward the red sedan, the children dashing ahead, when, looking about, she said, "It's so peaceful out here, so still. Like things used to be."

He turned his head, alert, hopeful.

She said no more; by then they had reached the car. She thanked him again, calling him Mr. Colter, thanking him so profusely that Sam was embarrassed.

"Come back. I'll be training my horse." He winked at the kids. "Next time we'll have soda pop."

He stood in the windy yard, watching the long sedan dusting in the direction of Red Mound. Was he any closer? Did Maggie trust him? He couldn't tell for certain, but he decided that today was a beginning.

Sam was saddling next morning when he heard a flivver come rattling and engine-popping and squeaking into the yard. He craned his head and saw Dee Oden. Sam continued saddling.

"Didn't expect you back for a while," Sam said, cinching up, when Oden came to the corral. "Maybe not at all."

"Didn't say I wasn't." The slim face grimaced-half apology, half chagrin. "Guess I figured I wasn't ready for a big race. Didn't want you to risk your money on a green jock."

"Any race is a risk," Sam told him, and the insight

occurred to him that Matt Colter could be talking, because you echoed what you had learned and passed it on, building on it as you learned on your own. "There are days when the best horse can't seem to run up to his potential. You never know. And there are days when they'll surprise you. Too, a horse can be playful and ready one evening, a sick peckerwood the next morning."

"You still need a jock?"

Sam faced him, his interest close and sharp. His eyes found a different Dee Oden, humbled and boyish, one that inspired liking and confidence. "Just going out," Sam said. "Let's see how you two hit it off."

In the pasture, when Oden was mounted, Sam said, "This horse won't make any mistakes. He knows what he's on the track for. Comes from breeding and training and winning. He loves to run. If you dropped the reins on him or lost your seat, he'd go on and do his damndest . . . But he has one peculiarity: He hates the bat. He resents being beat on. So let him run his own race as much as you can. If there's a horse ahead of him, he'll run like hell to catch up and pass. If he gets a good lead, he won't stop and wait for the pack to catch up. He's a competitor. He's thinkin' of where the wire is . . . I want you to work him out slow and easy, down and back. Walk and trot."

Oden looked tense. He took the horse away, walking as instructed. About halfway to the end of the stretch, Sam saw him quicken to a trot. At the end of the course, he reined to come back; but, instead of striding straight, the horse began to resent the hold.

Hands on hips, Sam watched every move, worried about the knees and the cannons. When Oden drew up, the gelding was still contesting the bit. Oden said, "He's a salty horse. He's ready. I like the way he moves."

"Except for one thing," Sam said critically. "You're tryin' to manhandle him, force him-don't. He's got a sensitive mouth. Ease up on your hold. When you get turned, break him out into a gallop. If he wants to run, let him open up a way. I was still kind of worried about him, but I'm not now."

"Believe you're sorta sentimental about your horse."

"I am—because he's honest. I respect him. Sentimental, sure. But, like I said, I'm particular, too."

And so the early morning passed.

Sam walked his horse by hand to the pasture gate, opened it, and led him to the corral and unsaddled and laid on the cooling blanket. Turning to Oden, he said, "You worked him out O.K., Dee. Job's yours—if you want it."

"I sure do."

"Good-then it's settled." Sam extended his hand; they shook. "We'll need to work on the break, the way this horse likes to push off, because the break is everything in a short race."

"You bet, Sam."

"Come up to the house and we'll talk turkey." Sam gave him a slow-breaking grin. "See how rich you'll be on a brush-track rider's pay."

After Oden had rattled off to town, Sam puttered around the rest of the morning, idling, procrastinating. Something bothered him, something obscure, more feeling than fact. He decided it was Dee's turnabout attitude, his complete agreeableness compared to the other day. Why? There had to be a reason. Sam thought about it some more. A man had to be fair, though. He had to take into consideration what Dee had gone through over Holly Abbott, and the load Dee still carried and would carry for a long time. And what was Sam waiting for? His horse was sound.

Sam Colter got moving.

At the Osage Hotel he called the Vail ranch. A woman answered—Fay. She sounded surprised that he was calling. Yes, Hank was there. He'd be there all afternoon. Come on out, Sam. Glad you called.

Fay met him at the door. "Come in, Sam."

Just the way she said it made him hold his glance on her. She wore a tight-fitting blue-and-white dress. Her face was smooth and tanned, and she showed a hopeful smile. He noticed the quick search of her eyes, behind them the shadow of her discontent.

Chattering, she seemed to brush against him in the hallway as she ushered him to Vail's office, which, like the vast trophy room, was an extension of the man himself: austere and efficient, on the walls a polished saddle gun, a framed painting of his stallion Tomahawk at proud stance, an enormous buffalo head mounted on grained wood. Otherwise, the room looked bare. Ledgers in one corner supplied the only visible vestige of business.

Vail was standing at the broad window, his profile clean-cut, his lean jaw and high-bridged nose silhouetted, his arms folded, his back straight, while he seemingly contemplated the sweeping spread of his holdings.

When Sam and Fay entered, Vail appeared to stand yet an additional moment by the window before he turned to more mundane matters. He smiled his arena smile and thrust out his roper's hand, brown and firm and sure. "Come in, cowboy. Tie up. What's on your mind?"

"That match race."

"No better time to talk about it." Vail cast his wife a direct look that said: Leave us. And, wordlessly, she left them.

"A drink?" Vail offered, not insisting, inasmuch as Vail wasn't much of a drinking man by Osage County standards. Sam had gathered that.

"Too early in the day for me," Sam declined.

Vail ran a restless hand through his hair, as straight and jet black as an Indian's. He came around the desk and lightly settled his athletic frame in a chair opposite Sam. "I'll run my Plunger horse."

"I hear he's a good one."

"One of the best, next to Tomahawk."

Sam abided the brag, smiling inwardly. But it wasn't mere touting. The man believed it himself, as if anything he possessed had to be the best; that was fundamental to his spectacular competence and image. Sam, keeping Fargo's admonitions in mind, guessed that Vail would prefer a long race, figuring such would be advantageous for his Thoroughbred-infused sprinters. Most brush-track sprints were three hundred yards or less, though now and then you would go a full quarter. By the same reckoning, why let Vail know that Slip Along was likewise a long sprinter? Let him find out on the track. Let him think he had the advantage.

"What do you say," Sam opened, playing it short, "to 100 dollars at 350 yards?"

"A hundred?" Vail's mouth curled disdain. "I wouldn't take my horse out of the barn for that little dab."

"Would you for 150?"

"I'll be frank with you, cowboy. That's chicken-feed money around here."

"Hmmnn." Sam rubbed his chin. "I'm not exactly in

the banking business either. But I'll go 175."

Insistence built in Vail's eyes. "Make it 225, cowboy"

"You're comin' in a mite high for a Texas brush buster. Tell you what I'll do. I'll go 200 even."

"You're on! But not for 350 yards. I'll run you three furlongs."

"Whoa, now." Sam leaned back and rested his chin on his hand. Was his horse ready to go that far? He felt himself beginning to hedge, and the old rule of matching your horse at his best distance steadied in his mind. "Three-fifty," he said.

"A quarter," Vail said stubbornly.

"I'll run you 400 yards," Sam came back, playing taken. "Even that's a fer piece for my old horse."

"It's a deal," Vail exclaimed, elated, and slapped his leg. "When you want to run?"

"About two weeks all right with you?"

"That's hunky with me. Fits in with our Sunday rodeo schedule, too. For the starter, I'd like to recommend Mitch Kell. He's started many a race out here. No complaints on him."

"Haw about Fargo Young?"

"Fargo's getting on in years," Vail said patronizingly. "He did all right the other day. Fair and square."

"You'd say so since your horse won."

"After going down at the break?"

"Fargo's unsure of himself at times. Mitch is steadier."

"I'll flip you for it."

Vail reached into a trouser pocket. He was shaking the coin between cupped hands. "You call it," he told Sam, covering the coin, then flipping it.

"Heads," Sam called.

Vail caught the spinning coin and slapped it on the back of his left hand. Vail grinned. Sam looked. It was tails. "Mitch Kell it is," he acknowledged.

"Now let's go down to the barns and look at Plunger."

They were at the door when out of the blue of his mind, Sam remembered and turned to Vail. "Tbere is one more thing. I want the right-hand lane."

Vail looked surprised.

"The left one's badly cupped in places," Sam said.

He expected Vail to suggest another flip of the coin, which Sam would not agree to, or to haggle and evade or even suggest a draw the day of the race. Vail spread his hands wide, an obliging gesture. "Take your choice, cowboy. Glad you reminded me. I'll have the boys drag the track down. Both lanes will be the same." He regarded Sam another moment, patronizing again. "You'll be close to the stands. If your horse is crowd-shy . . . ?"

"He's not. He loves company."

They walked down to the barns where Vail, with marked pride, showed Sam a gray stud of impressive proportions, a bigger horse than Tomahawk.

"Stands 15 hands, weighs 1,375 pounds," Vail began, reciting Plunger's credentials like a hard-times banker quoting interest rates, so it seemed to Sam. "This horse," Vail continued, much in the tone of a barker repeating a memorized spiel, "has never lost a match race and has never run out of the money in stakes races. Racked up twelve firsts, two seconds, and one third in fifteen starts. We've matched him up in Kansas, where he won by daylight both times at the quarter mile. One horse he beat was Big Medicine. Know you've heard of him. Fastest thing in Kansas. Plunger's the only horse ever to beat him . . . Took Plunger down to Louisiana, and he just about cleaned out the bayou boys. Ran the quarter in just a hair over twenty-three seconds. Gambling Man was the top horse down there. Plunger took him by a length. Threw dirt in his face all the way."

Sam, sensing that he was being given the "treatment," uttered a low whistle for Vail's benefit. "You've got me plumb scared."

"Plunger," Vail said, waxing more enthusiastic, "comes straight down the ladder from Copper Bottom on his dam's side, and his sire was Sir Timothy, foaled in England and brought to Kentucky as a yearling."

"Sounds like quality folks," Sam had to agree. He had heard his father speak of Copper Bottom, an early-day sprinting great. But Sir Timothy could be another "imported" phantom of Vail's, such as Fargo had snorted at. No matter, Plunger looked well-bred. And he heard Vail go on:

"I stress Plunger's breeding in case you might have some brood mares you want to book. Money back if the mare fails to stick."

"Got a few top mares left in Texas," Sam said. "Might see about that one of these days." Booking fees—that was what all the touting was about. Well, you couldn't fault a man for boosting his stud. Sam had yet to meet a bashful horse breeder.

While Vail continued to extoll Plunger's antecedents, Sam expressing a now and then "uh-huh" or "I see," a wizened little man led a horse by. Vail pointed him out as Pace McKee, his jockey. Sizing him up, Sam saw the print of many races written across the weathered and cagey face. Not only would young Dee be up against a good horse, but also a veteran jock would be in

Plunger's irons.

"Dee Oden's riding for me," Sam remarked.

"He worked for us a while."

Which took Sam by surprise, because Dee had denied ever riding for Vail. "Any trouble?" Sam asked.

"None at all. He's a good boy. Could have used him to help Pace with our young horses, but he wasn't steady. He drifts around too much. You know how some young cowboys are."

"Used to do a little of that myself."

They were trailing uphill toward the house when Sam saw a car appear suddenly on a road behind the ranch. It popped into view, a yellow coupe dusting down out of the unkempt hills, bristly with timber, slabbed with rock, a car driven rapidly and recklessly, bouncing in and out of the ruts.

Vail saw it also. He slowed his walk, openly displeased. "Here comes my rodeo man. Takes a car where a man ought to ride a horse," he said, as though he needed to explain.

The driver waved and honked as he roared up and stopped, racing the motor. Sam recognized Tug Lay. Lay lounged over the wheel. His mouth hung open. He weaved a little. It passed through Sam's mind that he had not seen the man when he wasn't pretty well loaded.

Vail's lean face expressed an old vexation. He looked hard at Lay. He snapped, "See you at the house," and walked ahead.

Lay's reply was a toss of his head. While he waited for Vail and Sam to pass in front of the car, Sam saw the man looking steadily at him, saw the broken grin that was more than the open-mouthed vacuity of a drunk.

At the steps leading to the house, Vail turned to Sam.

"Come in." A perfunctory invitation.

"I'd better drift along."

"We're all set."

"We are."

Vail held out his hand. His smile flashed. They shook.

Driving away, Sam saw Lay taking slow and careful steps up the long flight of stone to the great house. And he thought of the cryptic face, and as before he couldn't place it in the past. But it was back there, he knew.

Lay's coming out of the hills struck him as somehow odd. Upon reaching the brow of the rise that overlooked the ranch, Sam fixed his eyes on about the spot where Lay had appeared. That was rough country in there, too rough for stock. Vail had referred to Lay as his rodeo man. Yet Fay had said Lay was a hand around the ranch. There was a difference. He didn't fit either.

Sam drove on. Blamed if he wasn't getting as suspicious-natured as Scotty Hinton, who suspected everybody.

But before Sam crossed the pasture and rattled over the cattle guard, the road into those hills and the hills themselves occupied his mind once more. He turned north, away from Red Mound, and proceeded slowly, viewing Vail's spread and the broken column of hills. His purpose gathered momentum as he drove at twenty-five miles an hour. He was looking for a way into that ruggedness, maybe a gap. There was nothing to be seen along here. This was still Vail's buffalo pasture, five strands of barbed wire behind stout cedar posts closely spaced.

He cut speed even more, just looking, just watching, enjoying the vista, musing a little. There was everything within that fence that a cowman would want in life, and yet man always wanted more. The familiar imagery of hills adrift on a gentle sea rose to him.

He passed the buffalo fence comer and saw the beginning of three-strand wire, seeing whitefaces now, rolling fat on the bluestem. He never saw them that he did not think whitefaces were the perfect breed for the Osage grasslands. Like Fargo and his bright-red bay horses, he guessed he was prejudiced.

In his contemplation, Sam passed the pasture gate before he could stop. It opened on the dim trace of an old wagon road, which likely was the way to the ranch, coming from the north, before the highway was built. A man following it across the pasture would skirt the foot of the hills, and southwest into those hills was where Lay had come out.

Sam was quite thoughtful when he turned the touring car around, conscious of a rising excitement. By the time he drove home and fed his horse, the sun was down. Killing time until dark, he drove back to Red Mound and ate supper at Jimmy the Greek's and strolled to the hotel and back.

Summer twilight lingers late in the Osage. There was yet a glow over the hills at nine o'clock when he approached the pasture gate. Seeing headlights coming from the north, he did not stop. When the car passed him, he drove a short distance, whipped around, doubled back, snapped off his lights, and eased across the bar ditch. Lifting the wire hoop, he tossed the gate out of the way and drove through and closed the gate and followed the pale tracings of the wagon road.

The dark line of the hills crept closer. He almost ran over a cow bedded down in the road before she rose with a snort and bolted. Rocks began bumping and clattering against the underside of the touring car as he drove slowly in second gear. Far enough. He could knock out the pan and strand his car.

He left it there. At the last moment he remembered his handgun under the front seat. He set off southwest through the mellow light, soon wishing he was on horseback. He worked out of the rock clutter and passed through more cattle bedded down, continuing his drift southwest, while the starry night seemed to mark time. Later than his calculations made at the car, he reached the buffalo-pasture fence and followed it west. When it cornered at the foot of a hill, he started climbing, virtually feeling his way through the brush, stumbling over rocks. In the timber above him whippoorwills called; tonight those plaintive notes evoked loneliness.

His going seemed endless until he topped the backbone of the long hill. From here, southeast, he made out the scatter of lights at the Vail ranch; even at night the layout appeared big and formidable, and he thought how everything around Red Mound seemed to gravitate there.

Rested and his bearings in order, he turned south along the crest, welcoming the stronger light up here. At some vague point in his stumblings, he came against another fence. Not barbed wire, he found, feeling, but a high, hog-tight barricade. Standing on tiptoes, he touched barbs at the top.

There had to be a gate somewhere and there had to be a road leading to the gate he reasoned, following the fence to his left, downhill, which led him back into the tangles of brush and slippery rock slabs. He could feel runnels of sweat down his chest, and his booted feet were soring up. The fence angled off along the flank of the hill. He stumbled blindly along it; when the fence changed directions again, he was climbing and, surprisingly, the brush was thinning.

He heard a roar. He swung toward it and caught the sound of a truck laboring up a steep grade. He crouched. Moments and twin beams joggled uphill to his left on a rutted road not fifty yards away.

Understanding took him at the same instant: This was the road Lay had taken out of the hills and down to the ranch Sam watched the truck struggle to the crest and halt at the fence, watched a man leave the timber and unlock a length of chain on the wooden gate and swing it open. The truck passed through and halted again; its lights showed a wooden shack beside the road. Sam heard voices, indistinct while the idling truck motor chugged on. The guard closed the gate, and the truck rumbled ahead.

Sam, following the headlights, saw them continue north along the hilltop for a brief distance, then slant toward the west. They seemed to drop from sight immediately, and the hill was dark again, though he could hear the truck's motor changing, as though in low gear, and brakes protesting. Suddenly those sounds faded.

Circling away from the gate, Sam crossed the road below and worked back to the fence line. Now the guard was to his right. At times he seemed to hear a stirring, a kind of humming, in the direction where the truck had disappeared. He followed the fence a way and held up when the sound grew fainter.

He started climbing the fence where it was stapled to a post. Each time the wire squeaked, he paused. There were two strings of barbed wire at the top. He pushed his hat through, lifted the lower strand and eased under, the .45 like a rock grinding into his middle, the barbs digging into his back. Gingerly, he freed himself and stepped downward, hearing the squeal of the wire pulling against the staples. Clear, he dropped to the ground, snatched up his hat, and ran. A flashlight blinked at the guard hut. Sam dropped.

Flattened, he saw the guard walk to the gate and flash the light down the road, and left along the fence, and right, in Sam's direction.

He saw the light advance down the fence and waver on the post that he had just descended, waver, go on, and become fixed. Sam tensed for footsteps to come tramping down the fence. But the light snapped off. Sam waited, hearing the wind sighing through the timber.

At last, he pushed up and hastened on. Before long he came to a road that turned westward, and he followed its broad tracks, drawn by the stronger humming.

Sam saw the smoky glow before he heard the voices as the road dropped into the head of a shallow, V-shaped canyon. From its brushy rim he looked down in astonishment on a well-lighted, open-air shed and a congestion of steel barrels and a maze of copper coils. Fires burned under the barrels. Vapors rose. Sam inhaled the not unpleasant heavy mustiness of cooking mash. The humming came from an array of batteries under the shed that generated power for the electric lights. A spring-fed stream veined the floor of the canyon. The voices were those of workmen loading wooden cases into the back end of the truck. Rifles leaned against a stack of cases.

A man called, and the loading stopped. The man left the shed, holding a fruit jar on which he was screwing down the lid. He looked inside a case and set the jar therein. The other workmen laughed. The loading continued.

Well, as Sam could see, it was simple to figure why Lay, a known bootlegger, had driven out of these rugged hills: This was his supply source. Sure, Lay worked for Vail, but not as his "rodeo man," lining up stock and riders. And, of course, Vail knew about the still, which ran day and night. With his penchant for management, Vail probably supervised the operation and saw to its efficiency. Small wonder that Vail showed annoyance when Lay, carelessly, chose daylight to pick up a load, assuming he had, or even to drive out of the guarded area, when a ranch visitor might see and wonder.

Watching, Sam saw the boss man close and padlock the doors of the truck and toss the key to the driver, who climbed in, started the motor, shifted gears, and headed up the steep incline.

Fading back into the woods, Sam waited for the truck to pull by. When he heard it stop at the gate, he followed the road to where it angled south to the gate, and he hurried north to the fence, his mind racing. Tonight he'd had his first real peek behind the genial mask of the booming Osage. He could just see the federal alcohol boys hell-roaring in here and busting up that big still. Then he had second thoughts. Would a raid help or hinder the investigation? He'd talk to Scotty about it.

Around midnight he drove into the yard. After looking in on his horse, he went to the house. His mind was yet back in the guarded canyon. At least some aspects of the situation around Red Mound were beginning to hook up.

His first inkling that something was wrong alerted him when he saw the open back door, which he had left unlocked as usual but closed. Inside, he struck a match and lit the kerosene lamp on the kitchen table and held the lamp up, biting back his anger at what he saw.

The place was a wreck—drawers pulled out and contents dumped, including the flour bin in the old Hoover cabinet. He found the same trail of havoc in Fargo's modest little parlor: books pulled from the old-time, glassed-in case, the settee's cushions on the floor, the worn carpet ripped up. By all rights he ought to pay Fargo some damages. There was nothing here, he reminded himself, no credentials of any kind that linked him to the Bureau.

He paced back through the litter to the bedroom, trying to convince himself of the alternative of burglary. He held the lamp high, seeing the carcass of the overturned mattress, ripped and cut like a side of beef, the stuffing hanging out like a busted cotton sack, and the dresser drawers spilled, and, in plain sight on the dresser, his pocket watch and the ten-dollar bill that he had forgotten to take.

It wasn't robbery, so it was something else. And that, and its implications, he declined to think about further tonight.

He set about cleaning up the ruin.

CHAPTER 11

DAYLIGHT ADDED A FURTHER DIMENSION OF destruction, as if the methodical intruder had enjoyed ripping and dumping and scattering. Sam retraced his own steps from his first day in town. Had he slipped up somewhere? He didn't think so. Had he been too open with Maggie? He thought not. Besides, Osages weren't ones to talk. And with Dee Oden? Not when he considered what Dee had suffered.

Oden's prompt arrival broke Sam's circling thoughts. They took the horse to the pasture and worked him, and Sam liked the way young Oden followed instructions and handled the horse. Oden was getting the break down about right, learning to use the gelding's quickness without losing his seat.

"I've wised up to one thing," he told Sam. "That's hold onto your hair at the break—'cause he's gone!"

Last night kept coursing through Sam's mind after Oden left. What worried Sam most was that if his cover was known or suspected, so might the other agents be threatened. It was time he got in touch with Scotty.

In Red Mound, he bought a *Tulsa World* at the Osage Hotel and strolled to the post office, meanwhile looking for Hinton on the street. The town had donned its usual face of peace and innocence before his accusing eyes. Two middle-aged Indian women, their movements heavy, entered the Osage Mercantile. A businessman, coatless, sleeves turned at the elbows, a flutter of papers in one hand, stepped briskly into the bank. No one came out while Sam watched. Quiet. Very quiet. And he thought, the old renegade's resting again.

His mind slipped back to Red Mound's lasting shame—that stark piece of earth where the home of Ben and Grace Bear Claw Jordan had stood, blown to matchsticks that cold and windy March night in 1923; likewise the death site of pretty Holly Abbott. Bare except for mounds of rubble and the concrete foundation and the depression of the underground garage, where the nitro was placed. The lot belonged to Maggie as the next heir of her childless sister. Likely it would remain vacant unless she sold it to a white person, for an Osage would not build there after what had happened.

He dawdled away time at the post office while he penned a postcard to his mother, Letitia Colter, in Alice, Texas, written also for any snoopy eyes: *Dear Mama: Have met a few old friends like Fargo Young. He's still in business. Slip Along went down at the break, but won his first race. He's all right. Another match race coming up soon. Hot here, like you remember. Plenty windy. Hope you're feeling better. Love, Sam.*

After mailing the card, he loitered while reading the *World* . . . An Indian homicide at Wynona, south of Pawhuska. No suspects taken into custody yet . . . The Osage Tribal Council was protesting the prices some county merchants were charging restricted Indians . . . The self-styled Home Owners' Organization was stirring again. Composed of bankers and guardians and cattlemen who had purchased surface rights on the reservation, it was hurling the old threat of contesting extension of the tribe's mineral period, the main sustaining heritage left the Osages.

Reading about the HOO wakened his umbrage. The Osages were too easygoing. They ought to raise hell. Meet them head-on. Go after these pleasant-faced, hand-rubbing vultures, and he was not surprised at the depth of his reaction, for he felt these things.

Not spotting Hinton, he idled to the Sportsman's Billiards and shot a game of rotation with a friendly cowboy, lost as usual, and paid, and afterward loafed by the tobacco counter, smoking and watching the street. By now it was past eleven o'clock. He could wait no longer. He looked up Hinton's Insurance Agency in the phone book and gave the number to "central." An affable voice came on: "Hello. This is Scotty Hinton. What can I do for you?"

"This is Sam Colter, Mr. Hinton. I'd like to talk to you about a loan on my policy."

"Glad to. Why don't you drop by the office? I'm over the bank."

"I'll do that. Much obliged."

He climbed the wooden stairs to Hinton's office and turned down the long hallway, his boots clumping. Most of the attorneys' offices were open because of the heat. Voices hummed. One was unmistakably an Indian's. Hinton's door was likewise open. Sam entered and sat.

Talking toward the open door, Hinton, businesslike and genial, said, "About that loan on your policy, Mr. Colter. I think we can fix you up." At the same time, he slid a notepad and pencil across to Sam, who wrote, "Need to talk pronto. When can we meet?" He slid the pad back.

Hinton scribbled rapidly, returned the pad, and Sam read, "Tomorrow night—pens. Need time to call."

Sam, jogging his head, saw Hinton wad up the note and pocket it, to be destroyed later. Hinton said distinctly, "You'll need to bring your policy by so I can check it for the loan value. About how much you need?"

"Around a hundred, I guess."

"How old's the policy?"

"About seven years. It's a twenty-year pay."

"Should be enough in there, unless you have another loan against it."

"I don't have."

"By the way," Hinton said, in his best town booster voice, "I believe you're new around Red Mound?"

"Not exactly. Lived here before the war. My father was Matt Colter. He sold horses and mules. I've brought a short horse up from Texas. Beat Miss Whizzbang in his first match race."

"Say, I saw that! Some race."

"I've matched a race with Hank Vail's horse Plunger at the next Sunday rodeo."

"Well, I sure aim to see that! You betcher boots, young fellow. Glad you're back! Red Mound needs more young people. Too many wander off to places like Tulsa and Wichita, when there's more opportunity right here at home . . . Don't forget to bring in that policy. And if there's anything else I can do for you, Mr. Colter, just remember that Scotty Hinton Insurance is at your service. Yes, sireee!"

Clumping down the hall, Sam noticed more faces behind desks, faces that glanced up with interest when he passed. Scotty had laid it on pretty thick, and they'd taken in every word.

That evening Sam did something he had not done before: He turned his horse into the bluestem pasture for the night, concluding that was safer in view of the ransacking. As an added precaution he parked his car behind the barn, out of sight from the road or yard.

Restless, he sat in the cool darkness of the front porch. A high wailing—*el coyote*, singing off there, and another answering, now several. And the mysterious whippoorwills; they would call most of the night. Hearing the shrill cry of a killdeer disturbed in its grassy domain, he was reminded of an observation of his father's, "We're closer to the frontier than we realize." True, in Osage County, where the land was largely unspoiled. And that reminded Sam of his grandfather Colter, who as a young man had served with a Ranger company on the border, whose mind seemed forever fixed back then; sometimes dreaming in his cane-bottom rocker, he would snap up, savagely alert, watery old eyes darting, and whisper a low warning, "Watch for all signs—be especially on guard when you don't see or hear any." And the time-eroded face would be somewhat young again, for that moment.

Well, there were plenty of signs tonight. He was thinking of the ransacking. He switched his thoughts to Fay and her open discontent, and her unconcealed invitation of renewal. He supposed he ought to feel bitterness toward her, which he had once, and hurt, which also he had once, deeply; but he insisted to himself that that was rubbed out, as his Indian friends used to say of something gone, and that was so, he knew. But further, when he asked whether the roots of his old feeling still lived, ready to spring forth again, he shied away from answering.

As the night wore on, he realized that he was waiting, half expecting his ransacker to return, and hoping he would. The road had been silent for more than an hour, and still he waited. He stood and shifted the .45 to a more comfortable position.

He picked up the sound of a car, then, heading east from Red Mound. Not fast. Just purring along. He stepped to the end of the porch and sat, deciding that after the car passed he would go in to bed. Enough of this night-owling. He was letting it get to him. A question hammered. Why would his man venture back when he'd found nothing the first night? Unless—and the alternative crashed—it was to gun him down?

He could see the car's lights. Fargo's little ranch lay off a straight stretch of road; thus, usually, drivers were traveling fast when they passed. Except this driver didn't appear in the usual hurry.

Sam bunched his lips when the lights snapped off, while he continued to hear the drone of the car. That sent him off the porch and along the fence leading to the road, pausing some twenty yards from the road. If the driver swung into the yard, Sam would have him flanked.

He froze, faced west. Little by little he made out the dark hulk of the car coming through the gloom, still not fast, but deliberate. He turned his head as it approached. A sedan. He couldn't tell how many occupants.

A stringy tightness held Sam as the driver slowed to a crawl. Sam flung around, fully expecting the sedan to lurch through the open gate into the yard. *Damn you. You don't see my car. Come on.*

At the final instant, the driver stepped on the gas. A hundred yards or so down the road, Sam saw the lights flick on. He muttered to himself and drifted back to the porch, still waiting.

About fifteen minutes later, he heard a motor growling on the road to the east. Again he saw the eyes of the lights; again he saw them go out; again he heard the low-speed approach.

A wild impulse grabbed him. To wait by the bar ditch. If this bird slowed as he had on his first pass, to rush the car and jerk him out of it.

Hardly had he spurted toward the gate when he heard the driver accelerate. Spewing dust and gravel, the car whipped past the house. Sam stopped in his tracks, watching the headlights flash on well down the road, watching until they vanished.

He turned for the house, his thoughts settling and firming. Whoever, just couldn't make up his mind tonight. Peeling a blanket off his bed, he tramped to the barn and climbed to the haymow and took his sleep.

Sunlight warming his face woke him. He rolled up on an elbow and gazed out the haymow, the landscape and sky before him like a remembered favorite print: the great bowl of blue overhead, the serene hills. And his horse at the pasture gate, wanting his breakfast. The scene lost focus, as transient as a soft summer cloud, like a pleasant dream you tried vainly to call back, as last night and the night before clouded his thinking.

Young Oden didn't show up until about noon. By then Sam had long since worked the horse and turned him out and was fixing fence.

"What held you up?" Sam asked.

"Drove to a joint east of Ponca last night. Thought I'd listen around. Maybe get a line on who blew up the house. My jalopy broke down on the way back."

"Find out anything?"

A negative shake of the head.

"What you need is a good saddle horse," Sam said, guying him a little.

"Wish I had a good horse."

Oden had fallen into a mood. He hung his head and looked away, his light blue eyes discouraged and uncertain, in them the brink of bitter self-pity. He seemed thinner than yesterday.

Sam felt a stab of understanding. Dee had been through a private hell rarely experienced. His young hopes shattered, just as Sam's were once, only more so. Maybe Sam was being too rough on him. Yet, Dee had to learn responsibility, and there was something Sam had to clear up here and now. He said:

"We're matched against Plunger a week from next Sunday." The slim face showed neither surprise nor anticipation.

Sam intended to speak with consideration, but his voice carried an edge. "Hank Vail told me you worked for him once."

"What else did he tell you?" Oden asked, a tiny quiver of feeling scudding across his thin features.

"Said he let you go. Not that that's any of my business. Only you told me you never rode for Vail. Why, Dee?"

His equivocal face altered, boyish and appealing, the intense eyes meeting Sam's so openly that Sam almost regretted bringing up the matter. "If I'd told you I was canned, you wouldn't a-hired me."

"I found out anyway."

Oden's hand moved across his brows, a confessional gesture. "I'll tell you how it happened. I was snoopin' around at night, here and there, like last night, and got to work late one too many mornings. I don't blame Hank, hard a man as he is. He's got a ranch to run. Why keep a saddle bum like me around?"

Such self-pity Sam couldn't take. "And why run yourself down, Dee? That will never get you top wages. A man has to respect himself before another man will."

"You some kind of preacher?" Oden's voice flung a touchy resentment, yet he avoided Sam's eyes.

"Just telling you how it is-that's all. Get your dobber up, Dee. You'll never find Holly's murderer looking down at your boots. Hell—throw up your head and keep it there so you can see where the tracks got"

Painfully slow, Oden brought his head up. When he looked at Sam, some of his moodiness was dispelled. Sam read an openness he had not before, perhaps a willingness to talk. He asked softly, "Have you found out anything, Dee? Anything at all? Who might have the faintest motive to blow up the house? Anybody besides Rex Enright?"

"Seems you've always got a question." For once, he looked straight at Sam; then his voice dulled.

"Nothing—I just told you that."

"Any time you want to play detective is jake with me," Sam said. "Just remember, we've got a horse to get ready . . . Now you can lend a hand with this post while I staple the wire." He cuffed Oden lightly on the shoulder. "Then we'll put on the feed bag. You look like you could stand a good meal."

Oden left around mid-afternoon, fogging up the Red Mound road like a wild Indian on payment day. Sam kept thinking about him. A strange kid: hurt, moody, confused, erratic, overly sensitive. Like a man trying to rush off in all directions at once. Bitter one moment, drowning in sorrow and self-pity, obliging and hard-sweating the next. But a good hand with horses. A damned good hand.

While Sam's thoughts ran ahead to tonight's rendezvous, he occupied himself going over the rundown place. Fargo's barn needed shoring up on the north side, and there were more weak spats in the pasture fence that he couldn't get to today.

He was making his way up from below the barn when he heard the car enter the yard. It had a smooth and powerful purr, like a mewing cat. A horn honked.

He hurried, hoping to see Maggie Burk and her kids, though Maggie wouldn't announce her arrival by honking.

In place of Maggie's red Cadillac sedan, he found a brand-new roadster, gleaming white, top down. Fay Vail sat behind the wheel. She was alone.

She spied him just as he saw her. She waggled him a carefree wave. Sam held up. He wanted to see her and he didn't want to see her, not alone. He wasn't afraid of her, he was afraid of himself. He hesitated another moment, then waved and came ahead.

Arms smooth and shapely draped over the wheel, dark head canted toward him, long-lashed eyes paying him a strong interest, she waited for him in anticipation of his approval. Her new dress (her dresses always looked new to him), white with tiny blue flowers, and cut low in front, set off the gray-green depths of her eyes.

Sam glanced back and forth over the sleek machine and whistled. "Hey, what's this?"

"A Marmon. Got it in Tulsa this morning."

"Little present from Hank, I guess?"

"Other way around. From Fay to Fay." She slanted him an exaggerated, provocative look. "Care to go for a ride?"

His hesitation was no more than momentary, but he saw that she noticed; then he was saying, "Don't mind if I do."

She gunned the motor while he was walking around, and when he was in, she shifted gears and backed up roaring and tore out of the yard, heading east, streaming dust. Her wind-whipped hair sweeping back laid bare the bold silhouette of her face, the fullness of her mouth. Her short skirt kept climbing above her bare knees; in vain, she kept pulling it down.

The landscape began to blur by faster and faster. He glanced at the speedometer and saw that they were pushing seventy. He yelled at her, "You'll burn up the motor if you don't slow down."

With a sidelong glance at him of pretended pique, she reduced speed; now they could talk without shouting. "Do you really like it, Sam?"

He couldn't miss her childlike appeal for approval, her need for attention, for he knew her well. "Right nice little jalopy," he said, wanting to tease her. "I thought

Hank got it for your birthday." And the second he said that he realized his error, because she took it up: "Sam—you remembered!," and her expression deepened. She kept looking at him.

Countering, he asked, "Wonder what Hank would do if he saw us together out here?"

"He won't. He's in Pawhuska on a deal until late. If he did, it wouldn't matter. He doesn't care."

"Wouldn't bet on that if you gave me ten-to-one odds. I can't see Hank Vail letting anybody have anything of his, even if he didn't want it. I don't believe you."

She drove on a way, and her voice reached him as unusually thoughtful. "You're a pretty good judge of men, Sam—yes, you are. But you don't know a damn thing about women."

He laughed outright at her candor. "You know, I have to agree with you." She joined in the laughter, which seemed to break the strain between them. They were past the long, level stretch by now, coming to a scattering of wooded hills. She drove even slower, apparently not aware of it. She had quit pulling at her short skirt, unmindful of her bare thighs. She said suddenly, "I still feel terrible about everything."

"I thought we cleared that up once and for all."

"I can't forget it."

"Why can't you?"

"Because it was selfish and cruel."

"Like I said, quit blaming yourself."

"I can't."

"Time you did. We're all vulnerable through our emotions and needs, especially when we're young. It just happened. Leave it at that." He was beginning to feel wary and uncomfortable. He sat in silence, sensing his mistake in coming.

She regarded him so long and so intently that she let the roadster stray, and the right side started bumping along the rim of the ditch. With a quick turn she righted the car, and her eyes on him acquired a yet deeper engrossment. "I'm afraid you don't understand, Sam."

He chose to ignore that not-to-veiled meaning. "You've got everything a woman would want. Why don't you try harder to be happy?"

"I have. Today I bought this car. But it's not going to make me happy. I don't need *things*."

Despite his self-restraint that affected him, and suddenly he was on treacherous ground. One wrong involvement and he'd be in so deep he could wreck the entire investigation, bringing Scotty and Blue and Gene down with him. Shaking his head, he said, "You told me at the hotel you came to set things straight. You did. Leave it there."

"But I was wrong. I found out I hadn't. Not in my own mind."

They passed the loading pens and afterward the Indian cemetery and came to a north-south road. Sam expected her to turn around and head back. Without pausing, she drove deeper into the hills.

"Did Hank tell you he'd matched Plunger against my horse?" he asked, shifting the conversation.

"He told me, and you'll lose." She was being petulant, he saw, because he had changed the subject.

"Why so sure?"

"He never matches a race unless he's sure he can win. He doesn't think your horse can go four hundred yards."

"Did you know there's a lot of betting going on? That Hank is offering odds? That there's considerable Indian money on your horse?"

"News to me."

"Maggie Burk told me. We're good friends. She told me how nice you were to her and the kids that day on the road. She likes you, so she's bet on your horse. It's that simple. You know how Indians are."

"I know they're loyal to their friends. And I know I don't like what I've heard happened to the Bear Claw family."

"Maggie's been through hell. She's so sad."

There was his opening. "Tell me something, Fay. Who could've killed Elsie? Who could've blown up the Jordan house, and why?"

"Why"—her voice seemed to catch—"are you asking me?" She let the Marmon lose speed until it was lugging upgrade. She shifted into second gear and drove on, faster.

"You forget I've been gone eight years," Sam reminded her. "You've been here all the time. You know a great many people. You've had to hear something."

Fay wheeled the lithe roadster around a sharp curve and kicked it out a way, afterward easing off to conversational speed. Her voice came out precise and careful:

"It's being said that Rex Enright blew up the house, or had it done, though I hate to repeat that. It's a terrible thing to say."

The old, worn-out story bandied about even at the Sportsman's Billiards! He overcame the impulse to mock her. When she didn't elaborate, he pursued in his roundabout way. "Enright—Rex Enright, the roper? Didn't he and Tug Lay rub fur at your party?"

She nodded.

"Why would Enright blow up the house or have it

done? Why would anybody?"

"Money, I guess. What else? Maybe hatred?"

"You seem convinced he did?"

"I'm just repeating what I've heard," she amended distinctly, holding her eyes on the road. "You asked me."

"You said money. Has anybody figured out how Enright would profit?"

"To keep from paying a debt, maybe."

"He would still owe the estate, if it's a debt of record."

"Maybe it wasn't."

"Guess Grace's headright went to Maggie?"

"Who else? She's next of kin."

He was getting nowhere. "What about poor Elsie? Who are they saying murdered her?"

"You've got me there." When she turned her head, he saw a weary irritation. "Aren't you being awfully nosy, Sam?"

"Time somebody was. And there's Antwine Cloud-Walker. I heard what happened to him." Sam was getting angry again. "We were in the Army together. Antwine got the DSC. A national hero. He went through all that—came home and was murdered. Makes me mad as hell that nothing's been done."

"There were investigations. I know that. I mean the county did, and I heard that the state sent people in."

"But no charges filed."

Receiving no further response from her, he did not persist. He wondered if she knew anything. He turned away to watch the range country fleeting by. It lifted his cynicism a little. A subtle contentment reached him, a reawakening. He turned to find her watching him covertly, in the gray-green eyes that mixture of enigma and warmth.

By this time they were quite deep into the timbered hills and rolling pastureland, and the afternoon was waning. just when he thought she would go no farther, she made a sudden turn across a cattle guard and continued on without explanation.

"Where the devil you going?" he asked, more curious than surprised.

"You'll see," she said, a touch of color in her cheeks.

He settled back, his pulse beating a bit faster, noting the absence of recent car tracks on the pasture road, which she followed confidently, on through a shallow gap, on across a sweep of prairie, and finally off the road into a park-like cluster of stubby oaks. Within the shade, she stopped and cut the motor, exclaiming, "We're on one of Maggie's ranches. Sometimes we bring the kids out here for picnics. There's even a little spring over there."

Sam opened the door and strolled about, seeing the blackened circle of a campfire and, at the base of an outcrop of sandstone, the sparkle of the spring, which formed a glistening pool, which wandered happily downslope, until lost in the pristine prairie, eventually to join the dark green of the creek he saw curving away in the clear distance. He watched for filling moments, taking in the vista of prairie and hills and sky, feeling the peace and the strength here. The emptiness puzzled him, had vaguely since they had left the main road. He returned to the car.

She was touching a dainty powder puff to her face. She put it away in a beaded purse and turned her head, meeting his eyes, and he saw her open smile, free of any pretense, like a light showing the perfection of her face. There was no evasion. In that briefness, she was nineteen again, natural and warm. He shook off the perception.

He said, "Good country through here . . . wonder why it's not stocked?" and leaned on the car door.

"Tote Burk's not much of a cowman. Too far from town."

He let the silence swell between them, hoping she might add something about Burk. She did not—was it caution?—and that was one of the qualities about this older Fay, this full-bodied Fay, that bothered him. He said, "I don't remember Tate. When did he come to the Osage?"

"About the time you left, I think. I know he married Maggie about then."

"What did he do before that?"

Her you-should-know look rebuked him. "What you would expect—nothing."

"Where's he from?"

"I have no idea." She reproved him mildly with her eloquent eyes, her rich voice. "Why the sudden interest in Tate? To me he's a very boring subject"

"Just chinking in some gaps. You forget how long I've been gone."

"Need you remind me?" Her reproof vanished, which, he divined, signaled the end of the Tate Burk interrogation.

He considered her through frank eyes. "Fay, why did you come here?"

"So we can talk." But her following smile was nervous. "We've done plenty of that already."

"You still don't understand."

"Guess I don't."

"It's pretty plain. I need you, Sam."

"Whoa, now!" He was thunderstruck. "You don't

need me. You have everything."

She sent him the deepest of looks, and over him swept a pounding. He could feel the blood creeping up his neck and face like a rash.

"Everything, you say?"

"You have Hank," he reminded her, forcing steadiness into his voice. "Don't you two ever talk?"

"Yes . . . about cattle, horses, land, grass, water, wind, brush, fences, barns—"

"Isn't that what a rancher talks about mostly? It's his life."

"Is that enough?"

"Depends on the woman, I guess."

"So you do see what I mean?" Her high-boned face was a mirror of her discontent and of her unconcealed need. He saw all that; it was true. She was unhappy, unhappy as hell. Yet she baffled him, as if he saw two contradictory persons: one appealing and open, the other only partly defined, veiled and elusive.

He felt the tug and pull of old emotions, and hard upon those stirrings, like a fist jarring him into awareness, the reason for his being in the Osage. What did she know? She was too close to the center of the frenzy around Red Mound not to know more than the worn generalities she had echoed. Other names, other motives. He didn't like the position in which he found himself at this moment. He could insist that they leave, else he could stay at her whim and something might fall.

Therefore, when she fumbled in the side pocket on the driver's door and came up dangling a pint and a tin cup, murmuring, "Here's some honest-to-God Kentucky whiskey, not that rotgut Hank—" and paused in time, he had to smile. "Will you get us some water, please? We'll have a nip or two, then go. I promise, Sam."

"What's the hurry?"

He took the cup and went to the spring and back and slipped in beside her, feeling far from the calm front he wore. She held out the bottle. He uncorked it and handed it back.

"Here's dust in your eye," she toasted him, and sipped, grimaced, chased the whiskey with water, wiped the mouth of the bottle with a handkerchief, and passed the bottle to Sam.

"Here's to feathers in the wind," he said, and took a short pull. It was hot but sweet. He had tasted worse.

"Now, what would that mean?" she laughed, tilting her head back, her provocative eyes on him.

"To peace in the Osage."

"I'll drink to that, though I'd rather not think of such things right now."

They lit cigarettes and smoked in silence.

"Sam," she said, after another drink, "I can't believe you came back just to match some races."

"Red Mound is home to me. I like the country. Wanted to see it again. To be honest, I was plumb homesick."

"There was no other reason?" she asked softly.

He let that implication slide by. "I might settle around here, if I can find a place I can afford to buy."

She sat up, at once enthusiastic. "Like Fargo Young's?"

"Something about that size. It would have to be reasonable."

"Maybe I could help you buy a bigger place? Big enough to run cattle? Fargo's wouldn't support but a few head. It's more like a small horse ranch. Maybe I could, Sam?"

"Think Hank would like that?"

"Might," she said, laughing, "if he had first mortgage."

His smile was dry. "I kinda doubt that Hank would go for such a deal. I can just see him peering down the barrel of one of his telescopic rifles—me in the cross hairs."

"Maybe," she persisted, turning fully toward him, "I could swing it on my own. I'm a pretty fair business woman, I think. Hank has given me cattle. I've made money. I keep Hank's books at the house."

Then, he thought, his mind steadying, you know about the still and the trucks hauling the stuff at night—you'd have to. And behind those big eyes of yours, which look as innocent as a child's, you know a great deal more about Tug Lay than you let on. In reverse, he felt a flare of anger that Vail would involve her. He leaned back, realizing that he was making excuses for her, wanting her out of it, unhurt. He said, "Much obliged, Fay. But I couldn't let you do that. Besides, it's a little early yet. I haven't decided what I'll do."

"Well," she said flatly, "you won't get rich matching brush races."

"Hadn't aimed to. Figured while I was looking around I might pick up a few bucks with my old horse." He noticed that the drinking cup was empty. He should go far more water, but a lassitude gripped him, and he didn't move.

She said, in a voice low and recalling, "You haven't changed a bit—you never wanted to be beholden to anyone," and swayed toward him.

He had no reply. He was beginning to feel the drinks and an increasing awareness of her. He recognized the drift of her perfume—jasmine, he thought, the same she had on that night at the hotel. He could hear the rhapsodic tinkling of the leaves in the wind, and the voice of the wind going off whimpering. He could see the dappled shade on the long hood of the roadster.

She spoke again, with an intimacy. "I'm glad you'd come out here with me, Sam. It means a lot just to talk to someone."

"You're not trying to be happy."

"How can I be when I'm not?"

"Sometimes we have to work at it."

"I've tried that, too."

"You could go away."

"Go away . . . just when you've come back?"

Her face was quite close, in shadow, blurred, softly outlined. She was waiting, He leaned in and kissed her lightly on the lips. "For old times," he said, intending to draw back.

To the contrary, he found his arms around her and he was drawing her roughly to him, feeling the smoothness of her body beneath her thin dress. As she met his kiss with parted lips, her arms slipped around him and her whole body seemed to flow into his. His breath came and went unevenly.

Almost at once he felt her jerk back. He saw the softness drain from her face, and the sudden trace of hardness underneath. She stared into his eyes, her brows knitting, and then downward, and he knew even before she burst out, "You've got a gun!"

The .45 inside his belt! He had put it on when he finished working on the fence. His voice was as unconcerned as be could couch it. "Sure. The same one you saw at the hotel. My house was ransacked the other night. We left so suddenly I forgot to leave it."

The moment was over, leaving him the incompleteness of relief and regret. She pushed back farther on the seat, perceptibly upset. "Guns frighten me," she said, touching a hand to her throat.

"I hate the damned things myself, but sometimes a man has to carry one."

"I'm afraid."

"Afraid of what?" He had a wild surge of tenderness for her, and he threw an arm around her. She felt cold to his touch.

"It's nothing," she said, shaking her head.

"It's not if you're afraid. Tell me about it."

A visible change moved into her face and stayed there, dissolving the soft lines, spoiling the illusion and the mystery that he had glimpsed and that had drawn him to her again. He saw again the suggestion of underlying tautness. He let his arm fall.

"It's getting late," she said, sounding tired. "I've kept you out long enough." Deliberately, she put the bottle and cup back in the side pocket and, casting him a final look, she started the roadster and backed out.

She drove in silence for a long way. But before they reached Fargo's she was chatting again. Sam got out and closed the door, studying her face. "You all right?"

She shrugged as if it didn't matter, and, seeing her glittering smile, and the evasiveness again, he knew that she was herself once more. "That last kiss didn't seem like just for old times, Sam. It was sweet and tender."

That, and she roared off fast, slamming the Marmon into second gear when she turned onto the road.

Watching the roadster's wake of dust, drifting like smoke on the wind, he concluded that he had played his hand badly. Still, he could be wrong. Maybe she knew nothing beyond Vail's whiskey-making and whiskey-running enterprise. He hoped, doubting even as he hoped, that her involvement went no further. So nothing had been gained. Just old feelings raked up. No fulfillment. And what could she be afraid of, married to the biggest man in the county?

Her shock at discovery of the handgun was understandable, yet he sensed more than that behind it. Was it because she doubted him for the first time, just as he had begun to doubt her?

CHAPTER 12

BITS OF THE AFTERNOON KEPT STRAYING IN AND OUT of his head while he drove through the wind-whimpering darkness, bound for the loading pens; even when he focused on other matters, like what he had to report tonight, Fay and the puzzles she posed weren't far away, like dim faces pressing against the window of his mind, asking to be let in, pleading to be understood. *I need you, Sam.*

He seemed to fall into an abstract musing, which was unusual for him, for generally there were duties close at hand to be done. Despite his careful self-control, Fay had slipped past his guard. She had touched him, reached him, which he hadn't thought possible again, and possibly he had reached her. The past reformed before him: picnics they'd gone on, school dances they'd attended, so strictly chaperoned. A bright blue ribbon in her dark hair. Unreal now. Reality: What was it? Was death the only reality? He'd seen too much of that—too many young faces back there. You couldn't change the past, but you could keep it in perspective; most times he did, but tonight he couldn't somehow. A man like himself followed the course of duty; that was his main drive. For a woman like Fay (or most any woman, he supposed) it was love and someone listening. Ilad he listened enough? *You don't understand, Sam.*

He stopped short. By God, he'd better straighten himself out damned quick.

Seeing the cattle guard ahead and no one behind him or coming, he switched off his lights and turned in, rattling across, taking the dim tracks to the pens. He saw two cars, Scotty Hinton's and Gene Poole's. He was chatting with them when Blue Sublette powered up in a Packard sedan.

"Well, Sam, what is it?" Hinton asked after Sublette joined them.

Concisely, Sam began to sketch what had happened, from the night he was run off the road east of Red Mound—and spotting Kirk Singer's car in town bearing the telltale dents, and tailing Singer to the bootlegger's, and Singer ordering Tug Lay, roaring drunk, taken to Vail's ranch, and seeing Lay drive out of the hills behind Vail's, and finding the still in the canyon-to the ransacking destruction of Fargo's house.

"Whew!" Hinton muttered. "You've been getting around. Are you sure Singer was the one?"

"Positive. I've got his paint on my car. He denied it, naturally. Claimed some kids took his car for a joyride that night. Then he offered to have mine fixed."

"You've identified the car but not the driver."

"I saw two men in the car. I figure Singer would be driving his own car. The other man probably was Tug Lay."

"Why him?"

"They run together, don't they? Singer's generally in the background, always the one who takes over when Lay gets drunk. There's another reason. I've said this before: I've run across Lay somewhere. Probably in Texas. But a piece is missing. I can't put it together yet"

"Think Lay's recognized you?"

"Got a hunch he has. Otherwise, why would he and Singer try to wreck me?"

"Assuming it was Singer and Lay. Might have been kids driving the car. If Lay knew you in Texas, it was on the other side of the law. In which case your cover is worth about two whoops an' a holler." Hinton struck a match and cupped the flame in his hands, lighting a cigarette. He snapped the dead match. "We can't let this go by. Tell you what, Sam, I'll start some backtracking on Mr. Tug Lay in Texas. Take some time. Lay could be an alias. Meantime, you stay away from Vail's."

"Can't do it. I've matched a race with Vail a week from Sunday."

"Go ahead, then. Sure. But steer clear of Lay."

"Scotty, I'd like to make a suggestion. Let's keep the still to ourselves for a while."

"Think I know what you're getting at."

"A raid won't help us. If we tell the county, somebody will tip Vail off in advance—you know that—and if the federal alcohol boys bust things up good, we'll have more people with lockjaw than we have now."

"All right," Hinton conceded. "What's new up around Burbank, Gene?"

"About the same. I've noticed the farther you ride from Red Mound, the colder the trail seems to get. I've listened till my ears are bent, and I've told my old stories so many times I've got calf slobbers—and haven't picked up a single new lead."

"Nothing on Singer?"

"Not a smell, though what Sam said clears up some of

the smoke. I'd say Singer sides Lay because he's protecting his whiskey supply line to the oil fields around Blackjack. Big stakes. I've inquired about Singer around Burbank and among the ranchers, but nobody has cut clear sign on him. All they know is he runs that joint in Blackjack—whiskey, gambling, girls . . . dope, too, I've heard. Tell you what he puts me in mind of, Scotty, and that's an old-time bounty hunter. Leaves no tracks."

Hinton seemed to run that through his mind, back and forth. "Gene," he snapped, as if coming to a sudden decision, "I want you to shift over to Blackjack and start bird-dogging Singer."

"On my expense account? That calls for gamblin' and buyin' whiskey and talkin' to the girls."

"You won't mind the last part so much, will you? I'll see that more expense money reaches your general delivery. Believe you'd better keep your headquarters at Burbank. As a cattle buyer, you go to Blackjack for your fun. Give Singer plenty of rein," Hinton cautioned. "Just get acquainted. Play it loose and easy. Understand? No Ranger heroics."

"Don't worry. I aim to live to a crotchety old age in Texas."

Hinton turned to Sublette. "What's the word around Hominy and Pawhuska?"

"Tribal Council is thinking about posting a reward in the Cloud-Walker case."

"Doubt if that will help. John Cloud-Walker has already put up five thousand. Council posted rewards in the two Bear Claw cases, too. Nothing's happened."

"Hell," Sublette rumbled, "people are afraid to talk."

"What's more," said Hinton, his voice shading off to a mocking anticipation, "sometimes they get an unusual hankering to travel." He paused. "This just floated up to the surface in town. There was a drifting cowboy named Rusty Dunlap. Rode for the Ives ranch northwest of Red Mound. He was riding fence the day Antwine Cloud-Walker was murdered out there in early May. Rusty let that word drop at the Sportsman's Billiards. Not long after, seems he took a sudden craving to see the sights in Old Mexico . . . Was to get a wad of money. More than he'd ever seen or likely will see again. You can bet he won't come back to the Osage."

"So Dunlap saw who shot Antwine?" Sam said.

"Or hinted he did. Maybe saw the guy driving off. I've asked the Bureau to check with Mexican border authorities. Find him, we might have the key that turns the lock."

A car's roar swelled on the road west of the pens, and the four men grew still, turned that direction. The roar climbed to a higher pitch, held, unbroken, passed the cattle guard, and gradually ebbed to a murmur on the night wind.

"There's another new development from my end," Hinton said. "Maggie Bear Claw Burk is just about ready to give husband Tate his walking papers. One of my associates down the hall is handling the matter. Nothing filed yet. But it's in the making. My associate will make a nice, fat fee, and Tate Burk, who never had it so good, will lose his plush seat on the gravy train . . . Even an Indian woman has her limits. Before long squawman Tate will be plying that gold toothpick after rabbit stew instead of steak and potatoes."

Sam reflected on that, surprised. At last Maggie was showing some fight! Hinton's continuing factual voice cut short his thoughts:

"I keep hearing that Billy Gault was offered big money to leave the state—that was before he and Nora got hitched—but wisely he refused, knowing if he did he'd look even more guilty. Now that he and Nora are married, he's sitting pretty."

"An offer?" Sam asked.

"A bribe. It was done indirectly, you might say-through the mail. No names. Nothing you could trace. Money waiting for him at a certain place. Same way, I figure, Rusty Dunlap was offered his see Mexico money, with the broad hint that that would benefit his health . . . Which reminds me: I did some checking on land titles at the county courthouse. Although Antwine Cloud-Walker was murdered on the Ives ranch, it was on pasture leased from a fullblood woman named Rose Moon, who's a ward of the federal government. Know what that means? We've got a case that can go to federal court. Anything more, boys?"

No one spoke. To Sam it was as if they were going over and over the same cold, divergent tracks that led nowhere. Always dealing with suppositions. If they brought Rusty Dunlap back from Mexico? If . . . His backlog of frustrations broke, apparently spilling over to Poole and Sublette and gripping them with an identical muteness. "Guess it's time to go," Hinton said.

They were near their cars when Hinton swung around, and his voice, meant for Sam, conveyed an entirely different tone, an interrogative sharpness. "Ever talk to Fay Vail?"

"Just this afternoon."

"Well—," in a manner that said Sam ought to have volunteered such information.

"Nothing new." Not her upset when she had discovered the handgun. Not her fear. Not the complicated fear she wouldn't talk about and had tried to shrug off. Not her careful caution about names. He had acted instinctively, out of the deep-seated past. He said, "The only name she mentioned was Enright's . . . old stuff," and was glad Scotty couldn't see his face.

"I see," though Hinton was an extra moment answering. "Keep at it, Sam. I'll be at Vail's for the race. Good night."

In the days that followed, Sam readied his horse and avoided Red Mound except to go in for feed and groceries. Slip Along, a hearty eater, could put away ten quarts of mixed grain and bran a day, in addition to hay. The smoky heat of August clutched the hills during the afternoons. Sam made his bed in the haymow near his horse, alert for nocturnal intruders who never came.

Dee Oden hadn't missed a day. Sam continued to instruct him, to emphasize the break.

"You break on top," Sam told him, "and this horse will be hard to beat. He was born to run, so let him run his race. The few times he's lost it was never falling back, it was always coming up."

What did Dee know about Plunger?

"Big and rough. He'll top thirteen hundred pounds. Stands fifteen hands. Strongest horse I ever saw. Rank at times. He finishes hard."

"How is he on the break?"

"Quick and rough."

"Vail told me Plunger has never run out of the money."

"That's what they say."

One afternoon, while Sam was patching up around the barn, Maggie and the children drove out to Fargo's.

"They just had to see Slip Along," she explained in apology when Sam came out to the car. "He's all they talk about. We won't stay but a minute."

"And hurt his feelings? Slip Along had his workout early this morning, when it was cool. He's just loafin' now. You kids like another ride?"

"That's a bother," she objected.

Sam opened the backseat door before she could say more. "Come on, you kids."

He herded them to the corral, saddled the horse, and mounted them, the little girl in front, and led them around and around. Afterward, like before, he had them take turns handling the reins, and when that was over he invited them to the porch and served red soda pop, cooled in the well.

"Sam. . ." Richard began.

"It's *Mr. Colter,"* his mother corrected him immediately. "You know you don't call older people by their first names."

"What is it now?" Sam encouraged him. "How . . . how did Slip Along get his name?"

"So that's what's bothering you? Well, there's a story how that came about." He pursed his lips and frowned and gazed off, a teasing delay that turned the children impatient. Then, finally: "At first my folks couldn't decide on a name for him. My father wanted to call him Baldy's Boy, after Slip Along's daddy, whose name was Old Baldy. But my mother didn't like that. Several months went by and they still didn't have a name. They kept calling him Little No Name."

"Why didn't you name him?"

"I was in the Army. In France."

"Where was Little No Name?"

"In Texas. One afternoon it clouded up and looked like rain. The mares and their colts were out in the pasture-the colts down by the pond, and their mammies up toward the ranch house. By this time Little No Name was about three months old and pretty shaggy, and here he was, just a long-legged little fella without a name.

"My mother always worried about the horses when it stormed. She was out on the back porch, watching, when the wind came up, and there was a big roll of thunder. That was when the colts decided they'd better get close to their mammies . . . You can tell fairly early if a horse is going to be a good runner by the way he moves, how quick he is . . . Well, the colts took off running. Little No Name was last. Pretty soon my mother noticed he was catching up. Taking long strides. Next thing she knew he was up with the bunch. Then he was out in front, the first to reach his mammy. He hadn't seemed to run hard. Just sorta slip along. Right then my mother said:

"That's it—that's what we'll call him. His name will be Slip Along."'

Delighted, Richard and May, their Indian eyes gleaming, sprang to their feet with coltish leaps and bounded away to view their favorite through the bars of the corral.

"I'll swear, those kids," Maggie condoned, shaking her head, while smiling. "All they talk about is Slip Along. Good for them to get out like this. Be around stock. We have places in the country, but we live in town most of the time."

"Kids need ponies and dogs," Sam said, hearing undefined longings in her voice, and guessed that Tate Burk spent little time with his family. "In the country they can begin to understand the cycle of life. See something being born and growing up. Something growing old and being looked after."

"That is good," she said solemnly, and fell silent.

He let the silence run. Was she thinking of her

mother, Julia Bear Claw, who also had died under mysterious circumstances? Of Elsie, of Grace? Maybe, at last, now, she would reveal her suspicions. He waited. Her sad eyes on the restful hills told him that she longed to find peace of mind somewhere with her little ones. Another moment and the distant look left her face, and he knew that she wasn't going to confide in him. How, he thought, can I bring her around to trusting me? He must jolt her out of her submissive acceptance, her seemingly Indian-like resignation to fate, the brooding melancholy of her crushing sorrows. How?

"I visited Antwine's father soon after I came back," he said, a certain forcefulness to his voice. "He's hired a bodyguard, an Indian veteran, has a big watchdog, and has strung 'fraid lights around his house. He says he's afraid some white man will sneak in and murder him."

Once again, her solemn nod. No word. Just her inscrutable face. Her Indian face.

He asked it abruptly, plunging in, his words blunt, "Are you afraid, Maggie?"

She turned her head and met his eyes. Instead of the angry affront he half expected, she said, "Yes, I'm afraid," and her voice pinched off.

He did not let up. "Of a certain person or persons?" while understanding softened his voice.

"It's more . . . more like dark cloud over these hills, this bad thing I feel. I reach out—but I can't touch it, but I sense it. It's there. I look and I don't see it, but it's there, I know. It is very close somewhere. Very close." Her voice had fallen lower, like a moan, he thought.

"There is no particular person? Just the cloud?"

She nodded, and he knew that she spoke truth. A surge of sympathy charged through him, behind it the whip of his anger. He felt his features harden. He said,

"Wish I knew who murdered my buddy Antwine," and saw her dark eyes take on a vigilance.

"What would you do?"

"I would try to work through the law. Give authorities what evidence I had, hoping there was enough for the county attorney to file a murder charge."

"If county did nothing?"

"I would go to the Federal Bureau of Investigation in Oklahoma City. Tell them all I knew. They would help. No, I would do that first. I wouldn't go to the county."

She shuddered and leaned away from him, staring down at her brown hands, which she clasped and unclasped.

"I would do that, too, if I knew who killed Elsie and blew up the house," he said. "I would do that. I would go to the FBI." There it was. He had told her, tried to give her strength.

Briefly, he saw her impulse to speak. He saw it like a feeble awakening on her heavy face, extinguished as she said, with the old resignation, "So many bad things have happened . . ." Her voice trailed off.

She had sealed herself off again. He sensed that as he heard the children romping up from the corral. He got it out quickly then, yet softly, "If you ever need a friend, Maggie, you can count on me. Remember that."

By now the children had reached the porch, laughing and talking in excited gushes, calling Maggie "Mama." How big Slip Along was. How he looked at them. Richard had even dared pull some grass under the pasture fence and feed it to Slip Along. Mama, he did that!

Maggie, smiling at them, understanding them, enveloped them in her arms. Rising, she told them, "You thank Mr. Colter, now," which they did, shrilly, and when they ran to the red sedan, she said, "Thank you, Sam. What you said."

Her voice, dulling again, betrayed that she had lapsed into her impenetrable state, the damnable deadlock within herself that so frustrated and nettled him.

She went heavily to the car and got in. Richard and May waved. Sam waved back. Lord, how he enjoyed them! Shrill farewells. Maggie drove away.

Was he any closer? Did she trust him, a white man?

His mind was heavy as he walked back to the house. Tomorrow was Sunday, race day.

CHAPTER 13

AROUND ELEVEN O'CLOCK SAM LOADED HIS HORSE and tack and headed for Vail's Forked Lightning Ranch. He was leaving earlier than he had the day they beat Miss Whizzbang, when he timed his arrival after the rodeo started. Today he wanted to be set up before the crowd arrived, in time to settle his horse down just right and walk over the track alone. Dee Oden would join him later.

Passing the great house, he saw four cars there: Lay's yellow coupe, Singer's Lincoln, Vail's Cadillac touring car, and Fay's white Marmon. *All present and accounted for, sir,* thinking of the three men. He had expected to see Fay again at Fargo's, and had dreaded her coming in a way. His thoughts turned backward to their ride and those moments parked in the woods near the spring. So near. Like when they had ached to run off and get married that time. Only he was so blamed poor, they couldn't.

Although Sam Colter wasn't a superstitious man,

sometimes he pondered whether the marginal difference between living and dying was not foreordained. The man next to you gets a bullet, while you go untouched in a hail of machine-gun fire. A grenade's angry burst in the trench. A man cries out: *I'm hit, Sam—I'm hit!* You don't get a scratch. Like in the Ninety-first Psalm. The words rose to his lips like rote: *A thousand shall fall at thy side, and ten thousand at thy right hand; but it shall not come nigh thee.* It had not come to one Samuel Travis Colter for reasons beyond his mortal comprehension. Neither was it meant for Sam Colter and Fay Marcum to marry. Likewise, neither was it meant for them to make love the other day. There could be nothing between them, ever. You could not change what was precast, no more than you could bring back the young faces. And yet he had not loved another woman.

He pulled Slip Along's trailer into the shade of the little patch of blackjacks south of the track, and led him around and afterward fussed over him, using currycomb and brush.

"You know, pardner," Sam said, when finished, "you're not a badlookin' *hombre* when you get your hair combed and you're all slicked up.

Leaving his horse, he walked to the track and paced it from the four-hundred-yard starting line to the finish. True to his word, Vail had dragged and rolled it, filling and smoothing the cupped places. Somehow Sam hadn't expected that.

When the rodeo crowd began arriving around one o'clock, he experienced the onset of nervousness. In contrast, Slip Along stood like a gentle saddle horse, patiently waiting, seeming to doze and dream, moving only to switch flies. Sam, fidgeting, let him have a few sips of water from the bucket. Next, he brushed him again; next, he checked Slip Along's new shoes, tacked on in town at a blacksmith friend of Fargo's. The horse had sound feet; been lucky that way, always an easy keeper.

As the afternoon lengthened, Fargo Young strode over, dressed in his race-day best and looking serious. "I see you're all set," he observed, eyeing the horse. "Bets are right brisk. Hank Vail figures he can win, else he wouldn't be givin' three to one."

"Three to one! I'll just take some of that. Can you place it for me?"

"Plenty of time. Vail's had a man takin' bets all afternoon at the rodeo."

Sam, passing him a twenty-dollar bill, said, "Sorry you're not the starter, Fargo. Vail insisted on Mitch Kell. I wanted you. We flipped and I lost."

"Never mind."

"Who is this Mitch Kell, anyway?"

"Runs a hock shop in town, off on a side street. Takes in Indian blankets and jewelry and such up front. Peddles a little whiskey out the back door."

That links up, Sam thought, thinking of Lay and the still. "Where does Kell shape up as a starter?"

"Claims he's worked the big tracks in Missouri."

"I'm impressed with some of the people Vail keeps around him," Sam said, his mouth twisting. "Like this Tug Lay. Know anything about him? Where he's from?"

"Popped up around here a few years back. All I know. That and he bootlegs. Works the Indian trade." Fargo seemed to dismiss the subject as unimportant. He looked around, then said, "Pace McKee may try to carry your horse to the outside. He's pretty slick with it. He's done it before, here, with Plunger. Or he may try to crowd your horse at the break. Claims it's just Plunger's nature. Him bein' so big an' hard to handle."

"You believe all that?"

"Was I born yesterday?"

"This looks more and more like an old-time brush race, where a man had better hold onto his shirt. Have you seen Dee?"

"No." Fargo wore a surprised look. "Figured he'd been around by now."

Sam was scowling. "If McKee deliberately bumps my horse at the break, Vail's gonna hear about it."

Fargo snorted like a wild horse. "Man takes his chances on a brush track. You know that, Sam. If your horse breaks fast, you won't have to worry much. Anyway, figured I'd better warn you."

"Much obliged, Fargo, old friend."

Fargo beamed. He was living again, Sam saw, in his inseparable element of horses, his sound knowledge appreciated.

After Fargo left, Sam fretted out a dragging hour. Where was Dee Oden? Down to half an hour now before the race. Sam paced from his horse to the edge of the timber, watching the advance of the crowd leaving the rodeo, watching the distant flurry around Vail's barns. Sam saddled his horse, his anger gnawing.

Just minutes before race time, when Sam had decided he would have to ride, he saw a slim figure break running from the cars parked behind the rodeo stands. Dee Oden at last, carrying his riding boots.

Breathless, Oden ran up. His face was flushed, and his eyes were worried. Before he could mumble excuses, Sam tore into him. "Where the hell you been?"

"My old jalopy again. Damn it to hell!"

Sam's angry eyes, never leaving the thin features, saw Oden avert his gaze and hang his head, and after a moment look up in that hurt and ingratiating manner of his. "I'm sorry, Sam. Just couldn't help it. That old jalopy—"

"Damned if I'm not gonna buy you a mule to ride so you can be on time," Sam shot back, and relented a mite, shutting off his flow of hot words as he thought of the time. "Get ready. I see they're bringing Plunger over."

Oden sat on the running board of the touring car and struggled off his cowboy boots while Sam checked the saddle cinch for the last time. When Sam glanced around, young Oden had on his light riding boots and stood ready and hatless. His straw-colored hair, cut raggedly and short and falling across his forehead, created the impression of a boy in his early teens.

"Let's go," Sam said, hearing the announcer bawling the distance and the names of the horses and owners and jockeys. When Oden was mounted, Sam took the reins and walked Slip Along toward the track. At the moment Vail, astride a bald-faced chestnut, was leading the gray Plunger, McKee up, before the applauding crowd.

Suddenly remembering, Sam spoke over his shoulder. "McKee may try to crowd you at the break or carry you to the outside down the stretch."

Oden didn't answer.

Sam snapped around. "You hear what I said?"

"Yeah."

"Then speak up!"

"I was thinkin' about the break."

"About time you did. You just break this horse on top. He knows what to do."

Sam came to the track, hearing the murmur of the

crowd, feeling the familiar tenseness. He went a little cold when he saw a Vail cowboy, dressed up like the Fourth of July, in the judge's box at the finish line. That was one item Sam had forgotten. Well, he was learning! He just hoped Vail's man didn't have to decide a nose finish.

Sam moved on, and as he started to lead his horse before the chattering, shifting crowd, somebody whooped, somebody clapped, and somebody hollered, "Come on—Slip Along!," which suddenly established the crowd's mood. Applause. It rose louder, it became general, as well as the whooping and hollering. A sensation of warmth turned Sam, and he understood when he saw the Indians: enough for a big stomp dance.

As if not to be outdone, Slip Along threw up his head in recognition, the Botch ear hanging, and regarded the crowd curiously, if not warmly, and ambled on toward the starting line.

Kell, the day's official starter, was chafing at the slight delay. A brisk, restless man somewhere in his forties, tending to heaviness. His dark brown suit and his dark brown western hat, combined with his cheerless impatience, put Sam in mind of a casket salesman hurrying to catch a town's one train a day.

Kell raised his voice at Sam. "I want this short and sweet. When I drop my hat, the race is on." He turned pompously to take his position at the starting line drawn across the track.

Down the track some twenty yards, Vail had released Plunger, and McKee was walking the fractious gray stud. An uneasiness prickled Sam when he studied the veteran little jockey. McKee sat his horse like a crab, his alert face a mask of caginess.

Sudden heat fanned Sam's face. There was no call for

Kell's high-and-mighty curtness. Patience and coolness and horse savvy, not hurry, were the essentials of a fair starter. A man like Fargo Young.

"I think I know how a race is supposed to start," Sam informed Kell, speaking as Vail rode back and dismounted off the track where he could observe the start. "But if there's a bump at the break and either horse gets knocked down, I want another start. Got it?"

"I'll take care of the start," Kell said uncomfortably. "Just get your horse ready."

"He's ready—he's been ready," Sam said and walked on.

"Hey, cowboy," Vail called to him. "I know how you feel. Hell, I don't know what that revved-up Plunger horse of mine'll do—run or fly."

Sam had gone but a few steps when a deeper meaning sank home. Hell, he was being given the "treatment." Vail was playing up Plunger's wildness as an excuse preliminary to McKee's trying to rough Slip Along.

No matter, Sam thought. From here on it was up to Dee. He'd just have to outrun the other horse. Muttering a "Good luck," Sam handed the reins to Oden, who walked the gelding on a way preparatory to flanking McKee, coming up on Plunger, to approach the starting line.

Sam stared in utter astonishment when Oden reined Slip Along about to come even with Plunger, when he saw Oden at that late moment reach inside his right boot and pull out a leather bat.

"Hold it!" Sam shouted, striding to his horse. Furiously, he snatched the bat from Oden's hand and heaved it. "I told you no bat! Never use a bat on this horse!" he was raging. "What's got into you, Dee? You out of your head?" He was struggling inwardly not to jerk the boy off the saddle.

"Just figured I might need it today against Plunger," Oden said, and put on his hangdog look.

"Never, by God! Never!"

"Say, Colter"—Kell's abrasive voice struck between them—"you intend to run this race or forfeit?"

Sam was sorting out alternatives. If he rode in Dee's place, he'd be handicapping his horse some thirty pounds. Now, without the bat, Slip Along had a better chance with Dee up, if Dee rode a strong race. He looked straight into Oden's face.

"Dee," Sam said, as flat and final as he could make it, "you ride this horse-and you ride him right!" He stepped clear, seeing the surprise on Oden's face.

Sam watched the horses cavort to the line. Plunger was acting up, yet nowise the uncontrollable terror Vail had implied. Slip Along was behaving quietly as usual, keyed for the first jump. But Dee should move up. He was a head behind McKee, and he should bring his horse sideways enough so Slip Along could push off at the break. Kell's hat dropped like a dark-brown blur.

They were off! A sudden start. Too sudden.

Sam bit his lip. Dee was caught with his horse flat-footed, missing the advantage that could have been his. A clean break, though. No bumping. That was something.

Sam scowled as Plunger jumped in front, getting away fast, half a length ahead, moving powerfully. Standing in the bloom of dust, Sam leaned forward, hands clenched, as if he might lend impetus to his horse. The starting line was the worst possible place to watch a race. He could hear the cow-country crowd beginning to find its partisan voice now.

Plunger held his lead to the first furlong stake, but

Slip Along was coming up. Sam saw him close suddenly. For about fifty yards they appeared to run head to head.

McKee started to bring Plunger across, and Sam flinched, fearing for his horse. It was happening. McKee was going to force Slip Along to the outside. If Dee didn't give ground, McKee would bump him and break the gelding's stride or possibly knock him down.

But as McKee bored in, Sam saw his own horse leveling out, running lower and lower, striding longer. Dee was letting him run his race. Finally! *Take him on, Dee! Let him go!*

Now McKee straightened Plunger. He had to. Slip Along wasn't even. Wasn't there. He was out in front. McKee's right hand flashed up and down. He was going to the bat. He'd lost valuable ground veering over.

Now Plunger was challenging, sprinting like a gray ghost through the dust. McKee's bat never ceasing. The crowd standing and yelling and whooping.

Sam lost clarity of the race through the dusty haze. He saw the blurred shapes streak past the judge's stand, and he thought his horse had a chance, maybe. Maybe not, the way Plunger had come up with heart under lashing. Hearing a thudding close by, he saw Vail tearing off down the track on the chestnut.

Sam felt weak. He hastened, half dreading, half anticipating.

He still hadn't reached the stands when he saw the horses turning and circling back. He noted with satisfaction that his horse still wanted to run.

Fargo Young rushed up, shouting and hopping, "Boy, howdy! Your horse by half a length! We saw Old Baldy and Peter McCue out there today, you bet we did! See you in a whipstitch!"

Sam's eyes were moist. He hurried on, aware of a heady elation. Looking for the horses again, he saw McKee rein Plunger off the track and head for the barns.

Oden was standing up in the irons, a set grin on his face. When he dismounted, the crowd flowed around him and slapped him on the back and shook his hand and admired the horse.

Sam held back. Let Dee enjoy his victory. Might be the very thing he needed to lift him out of his doldrums. Sam turned at a touch on his arm. Maggie Burk was smiling as he had never seen her smile. She had to yell for him to hear:

"I bet on Slip Along. First time I ever won a bet off Hank. He lost his shirt today." She left him to make her way toward Oden and the horse.

Fargo jostled up and shoved a handful of greenbacks at Sam, who tried to press one in Fargo's hand. "Cleaned up some myself," Fargo chuckled throatily, warding off Sam's hand. "Reckon I know horseflesh. Your horse was pulling away at the finish, comin' like a bat outa Carlsbad."

Sam waited until the well-wishers had thinned out before he went up to Oden and shook hands. "Nice ride, Dee. You beat a pretty good horse today. Let's go home." Other details, like the bat and the late break, could be chewed on later. But by the time they walked to the trailer, Sam hadn't the heart to take Oden to task. The boy had won, hadn't he?

When Oden changed boots and stood up, Sam paid him and said, "See you in a few days, Dee. You turned him loose at the right time."

Oden smiled his thanks and headed for the stands where his jalopy was parked.

Sam watched thoughtfully after him, thinking, *Mighty*

quiet after riding such a *good race. Most kids would be swaggering around.*

Sam unsaddled and watered his horse and was draping on the cooling blanket when Vail rode up. The sight of him raked anew McKee's attempted rough ride. Now, Sam decided, was prime time to clear the air.

"Congratulations, cowboy," Vail greeted. "Didn't figure that old horse of yours could go four hundred yards like he did. I take my hat off to him." He did so, with a flourish. He appeared to be taking his loss in good humor as he handed Sam his winnings. "Would you sell that horse, cowboy?"

"He's part of the family," Sam answered, shaking his head.

"Would a thousand dollars interest you? That's a heap of money for a gelding."

"It is. But I can't take it."

"Was afraid of that."

Vail was guiding the conversation along genial lines that Sam resented. Sam had the feeling that Vail wished to avoid the obvious. Sam spoke bluntly:

"McKee tried to carry my horse out. It was deliberate, Hank. You saw it."

Vail's brows wrinkled instant disapproval. "I saw him draw over, if that's what you mean. I asked Pace about it, too, you bet. He said Plunger pulled over him. Lugged hard. Plunger is a mighty rough horse."

"I'd say McKee did the pulling over. It was deliberate."

Vail shrugged, his geniality tapering off. "That's one of the chances a man takes. I've taken mine many a time."

"Point is it looked deliberate."

"Pace said it wasn't. That's all I can say." Vail's

attention shifted from Sam to the horse and back. His lean face seemed to become leaner. His eyes flung out a vying. "Later . . . say in September . . . I might match Tomahawk against your horse. Think you might be interested?"

"Maybe."

Vail's voice hardened. "Maybe's good enough for me right now. I figure Tomahawk can take your horse at any distance."

A hot wind seemed to whirl up through Sam and into his voice. "There's an old saying among horsemen down in Texas. That an ounce of performance beats a pound of hot air."

"I'll be in touch, cowboy." Giving his arena wave, Vail reared the chestnut around and spurred into a run.

CHAPTER 14

THEY WERE MEETING AGAIN, THIS TIME AT THE INDIAN cemetery, under a mid-August moon. Tonight Sublette, Poole, and Sam waited on Hinton. A rising wind blew its parched breath through the blackjacks, rattling the leaves, promising no relief.

"Hot and dry," Poole observed, speaking as a cowman. "Grass is holding up, though. Wonder what's up?"

"Scotty called me at Hominy this afternoon," Sublette said. "Said be here for certain. Funny thing, said he was calling from Pawnee."

"He seemed in a big hurry when I saw him in town this morning on the street," Sam said.

A car was approaching fast from the west on the main road below the wooded hill. Sam turned to listen. He knew the labored sound of that motor by now. It was Scotty's old coupe.

Hinton parked under the trees, slid out, and stepped quickly across. Without his usual prefacing small talk, he began. "We've had a turn or two in the case. May be something. May not amount to a hill of beans . . . Remember I told you about Rusty Dunlap, the drifting cowboy on the Ives ranch, who let slip that he was riding fence the day Antwine Cloud-Walker was murdered in the Ives pasture? That Dunlap was offered a bribe by mail to get out of the country, and took it?

"Well—the poor guy never saw Mexico. His body was found three days ago in a ravine west of Pawnee by some squirrel hunters . . . Some rough country in there . . . However, identification wasn't established until yesterday. Looked like it happened several months ago, about the time he was supposed to leave Red Mound. Been shot in the head three times. So the coroner's jury found."

"Any big money on him?" Poole asked.

"Not a dime. Not even a pocketknife. Not even a sack of Bull Durham. No identification. No ring. No belt buckle. No clothes. Even took the poor boy's boots. There was one little slipup, however. Dunlap's name was on the sweat band of his hat, found in some brush . . . You know how cowboys are; they like little personal things like that . . . The sheriff over there started calling around. Called Ponca City and Pawhuska. Somebody in the sheriff's office at Pawhuska called Red Mound . . . Happened that one of my down-the-hall lawyer associates had represented Dunlap in a minor matter, and that further established his identity and his job at the Ives ranch. I just wonder if Dunlap didn't go to the ravine for the payoff and was murdered there."

"And," Sam submitted, "whoever killed Antwine killed Dunlap. Or had it done."

"Now hold your horses for another puzzler," Hinton said. "Although I don't see any connection as yet with the Osage murders, it could be important." He paused, as if reconstructing the scene in his mind. "Tug Lay, Red Mound's leading bootlegger and supplier to various and sundry dives in the Osage oil fields, was found murdered in his car this morning south of town. Two shots in the head, two over the heart. A .45 was the weapon. Appeared he'd stopped on the road to powwow with somebody when he got it."

Poole broke in. "The head and the heart? Sounds like a professional killer. But wait and see, they'll call it hijacking."

"That's not all." Hinton took something from his inside coat pocket. "Anybody got a flashlight?"

"In my car," Sublette said, hastening there and back.

"Take a look at this," Hinton said. He knelt and clicked on the light, his body shielding the glare from passersby on the road.

The three crowded around. Sam, looking down, saw a man's prison-type photo.

"Mean anything to you, Sam?" Hinton asked after a moment.

Sam, staring at the beardless face, age middle or late twenties, noted the aggressive mien and the quarrelsome eyes. He stared at the closely cropped hair, at the slash of the irregular scar above the upper lip. But it was the assertive cast of the lean face that held him.

"You know him, all right," Hinton said.

As Hinton spoke, understanding crashed through Sam. "Why," he exploded, "that looks like Tug Lay . . . yet—"

"It is," clipped Hinton. "A younger Tug Lay at Huntsville prison. In for cattle stealing. On the records there his name is Roy Earl Lay—Tug was a nickname. Guess he liked that because it made him sound tough. He also traveled under aliases. You didn't recognize him here because he had covered up that scar with a full mustache and he wore his hair long, like an imitation Buffalo Bill, and he was much heavier—a sign of more provident times."

Events were coming into focus for Sam now, sliding together, fitting. "I might forget a name, but not a face."

"He also went by Roy Earl Quinn and Earl Roy Robb."

"I helped send him to prison," Sam recalled. "I testified against him. Yes, it was a cow-theft case. I was the chief witness."

"When was that?"

"About six years ago, when I was a Ranger. He'd changed so much here I couldn't place him. The name Lay just didn't hook up back there with the face. His case was routine. We worked on a lot of cases. But he remembered me. Guess I haven't changed much." Sam groaned at the realization.

"Important thing is, your cover could be gone."

"But 1 wasn't a threat to Lay's bootlegging."

"Wouldn't he want to get even? Run you off the road? Kill you if he could? Wouldn't Singer help him, being in the same racket?"

"Furthermore," Sublette said, "if Lay was involved in the Osage murders, he'd pass word first thing he'd known Sam as a Ranger. He'd see Sam as threat."

"That's what worries me," Hinton said. "How this affects the investigation, if it leaves Sam open. If Lay was involved, he was bound to have told others about

Sam, and we know more than one person figures in the killings. It's too well planned, the way they're exterminating the Bear Claw family."

A troubled silence settled upon them, unbroken until Hinton spoke. "Sam, I've a mind to take you off the case. You could be a marked man. If I knew for certain that Lay was implicated in the Osage murders, I'd order you out of here before daylight."

Which was what Sam was afraid Hinton would say. "If we knew he was," Sam argued. "But we don't. Listen, Scotty, I've talked to Maggie Burk again. She keeps bringing the kids out to Fargo's to see my horse. I think she trusts me. I'm positive she knows something—she just won't let go. She's afraid. She calls it her dark cloud. Before long, I believe, I hope, she'll tell me. You order me out of here now, she'll never talk. I'm willing to stay and take my chances."

"I better think about it," Hinton said, unconvinced. He turned to Poole. "Gene, you turning up anything around Blackjack?"

"I'm getting acquainted at Kirk's Place."

"You mean with Kirk Singer?"

"Nobody gets acquainted with Kirk Singer, except the girls. He keeps the trade at an arm's distance, me included. But he likes the money I throw around. I buy whiskey. I gamble some . . . and, believe me, it's not Hard to lose it up there . . . I take my losses like a good sport. All in fun . . . everything is wide open. There's a definite linkup between Blackjack and the Kansas City underworld. Singer's No. 1 girlfriend let the cat out of the bag one evening when she was high."

"Link? Specifically what?"

"The heroin they're bringing in. The girls. The greasy-haired gamblers. Man can hire him a sure-shot killer out of KC or other points back East, if he's got the money. Of course, the whiskey comes from Vail's operation. Why haul it from KC?"

"This girl? Who is she?"

"Sunny—that's all she goes by. I said girl—she's a woman. From some little town in Missouri. Good-looker. Blonde. Built like a million. I work at getting acquainted with her when Singer's not around. She's really a pretty good gal. Just got in with the wrong crowd a long time ago. Now it's too late to cut out, she thinks."

"You're getting soft-hearted, Gene."

"I'm beginnin' to think I am sometimes for this game."

"Just don't overplay your Hand, Gene. And remember, you're not up there to save the world." Hinton looked at Sublette. "I hope there are some new tracks over your way, Blue."

"Same old story. The Osages are waiting for the Great White Father to do something. They feel promises have been broken. They want action."

"How well I know. That's what I keep hearing from Oklahoma City." Hinton fell silent. When he spoke again, his voice relayed an older man's caution and concern. "I don't want any of you getting in over your heads. We'll meet here two weeks from tonight. It's . . . shall I say? . . . more private than the pens. Good night."

As they drifted toward their cars, Sam held up, sensing that Hinton had more to say to him, maybe a good deal more. And Hinton said:

"We'll let this ride a little while, Sam. But I don't like it."

A week following the meeting, Sam dropped in for a game at the Sportsman's Billiards—a listening post,

Hinton had described it soon after Sam's arrival, a sounding board of Red Mound's rough-and-tumble happenings, of ranch gossip and countywide violence, likewise a wellspring of rumors. Here gathered the town's leading domino players and pool sharks, carefree Indian youths, neighboring cowboys, rowdy oil field workers, town loafers, small-time gamblers, and pint-bottle bootleggers. Here Rusty Dunlap, perhaps out of self-importance, had made the mistake of remarking that he had ridden the Ives pasture the day of the Cloud-Walker murder, and here the story, speeding along many tributaries, had inevitably reached the ears of Antwine's killer. And here Sam came every few days.

This late afternoon the pool room had the hushed stillness of an elderly men's club. Two teen-aged Indian boys were playing a boring game of snooker. Only one domino table was occupied, and a heavyset man, middle thirties, loafed on a bench while he watched the Indians smoothly stroke their kills, their slim hands graceful on the green cloth of the six-pocket table.

When Sam idled back to the tables, he saw one of the youths glance up. A sudden interest cleaved his Roman-nosed face. Sam sat and watched the snooker duel, which ended directly. The youths stacked their cues, the loser paid the house man, and as they strolled past Sam to go out, the last one turned to him, grinning. "Slip Along your horse, ain't it?"

"That's right," said Sam, rising.

"Purty soon, you gonna match him against that Tomahawk?"

"Don't know yet," Sam replied, surprised that already the race was being talked. "Maybe."

"That Slip Along is good horse, ain't it?"

"A horse always looks good when he wins."

"Where you trainin' him, this horse?"

"Five miles east of town-Fargo Young's old place. Come out sometime."

"Hey, that's good. Thanks." He extended his hand. "I'm Tommy Buffalo Horn."

Sam received the old-time Indian handshake, the relaxed fingers lightly in Sam's palm. "Sam Colter's my name. Glad to make your acquaintance, Tommy. I used to live here before the war. Knew a lot of Osage boys. Antwine Cloud-Walker was a close friend. Did you know him?"

Buffalo Horn looked down. "My cousin."

"Sorry to hear what happened."

"Yeah."

"Come out sometime. Can't miss it. On the south side of the road. Little white house."

The tobacco-brown eyes retreated. The boy nodded and turned away, but Sam knew that he wouldn't come out.

"Like to shoot a game of rotation?" It was the heavy-set white man. "O.K."

"Say, a buck a game?"

"Might as well make it interesting," Sam agreed, selecting a cue stick.

Sam hadn't seen the man before. Neither did he appear to fit locally. Probably a salesman between calls, judging by his loud, doublebreasted plaid suit and gray felt hat worn low, his light blue silk shirt and polka-dot tie and shiny yellow shoes. A rather pallid face, round and heavy through the jaws, otherwise nondescript, and the body slack-looking. Still, he gave the effect of muscularity and agility. The eyes, peering out from under thick brows, had a washed-out quality, a flat look, yet also a concentrated look.

"Nice little town you got here," the stranger said, his bland voice devoid of any real interest.

"Livelier than it looks. They cut a pretty wide swath around here on Saturday night . . . Go ahead and break."

His hands, cueing up for a shot on the green cloth, were large and competent, the nails meticulously trimmed. He played well, if not methodically, now and then muttering over a shot. He won. Sam paid and would have hung up his stick had not the man suggested another game. A dull game that dragged along as Sam's opponent kept missing easy shots, shots he had made in the first game. Hardly a word was said. Sam won.

The stranger paid, nodded, and walked out.

"Who is that fellow?" Sam asked Tim, the house man.

"Never saw him till day before yesterday. Comes and goes. Sits mostly. Not very talkative, is he? You're the first fella he's played. Generally, he just watches. Got a room at the Osage. Takes his meals at Jimmy the Greek's."

Another of those fruitless days, Sam fretted, coming out on the street. Of going in circles, of being on the defensive, of waiting instead of taking action or knowing where to head, where to dig, where to prowl and listen.

On impulse, he drove north out of town for Ma's, mulling on the scene there with Singer and seeing Lay howling drunk. Sam drove with impatience, took the county road beyond Vail's into the wooded hills. Minutes later, he entered the pasture and followed the rutted road to the long shack, crouched defiantly in the blackjacks.

More cars today. None that Sam recognized. He had to park below the shack, and that was when he saw the road that circled around behind the building and the white Marmon roadster parked in the shade. Now what? Was Fay, whom he hadn't seen since the day of their eventful ride, here on "business" that Lay used to handle? It was obvious that Vail-made whiskey supplied the joint. He could feel his resistance to the thought, there because he did not want her involved, yet felt certain she was.

He stepped inside to the bell's warning tinkle and the undertone of voices. Fay wasn't up front. just some Indian youths, off by themselves in a corner, laughing and talking; two suit-dressed customers he took for Red Mound businessmen, drinking discreetly, and several sunburned oil field workers. Always forbidden on the reservation by federal law, whiskey had become "big medicine" in the Osage, to be drunk covertly and quickly. Even out here in the hills, customers seemed to converse in hushed tones.

The bell brought the dyed-haired woman to the counter. Her earthy eyes sized him up as he took a stool. Recognition came. "Figured you'd greased your moccasins and took off," she said. "First time you've been back." She swiped at sweat beading her face.

"That's right."

"Missed yourself a bunch of fun, bud. This is the best joint between Red Mound and Blackjack. Gonna serve eats when things get goin' good."

"You said that last time."

She ignored him. "Later on I might even put me in a dance hall out here. You know, kinda open pavilion-like. Seen one once at Bella Vista, Arkansas. Was out over a lake. Now, there's a resort!"

"You're a dreamer, Ma."

She poured him a shot. He laid down a dollar bill, and

she scuffed out of sight through dun-colored curtains that hadn't been there before. Moments after, Sam heard another woman's voice begin. Her tone was renewing, as if Sam's arrival had interrupted their conversation. Although the words were indistinct, the timbre was low-pitched and rich: Fay Vail's voice. The murmuring ran on while he lingered over the incredibly hot whiskey.

An oil field worker raised his voice. "Ma—we need another jug out here," and the woman shuffled out, took a pint to the table, collected, and scuffed to the rear.

Before long, Sam heard chairs scraping and a door opening and someone going out. Sudden decision impelling him, he came to his feet and was at the front door when he heard the woman complaining after him, "You forgot your drink again, bud."

He was standing beside his car when he saw Fay start the roadster and come purring around on the circling road. He walked out and waved. She braked suddenly, staring at him blankly, calling, "What're you doing out here?"

"Came for a drink? What about you?"

"Same thing. Ma has a little room in back for the fair sex." If Fay was drinking, she didn't show it. "Get in."

He opened the door and got in beside her.

She drove under the trees, but kept the motor running. He thought she seemed somewhat on edge, somewhat tense, and still surprised at finding him here. "You know, Sam, you could end up in the county jail if Ma got raided." She was trying to banter and not succeeding.

"She should be, that stuff she sells."

Her light laugh sounded more natural now. "Last week there was a holdup. Ma got cleaned out, and her customers lost their money and watches."

"I'm not worried. Still carry my handgun for hijackers."

"That!" She shivered, squeezing in her shoulders.

"Pretty handy to have along after what I heard happened to Tug Lay. Believe you said he worked for Hank?"

"Did off and on. Nothing regular."

"Figure it was a hijacking?"

"Maybe. We don't know what happened."

"No details?"

"I said we don't know."

"Was his money taken? His watch?"

She turned her annoyance on him. "Sam, you can be very insistent. I said we don't know."

"Just curious. In town they're saying he was shot four times—two over the heart, two in the head. That tell you anything?"

"What do you mean?" Irritation thinned her voice.

"Hijackers don't usually shoot their victims. Not so accurately, anyway. They just rob. Lay's murder has all the earmarks of a professional killing." She looked most appealing at the moment, her face shadowed, and a near hurt drifting like mist into her flawless features, as if he were unkind. But he did not let up. "Lay bootlegged—you know."

"If he did," she replied, unperturbed, "it was on the sly." She rested a hand on his knee. "I have to go now, Sam. Hank will be expecting me. I've been out most of the day, just riding around, looking at country." She paused, and her eyes mirrored a subtle inquiry. "Sometimes I go stargazing, only I don't like to alone. Went by your place one night, but you were gone."

"When was that?"

"Week ago last night."

A wariness tapped him, for that was the night of the meeting at the cemetery. "I was there till just before ten. Drove to town. Chinned with Jimmy the Greek for quite a spell."

She arched a doubting eyebrow. "That late?"

"Jimmy likes to talk horses." And equally doubting: "You go for drives that time of night?"

"Sometimes—when Hank's not home."

He threw up a hand in exasperation. "You and Maggie Burk. You drive and drive. Maggie and her kids. You—alone. What are you trying to run from—you and Maggie? What is it, Fay?"

She became absolutely still; for the merest fraction of time her face was open, free, natural, responsive, in that way that always affected him. It altered as swiftly, changed back, and she said, "I was just blue the other day."

"You told me you were afraid, and you're still going in circles. Why don't you get out of the Osage? Just leave?"

Her set expression told him nothing.

"What makes you afraid, Fay?"

"That day I was worried what Hank might say about buying this car. It is expensive, you know." Her half smile was unconvincing.

"What did he say?"

"Not a word."

He believed none of this, and he could not resist sarcasm. He said, "You didn't need me after all, then, did you?" and saw its effect strike her face.

She shifted into low gear, gunning the motor. He slid out and closed the door, making a distinct click, and looked across at her. "You were more honest the day we went riding," he said and stepped back.

Holding his gaze, she said, "Speaking of honesty, I went to Jimmy the Greek's after I left your place. It was about ten o'clock. I was there till eleven, talking to people. You never came in."

She gave a toss of her head and tore away, the Marmon's rear wheels spinning dust.

On the road to Red Mound, Sam took stock of what had happened. First, he had made the mistake of attempting to explain too much, if at all; second, he had been too specific as to time and place, and she had trapped him neatly. Fay baffled him; perhaps she always had. Her contradictions and inconsistencies formed in his mind: one moment warm and appealing, the way you liked a woman, the next seemingly playing some kind of obscure game. An entirely different woman from the one the day of the ride, then almost childlike in her need for approval, and love as well?

Twilight was hazing the rounded hills, darkening the patches of timber, making them secretive and unreal. He could imagine the early-night sounds. He scanned the sky. Clouding up a bit. Wouldn't be much moon tonight. Neither did the clouds mean rain, blessed if you got any this time of year in the Osage, and realized as he had often of late that he was musing out of the past, out of his longing to put down roots here. Dreaming, he was, when there could be no dreams, no fulfillment.

He switched on the headlights. The sobbing wind dropped off as if on signal. Turning south, he passed the turnoff to Vail's. Driving pokily through the early darkness of the warm August evening, he could see the mocking serenity of Red Mound's lights. When and how was it all going to end?

Something seemed to draw on his awareness from behind. A feeling of being followed. He looked and saw car lights, neither close nor far. Nothing wrong in that. Yet—and it came to him belatedly, just now breaking through the cloud of his mulling—he remembered a car behind him soon after he left Ma's and took the county road. As poky as he had been driving, he wondered why the driver hadn't passed him.

He sped up, and by the time he reached Red Mound he no longer saw the lights. Over his meal at the City Cafe, he listened to Jimmy the Greek's observations on Tug Lay's violent passing.

"It was over whiskey," the formidable Greek confided, his voice discreetly low. "A war over bad whiskey. Jimmy judges no man, but Tug Lay will not be mourned. Better if everybody drank good wine. Better if they remembered the proverb: 'A little wine for the stomach's sake.' They drink bad whiskey. They get drunk, they run off roads, they get killed, they shoot each other . . . Better if they drank wine." He shook his gray head. "Better, maybe, if Jimmy go back to old country, where not so many shootings."

"This town would starve if you left," Sam assured him.

Sam did not notice the car lights behind him until he was about two miles out of town; even then he would not have given them further thought had not this driver maintained the same careful interval as had the driver north of town.

His frustration built up. He was on the defensive again, reacting instead of taking the initiative. Why not find out whether he was being followed? And so, instead of turning in at Fargo's, he drove on at an unhurried thirty-five miles an hour. The car dropped back and stayed there. Sam was beginning to question his suspicion when suddenly the driver closed up, holding the same distance as before.

Sam had no doubts now, and he weighed his choices. He couldn't outrun anything but a Model T in the old touring car. He could stop on the road and see what happened. But why throw away his mobility?

Keeping on, he passed the John Cloud-Walker ranch. He passed the loading pens. Nothing changed behind him.

It came to him as he racketed down the hill west of the Indian cemetery and crossed the bridge over the creek, as he remembered how the little side road angled sharply to his left up to the wooded cemetery hill. He glanced back. His friend hadn't topped the hill yet. For a few more moments Sam would be out of sight.

Sam switched off his lights and gunned the touring car, tearing upgrade, turning and bouncing across the shallow bar ditch and onto the grassy cemetery road. In second gear, he rushed uphill and drove under the blackjacks, stopped, and looked back. His dust still fogged the main road up from the bridge. There was hardly any dust sign over the grassy cemetery road.

Shortly, he picked up the steady purring of the car, a big one by the sound of it. He saw the lights crest the hill west of the creek and slant downward. Suddenly, the big car accelerated. That meant the driver had lost Sam's lights. The roar of the car rebounded as it crossed the bridge and hurried on eastward.

Sam got out of his car, listening to the retreating sound. If the driver didn't backtrack, this meant nothing. If he did . . .

Not many minutes later he heard a humming out of the east. Bobbing headlights appeared. This time the driver was traveling much slower. Sam imagined him peering into the darkness. Sam went rigid when the driver neared the point of the dim cemetery road, then let down when the car passed. That told Sam something: An area man would know the cemetery road; likely, he would turn in and throw his lights on the timbered hill. This driver hadn't as much as paused. He was picking up speed now. While Sam watched, the driver crossed the bridge and roared on over the hill out of sight.

Galvanized into action, Sam started the motor and backed out. His purpose strengthened with the jerking of the touring car. Why not some bird-dogging on his own for a change?

Coming to the top of the hill past the creek, he saw the headlights turning northwest toward Red Mound. He kicked the touring car out.

Sam was within about fifty yards of the big car when he flipped on his lights. It was a sedan, a black sedan. Nothing changed for a count or two.

Whereupon, with a roar that Sam caught above the labor of the touring car, the sedan took off. Sam hit the clutch and shifted to second, gaining a little, quickly lost when the big car shot rapidly away.

Sam lost it in the muddy fog. About then the touring car started knocking, and he dropped back. That was a mistake, he knew now, turning on his lights just for the deviling joy of reversing the roles and playing the hunter. He had hoped to follow the sedan into town and get a look at the driver.

Entering Red Mound minutes later, scouting along Main Street, Sam saw two cars parked in front of the City Cafe: a roadster with the top down, and a Model T. Inside, Jimmy the Greek was talking to a couple of Indian boys. Scanning the side streets as he went, Sam drove to the end of Main and back. The sedan had vanished. He drove home.

His first thought was to park behind the barn, which he had after the ransacking incident. But why not put out some bait, and what was better than his car to announce that he was home?

Therefore, he parked in the yard, away from the house, where a passerby couldn't miss the touring car. After which, he looked in on his horse, tied in the barn, and climbed to his haymow perch. If company came, it would call at the house.

The night was hot and muggy, and the roving bands of clouds, straggling out of the southwest, shadowed the moon off and on, diffusing the light, creating an eerie effect. From the haymow Fargo's little house loomed as a soft gray blur, unreal, tethered tenuously to the ground. Sam settled himself by the door. The bones of the relic barn creaked. Below, his horse snuffled and stamped. A car rushed westward on the road. Later, he thought he heard one coming from town. But the hum receded, hushed, lost on the wind, and he heard it no more. Sam dozed.

He did not know when the sound first dimly registered on his consciousness, it was so faint, so intermittent. Not his horse nor the arthritic barn nor the wind. He heard it again, like a faint banging, in the vicinity of the house. He looked out on the yard and marked only the dark bulge of the touring car. Nothing moved there or around the house.

Whatever, Sam knew, it *was* a change in the night sounds, for he had not noticed it before.

He came down the ladder. Outside, starting to the gate, he remembered its squeal when opened. Turning to the rear of the pole corral, he climbed it and dropped to the ground. With the corral between him and the house, he went to the barbed-wire fence separating the house and pasture and let himself through.

The .45 automatic was in his hand as he worked along the fence line. When he came even with the far end of the house, past the back porch, he lifted the middle strand of wire and eased through. Some yards away stood the house, dark and fathomless. The playful wind had dropped to a mere whisper. At the corner of the house he slipped to his right and onto the porch. The old house stirred, barely audible. He waited. A short while and the frolicsome wind picked up again, gusting a little.

As it rose, a distinct banging broke Sam's tension. A banging from the kitchen. The back door. That was what had roused him. just that. He felt his relief, which lasted but an instant. Behind it a creeping coldness, because he had left the door closed.

A thought bore down: He wasn't going in there against the light. He would wait it out, just as someone was waiting for him.

Minutes after, though it seemed much longer, he pulled back to the corner of the house, trying to puzzle this out. He turned to the front of the house and came to the corner. His eyes were on the porch, which he saw was empty, and the front door, which he seldom used and which he saw was closed, when a vigilance yanked savagely at his senses.

Jerking toward the touring car, he glimpsed dim movement. Old reflexes took over as he hit the packed earth heaving up at him, as he rolled and saw muzzle flashes and heard the blasts.

Sam fired once, feeling the recoil jump in his hand, the roar of the .45 jamming his ears, then twice. You had to concentrate like hell to hit a man with a pistol at twenty feet. He heard a cry. There was the thump of a body crashing against the touring car's side and a flopping as it struck the running board and now the ground.

Sam stayed. He could see better. The gunman wasn't flopping so much now. When Sam heard a moan, he got up and stepped carefully over there, the .45 at the ready.

The gunman lay on his back, one knee drawn up, one arm flung out. Sam struck a match. A big man, well-dressed. Double-breasted plaid suit. Round-faced, heavy through the jaws. Sam toed the loose handgun away from the hand. The match burned his fingers. Striking another, he stared down at the pallid face, a dim recognition beginning to connect.

Kneeling, he pulled back the gray felt hat and knew the instant he saw the nondescript face, the washed-out eyes deepening in shock. Sam unbuttoned the suit coat and lit another match and frowned. The guy had taken two slugs high up. From his looks he wasn't going to be around Osage County much longer. A prompting hurried Sam, a coming back, an urgency. He made his voice rough:

"Who are you?"

"Go t'hell."

"Who hired you?"

A mumbled moan. Sam could hear the ragged breathing. In haste Sam said, "I'll take you to the hospital. But first-who hired you? I want his name. Talk—damn you!"

He got no response. Only a gasp. In the glow of another match, he saw a shudder pass over the fleshy face. The gunman was dead.

Sam stood and became stone-still, seeing the odds and ends joining, interlocking. A stranger in town. The friendly game of pool. Overhearing the conversation with the Indian boy. Sam giving his name and the location of Fargo's place. The trailing car after leaving Ma's. An out-of-town killer. An old pro. And he had damn near pulled it off, waiting there beside the touring car, after finding the house unoccupied. But where was his car? It had to be close. And now, Sam realized, he faced the disagreeable but vital must of removing the gunman and his car from around Fargo's. If he didn't, there would be a county investigation. That, coupled with the consequent publicity, might hinder the Osage probe and he would be taken off the case, his usefulness here at an end. Too, one Sam Colter had no witnesses to back up his self-defense story.

He hurried to the road. Peering through the murk toward Red Mound, he sighted the dark bulk of a car about a hundred yards away. Running back, he found car keys in the killer's coat.

The car turned out to be a Cadillac sedan, sleek and smelling new. He drove to the yard and lugged the heavy body to the front seat. Searching the gunman's clothing, he found a well-padded wallet, some change, a gold pocket watch, and a small notebook. No cards, no identification. He hesitated. Likely the county boys had no fingerprint man; nevertheless, you couldn't underestimate them. A simple matter to call in one from Tulsa. So he wiped the wallet and watch clean of his prints and put everything back except the notebook. Its disposition and the large-caliber revolver, which he wrapped in a handkerchief, would be for Scotty to decide and ponder over.

Sam drove east on the silent road. Some miles onward and he eased into the bar ditch and turned off the ignition and lights, wiped his prints off the dash instruments, the steering wheel, and the door handle, and left.

After crossing the fence, he set out for the long walk over pastureland to Fargo's, the first leg of another journey tonight.

CHAPTER 15

IT WAS CLOSE TO THREE O'CLOCK WHEN SAM, DRIVING fast, entered the outskirts of Red Mound. The houses showed no lights, and the streets were deserted. He gave in to a moment of temper, thinking of concession in the midst of murder—murder that had gone unchecked for years. Merchants, snoring blissfully, would rise in the morning and open their stores and go about their business as if nothing had ever disturbed the tranquility of Red Mound. Not even the Jordan house blowup and three dead had ruffled its complacency. Four men were doing the town's dirty work, in fact the whole county's, and taking the chances.

Looking back on the gunfight, Sam had no sympathy for the professional who had stalked him. Had Sam not acted instinctively and flung himself flat, he would be lying dead in Fargo's front yard now. He had thought to look for blood on the ground by the touring car and found a dark stain and two empty cartridges. Taking a shovel, he scooped the dirt and tossed it on the floor of the corral, and afterward he drove the car back and forth over the place. Then, searching by the house, he picked up his three empty .45 casings.

He slowed dawn coming onto Main. It was deserted, too. Jimmy the Greek closed at midnight except on Saturday, which was dance night at the Legion Hut. Turning off Main, Sam felt his dread begin to mount. His immediate concern was not what had occurred tonight, but what tough little Scotty Hinton would do about Sam Colter's future role in the Osage investigation.

Hinton's modest house, where he lived alone, dozed beneath elms on a quiet street at the western edge of town. Sam parked in front and went to the door and rapped lightly. He had no more than ceased when Hinton let him in and, without a word, led to a back room and drew the blinds before turning on a desk lamp.

Tersely, Sam described the gunfight and what he had done with the killers body, and prior occurrences leading up to the shooting, and ended by handing Hinton the revolver and the notebook.

"I've been expecting something like this," Hinton said, and commenced flipping through the notebook. "Some names in here. We'll check them out through Oklahoma City." He laid down the notebook. "This toy cannon is probably stolen. Looks like some foreign make. If his prints are on file, we can identify him. Couldn't say that till recently. Bureau's now the chief repository for mutual interchange of fingerprint data for all U.S. law-enforcement agencies . . . Did you think to look at the license plate?"

"Missed that. I should have."

"I'll find out today when the county boys hit town. I can always inquire on the excuse it might be one of my policyholders. A plain hired killer, Sam. No identification, naturally. A wad of bills on him big enough to choke a mule. This bird could have slipped in here from a dozen places. Point is, your cover is all shot to hell."

Sam got ready. It was coming.

"The time has come for you to get off the case,"

Hinton told him. Shaking his head, Sam said, "Not yet, Scotty. Not yet."

"Might very well save your life. We can shift in another man. Brief him on what's happened."

"Look kind of suspicious, won't it, if I pull out of a sudden?" He was fumbling for valid arguments. "Right after a shooting. And just when I'm getting my ear to the ground at Vail's and matching some races."

Hinton's stony expression didn't weaken. "I could order you off tonight, which is what I ought to do for your own safety."

"I guess this case has got to me, Scotty. I feel a personal obligation to see it through. Antwine Cloud-Walker is one reason. And the Osage is home. I don't like what's happened to it. This is fine country. Besides, I hate to run."

"You wouldn't be running. It's common-sense procedure when an agent's identity is exposed to move him out. He's no longer useful."

"But it's not public knowledge."

"Somebody knows—the man who hired that killer. He'll probably hire another one."

"Not for a while," Sam argued. "He'll pull in his horns. See what the county finds out. Moreover, he's just been out a hunk of money. We've still got some rope left, Scotty."

"Not much. I keep thinking about Lay and Singer."

"All we had on Lay was his bootlegging."

"And that he recognized you, and now Singer knows who you are. I believe you're the one who said the whiskey operation might link to the Osage murders." Hinton drove a tight half smile back at him, which told Sam he was losing ground. "Let's go back to the person or persons who hired tonight's killer. He got onto you through Tug Lay. How else would he know? He's afraid you're an undercover man, whether it's whiskey or dead Indians. You're a threat to him, like Blue said." Hinton's voice fairly crackled: "You're wide open—you're fair game. I want you off the case, Sam. We've just had one turkey shoot."

Sam took it in painful silence, let down and struggling to organize and counter his thoughts. So he was through. And as he looked at that, still refusing to accept it, and events and people these past weeks came trooping through his mind, he saw with absolute clarity what he had not earlier.

"Scotty," he said, "the key to this entire investigation wasn't Tug Lay. It's not Kirk Singer. It's not the man or men who hired the killer, though Singer could well be that person." He let his mind fill further, and then he went on. "It's Maggie Burk. Someday—and before very long—I believe she will talk, and it will be to me. When she does the case will break."

"What makes you think she'll talk? All these years she's never said one word."

"It's me, Scotty—me. Because I think she trusts me. If she ever talks, I believe it will be to me—me alone." Sam was surprised at his impassioned voice. He didn't sound like himself.

"That still leaves you on the hot spot."

"What if it does? I want to stay. I think I'm needed."

Hinton kept looking at him. His gaze was like a file. "What if she doesn't talk?"

"I have to hope the other way."

Suddenly, Hinton slapped his thigh. "All right. You stay—under one condition—and I mean it, Sam. You make no major moves without my O.K. No more prowling around in Vail's hills at night. No more jaunts to Ma's. No more night trips to town. You're strictly a short-horse man. Understand?"

"I understand."

"Now get the hell out of here before my neighbors think I'm bootlegging on the side."

Sam slept in Fargo's house the rest of that night. Next morning, while he and Dee Oden worked Slip Along on the pasture track, the passing of an unusual number of cars on the road to and from Red Mound arrested Sam's attention. Later, a hearse sped out and returned slowly.

It was late morning when a four-door sedan pulled into the yard. By then Sam and Oden were in the corral, still fussing over the horse. The lettering on the panels of the sedan's front doors proclaimed: OSAGE COUNTY SHERIFFS OFFICE. A man pulled himself out, big-hatted, hung-bellied. He wore his inner pants legs tucked inside hand-tooled boots, and an enormous revolver wobbled on his right hip. He waved amiably and took short, boot-tight steps over to the corral.

"Mornin', boys."

"Morning," Sam said, knowing what was coming.

"You boys hear any shootin' on east down the road last night?"

"I didn't," Sam volunteered. "What happened?"

"Got us another dead man in a car." He seemed a trifle embarrassed, but not apologetic.

"Who is it?" Oden asked.

"Don't know yet. Some stranger. Why I'm askin' questions." He pinned an inquiry on Sam. "You didn't hear a thing?"

"No shots. Heard cars. Did you stop by John Cloud-Walker's?"

"We talked to John. He didn't hear anything either.

Could be this fella was shot someplace else and—uh, left down the road."

"Another hijacking?" Sam asked, projecting the usual.

"Him with a roll of bills on 'im you could stop up a well with?": His friendly eyes, straying to the horse, kindled a bright interest. He seemed thoughtful when he turned to Sam. "Mind if I look around a bit?"

"Not at all," Sam said, worrying about the two bullet holes in the north side of the house at the level of a man's chest, just inches apart.

He watched while the lawman, in his hobbling walk, went to the road and looked up and down the bar ditch, and went over the yard, back and forth, now and then kicking at a clod, and went back, disappearing behind the house. When he appeared at the northwest corner of the house, which Sam had rounded just before he became aware of the gunman, the lawman looked long and thoughtfully this way, so long that Sam began to wonder. Even more when the lawman tight-stepped straight across to the corral and looked through the bars.

"Figured I recognized that horse," the man said, pleased with himself, a keenness coming to his eyes. "He beat that Plunger horse out at Vail's." As Sam nodded, the other smiled and offered his hand. "I'm Alf Scholl from Pawhuska. One of the deputies." He grimaced. "Seems like we got more business than we can handle."

"I'm Sam Colter. This is Dee Oden. He rides my horse."

"What I'm gettin' around to," said Scholl, grinning, "is I got a horse that can stir the dust a little."

Sam kept still and grinned at the almost fraternal approach of a proud horse-owner looking for a match race.

"As a matter of fact," Scholl continued, "I might just be agreeable to runnin' you."

"That's kind of interesting," Sam replied, enjoying the circling talk.

Scholl leaned on the fence and dug one forefinger at the wood. "Might make it more interesting."

"Well, Mr. Scholl," Sam said, slowly rubbing the side of his nose, "about how far and about how much you got in mind?"

"Oh, say, 220 yards for 75 dollars. How's that strike you, Mr. Colter?"

"Horse feed's a little high these days," Sam dickered, smiling to himself at their formality. "Would you go 100?"

Scholl cocked a skyward eye. "Believe I can manage that."

"At Vail's?"

"No, Pawhuska. At the fairgrounds south of town. Ed Rowden starts most of the races. He's fair."

"When would you like to run this race?"

"How does next Saturday set with you? There'll be three or four other match races. If that's too soon, maybe the Saturday after?" Since Scholl had seen Slip Along's poor start against Plunger, Sam was thinking, the man must have a quick breaker and be figuring his horse could barrel the one furlong before the gelding got rolling. "You got yourself a race, Mr. Scholl," Sam said, holding out his hand.

"Alf—just plain Alf," said Scholl, as congenial as could be.

"You know anything about Scholl's horse?" Sam asked Oden after the deputy had gone.

"He's got a blue roan stud he's mighty high on.

Breaks awful fast. Never runs him over one furlong."

"I think I see why," Sam said, with misgivings. He had agreed to the race for no other reason than to draw Scholl's attention off the shooting.

Sam practiced Oden on the break the rest of the week. Horse and rider paired off much better by now, and Sam could see improvement as he worked them on the getaway time and again.

Although Sam hadn't brought up the incident of the bat since the victory over Plunger, deciding the point was made and settled, he continued to puzzle over it. Oden's excuse had sounded lame. Sam could attribute it only to impulse and inexperience.

The bat occurred to Sam again, just for a fleetness, the afternoon of the race at Pawhuska, while he was leading his horse toward the starting line. Then, mindful of the all-important break, he forgot it.

Slip Along appeared rangy beside Scholl's chunky Blue Dog. Young Oden looked grimly determined when Sam handed him the reins and stepped clear. Oden settled himself, hands clenched. Those are good hands, Sam thought.

The horses approached the line. Oden was ready this time. He angled Slip Along a bit for the shove-off break. The horses were even. The starter's hand dropped simultaneously with his shout.

Both horses broke like bats out of Carlsbad. Sam couldn't have jumped his horse out any faster. Head to head they ran, masses of surging muscle, manes streaming, the crouched jockeys like extensions of their mounts. Slip Along was reaching his long stride earlier today, running straight, running true. When the blue roan's jockey went to the bat, Sam figured his horse was going to win.

In another breath, the horses were over the finish line. The race had tightened up at the very last, when Blue Dog came on gamely, driving hard. Sam wasn't so certain now.

Watching, fretting, he saw Slip Along still eager to run and Oden easing him up and turning him slowly, and when Oden stood up in the irons and waved, Sam let out a whoop and waved his hat.

Jogging back, Oden was grinning as Sam had never seen him. More than after beating Plunger. His flushed face was boyish and triumphant. The troubled bitterness, for once, was missing from his light-blue eyes.

"It was close," Oden said. "That stud can run." He swung down and handed the reins to Sam.

"You rode just right, Dec." Sam whapped him across the shoulders. "Got away clean and quick. We'd lost with a slow break. I'm proud of you."

The boy seemed to grow taller; then he looked away. Sam had begun to anger whenever he saw that giving-in expression.

He walked his horse around to the trailer, cooling him down, unsaddled, laid the blanket over the glistening back, and filled the water bucket. Afterward, he poured a canful of oats into a *morral* and slipped the nose-bag strap over Slip Along's head.

Before long, Alf Scholl came over. He shook hands and paid without a whimper. "Your horse," he said, trying to grin, "is the first to beat my Blue Dog off the break. Time you outrun Plunger, he didn't get off so good."

Sam agreed, nodding. "Dee says your horse was driving hard at the finish."

"First time he's lost here."

"I believe he can beat Plunger, if you could get Hank Vail to go the shorter distance."

"I won't race at Vail's," Scholl said, his good-natured face stiffening.

It was a straightforward remark. But, Sam saw, that was all Scholl was going to say as a deputy sheriff whose livelihood depended on the political connections of the sheriff who appointed him. Vail, undoubtedly, had broad political power around Red Mound among the racing crowd and ranchers and young cowboys. Enough said.

Scholl left, walking slowly, head down, and Sam understood. When your horse lost, you felt it two ways: for your horse, first, because of your inseparability from each other; then for yourself.

A score or more of whites and Indians began to collect, curious to see up close the horse that had beaten Blue Dog, the local favorite, in the feature race of the afternoon.

"I tell you, that was some little boss race. Blue Dog was a-comin' up, but he couldn't catch this ol' boy here."

"How close was it? I was down around the starting line."

"This horse won by half a length."

"What was the time?"

"I heard somebody say a shade under thirteen seconds."

"That's sure not lettin' the grass grow."

"The track was fast and hard—hard as flint. You can't even dent it with your boot heel. A wonder some horse didn't break down today."

Sam felt a common ground here. Some men visited with him and asked pertinent questions, and talked with young Oden, and they all took long looks at the horse and made comments.

During this time, Sam noticed a dandyish man sauntering up. Tate Burk: gray western hat set at a rakish angle, red-and-white checked shirt, and gold cufflinks the size of half dollars. He exuded the air of holding himself apart from the friendly chatter. The gold toothpick drooped between slack lips, and his smooth face, pink and full, wore the stamp of boredom. A short while later, when the talk dwindled and the little crowd wandered off, Burk slouched forward in his careless walk.

"Hank's here," he said, his tone that of one making an announcement of importance. "We're havin' a few drinks. You fellows like to join us?"

Sam started to decline, simply because he didn't like the man. On second thought, the invitation presented another chance to mingle and listen. He nodded his thanks and glanced at Oden, who said, "I'll stay with the horse." He had put on his cheerless face again.

As Sam walked along with Burk, they passed near a new Packard roadster, its top down. The young white girl sitting behind the wheel seemed self-conscious surrounded by such unaccustomed affluence. She was also impatient. She honked.

Burk threw her a careless wave. "Be back in a little bit, hon. Hold your horses." He sauntered on.

Burk entered an office behind the barns. Going in, Sam could hear Vail's voice. Vail paused, and his voice broadened in greeting, "Well, cowboy, your horse took the sugar again."

"It was close enough," Sam said, looking around. He knew none of the others. He had hoped to see Alf Scholl again. Vail, as the host, gestured to whiskey and glasses on a table. Sam poured himself a drink.

The conversation swung back between Vail and an elderly rancher whom Sam thought he recalled seeing at the great sandstone house the afternoon of the party early in July. Several other men sat around. Today Vail was touting for sale some yearling colts of running and saddle blood. He would describe a certain colt and its breeding, and sometimes draw in Burk, who would nod or add a few indifferent words. Burk really wasn't interested, that was apparent, and Sam recognized something that even Scotty Hinton hadn't mentioned: Burk deferred constantly to Vail, like a second fiddle. Vail dominated the squawman. Evidently they were partners in some stock arrangements, hence the sales spiel.

Finally, the rancher said, "Right now I got all the good young horses I need, Hank," and put down his glass and rose to go.

"Just so you know where the good colts are," Vail bantered, his smile widening. Turning to Sam, he was the Hank Vail of the Red Mound train station and the crowd flowing around him. The returning champion of the rodeo arena, expansive, clean-cut, leanly handsome, the embodiment of a man's man of action. He said:

"What about that match race, cowboy? Do I get another run at your horse?"

"Anytime—with one big exception."

"What's that?" Vail asked courteously.

"I won't take Mitch Kell as the starter."

"Got somebody else in mind?" His tone betrayed that he knew.

"You bet I have-Fargo Young."

Vail ducked his head in mock pain. "Old Fargo . . . he's far past his prime."

Sam was on his way to the door when Vail, his voice abruptly favoring, called after him, "Don't fast break on me like that. Tell you what I'll do. I'll think about Fargo. I will."

"Fair enough," Sam said, glancing back at him, unconvinced.

"We're getting closer, cowboy."

CHAPTER 16

SAM WAS THE FIRST TO ARRIVE AT THE RENDEZVOUS. He left the touring car and stood listening to the wind-singing blackjacks. Minutes passed. His mind felt so light it seemed to float through the night, removed from worldly violence. He thought of quiet waters and soft clouds and of oak leaves drifting down in the fall of the year. When a distant hum intruded, the sensations left him as if borne on the wind.

The new pulse was approaching from the west. He heard it descend the hill west of the creek, heard its reverberating din as it crossed the bridge, and then, in moments, ascending the cemetery hill: Scotty Hinton, traveling fast. Within minutes, Blue Sublette roared up in a sedan.

A mundane remark or two and Hinton moved to the night's business. "Sam, the prints on that revolver belong to a thug known as A. A. Riggs, more widely known as Trigger Riggs. Operated out of Detroit, Chicago, and Kansas City. A hired killer. One of the top professionals. His fee ranged from two thousand up. The boys at the Red Mound Funeral Home said they found eighteen hundred in Riggs' wallet."

"Guess I just rated a two-thousand-dollar job," Sam

said. His words, meant to be light, sounded flat to his ears. "Did you get a look at the license plate?"

"Stolen in Missouri. So was the car. Two of the names in the notebook checked out to underworld figures in Kansas City, Missouri."

"So the contact from around here was made through Kansas City?"

"I think you mean *contract*. Yes. Seems logical. Like Gene's been telling us, there's a pipeline from Blackjack to KC . . . Nobody's claimed the body yet. Likely nobody will."

"Occurs to me Riggs might have done in Tug Lay."

"Except he didn't show up in town until after Lay was shot."

"You're right. He didn't."

"Wonder what's holding Gene up? It's not like him to run late, let alone miss a meeting."

Sublette told of being invited to a Peyote meeting, of going to the sweat-lodge made of cedar saplings stripped and stuck in the ground and covered with canvas, of sitting naked in a circle while water was poured over hot stones piled in the center of the lodge, of drinking a mixture and then of sweat running down his forehead and body. Of taking a blanket and going outside, as the others did, one by one, and facing north and emptying his stomach, of returning to the lodge and taking his place in the circle again, and sitting there in silence for a long time and listening to the worshipers.

"John Cloud-Walker was there," Sublette said, his recalling voice calm and impressed. "John was weeping about Antwine. He said his heart was on the ground. He said he wanted to kill the white man who shot his son. The Road Man, I think he is called, said Antwine and the other Indians killed by white men had taken the wrong road, the white man's road. He said they drank whiskey and some took dope and some married white people. He said that was why they were killed. He was harsh because these Indians had tried to live like whites."

Sam stirred. "Did John name Antwine's killer?"

"No."

"Did they name any white men in the other cases?" Hinton asked.

"Not one. But I think they suspect certain white men. I feel they know. But what can they prove?"

"If they're afraid to go to the county attorney, they could tell the Osage agent or the Tribal Council," Hinton said crossly, his voice tired. "The Council has asked the Bureau to investigate. We could certainly use that information; even their suspicions would help."

"It's hard to explain, Scotty. This Peyote religion is a kind of mixture of the old Indian way of being in harmony with nature, and also Christianity, and it's also passive. To me it is. The Peyote worshipers believe a man must begin by throwing off evil from inside. They hate whiskey, they hate dope. They say Osages ought not to marry whites. They say let evil flow out of the body through sweat. It's symbolic. I know that afterward you feel good and clean and your mind is keen.

"Except for some modern conveniences, many older Indians live and dress as their fathers did. These old Indians are patient and enduring. They believe in retribution—that these bad white men will be punished. Their religion is very strong." Sublette's grunted laugh brushed self-ridicule. "Stronger than my medicine."

"I don't happen to share their patience," Hinton barked. "These bad white men will never be punished without leads, without cooperation from the Osages. I want you to work harder on your fullblood friends, Blue. Pin them down. They trust you or they wouldn't have invited you to a sweatlodge. That was a high honor."

"I'll keep trying, but don't expect too much. You can't force these people."

Conversation waned. By eleven-thirty Hinton sighed and gave up. "Guess Gene couldn't make it. This bothers me some, but I'm not worried. Gene can take care of himself. I don't know a man who's more capable. Let's go."

Therefore, the following afternoon when Hinton drove into the yard and got out and stood uncertainly beside the coupe, Sam knew instantly that something was wrong, quite wrong. Hinton had not shown himself at Fargo's before, deeming it wiser not to.

Sam's dread kept deepening and spreading as he walked to the car.

"You alone?" Hinton seemed to force his speech.

"Dee's not here. I'm resting my horse this week. Is something wrong, Scotty?"

Hinton looked visibly aged, drawn down to the very lean of his wiry body. A rising pain filled his face, dulled his eyes. For a very long moment he said no word. Finally, he spoke, his lips scarcely moving. "It's Gene, Sam—he's dead. Found yesterday in a tool shack south of Blackjack. Shot—" Hinton's voice cracked.

Sam stood stunned, robbed of thought, struggling emotionally to refute the impossible news, seeing the imprint of his own shock in Hinton's eyes. Sam jerked away and took one step, and another and another, and stopped, immobile, head hanging, arms limp. Something lumped in his stomach and rose to his chest and reached his throat. He choked. He could feel his face twisting and knotting, the wetness on his cheeks. Then he was weeping like a child, and he had the sledgehammer effect of reeling and absorbing not just one, but a rain of blows. And the lost young faces, ever in the background of his consciousness, flashed before his eyes. With the horror, the mud, the rain, the smells, the shrieking sounds, the moonscape fields, the cries. *("I'm hit, Sam-I'm hit!")*

He jerked around and came back. "How the hell did it happen, Scotty?"

"Don't know yet." Hinton swallowed. "Some girl at Blackjack called Gene's landlady in Burbank. Said she knew Gene . . . Gene had left my name with his landlady in case of an accident. Am surprised he did that. Was so open about it. Like . . . he had a premonition or something."

Sam was struggling to think. "This girl? Did she say who she was?"

"No.. . but. . :'

"You mean Sunny. Gene said she was Singer's girlfriend. Said she knew what was going on up there." Rage swept over Sam until he could taste it. He was trembling, aching to act. "What're we waiting on? Let's bring Singer in! Go get 'im!"

"Now, Sam, you just ease up a little. You're not going off half cocked. You listen to me!" Hinton, the tough-minded realist, had managed to recover his self-control. "I'm itching to take Singer in as much as you are. But we don't have evidence for a warrant. Not one scrap. A smart lawyer would spring him in five minutes. We don't know he murdered Gene. If we jump the gun, we could blow the whole Osage investigation—if

Singer is involved." He clamped his jaws. "I've called Blue at Hominy. He'll pick you up here. I want you two to hotfoot it to Blackjack and backtrack on Gene's movements. Everything. Talk to this Sunny."

"What about Singer?" Sam flung back.

"You'll have to use your own judgment, depending on what you dig tip."

"That's a helluva order! How far can we go?"

Hinton's face hardened, reddened. "How much leeway do you need? Want me to put it in writing?" The pain returned to his eyes. "I'm having Gene's body brought to Red Mound for an autopsy. Now I've got to make some arrangements, including a mighty tough phone call to a young lady in Texas."

Sam calmed down. That was Scotty, he acknowledged as Hinton drove off, bringing order out of the confusion of shock and grief. Somebody had to think straight at a time like this. And while Sam chafed, waiting for Sublette, the predestined way of looking at life bore upon him unmercifully. Neither was it meant for Gene Poole, a good and decent man who had tried to right dreadful wrongs in a strange and violent land, a man blessed with the rare gift of making people laugh, to have what he longed for most—love, family, home, peace of mind.

Blue Sublette was there within less than an hour, driving a borrowed purple Lincoln sedan. Neither man spoke until Red Mound's sprawl was in sight.

"I figure Gene walked into something," Sublette said, shaking his head. "Got blind-sided."

"Maybe somebody he knew."

Before Sam's critical eyes Red Mound appeared to stretch itself lazily and yawn, fat and content, oblivious of any wrongs. Today, in his intense bitterness, he detested the town even more.

Turning north, Sublette drove fast and doggedly. Now and then he passed a car, roaring by in a cloud of dust. Before many minutes they entered an interminable, clangorous oil field. Sublette eased up on the gas. "We'll look like a couple of bird hunters ready to fire, with dogs on point, if we don't simmer down," he said.

Where once was bald prairie roiled the boom town of Blackjack, an orderless massing and scattering of frame buildings and shacks and sheds and heavy equipment yards on the edge of a forest of wooden derricks crowding the sky as far as the eye could see. There wasn't a single tree. The continuous *clank-clunk* of cable drilling tools making holes pounded Sam's ears. The sulfurous smell of crude oil rankled the hot air. Antlike figures toiled on distant rig towers and swarmed on rig floors. Dust laid a brownish pall over the rough street down which Sublette drove, stirred by cars and trucks and teams of stout workhorses, matched teams wearing brass-studded collars and white rings on their black harness, proud, handsome, head-tossing animals hauling derrick timbers, bull wheels, pipe, tubing, pumps.

Sublette had to pull over to let a six-team outfit lumber past, a bailer, chained on the wagon frame, swaying and nodding like a rotund idol.

Here, Sam was thinking, is the eye of the frenzy.

When the first false-fronted stores grew alongside, traffic thickened and crawled. Cars, parked with abandon in the ditches on both sides, narrowed passage on the street. On the board sidewalks an eddy of bodies moved and paused, then moved again. These were rough-clad men—jostling, standing, watching, talking, smoking, going in, coming out, their voices an insistent babble. Sam saw no women. He heard shouts. There was a milling over there, a fight. A man went down. Sublette drove on. A mingling of gasoline fumes and dust, and frying meat and coffee competed now for dominance with the heavy crude-oil smell.

One building stood out above the others. A long, two-story wooden structure. Over the boardwalk a sign read: KIRK'S PLACE.

"There it is," Sam said, feeling every muscle in him grow tense. Sublette drove on a way to find room to park. Climbing out, he took a hitch at his trousers and set his hat; he was a slim-hipped man whose weight rode his shoulders and arms. Their boots raised hollow sounds on the boardwalk to Kirk's Place. Sublette had to duck as they entered.

Sam looked around at the tables, not expecting men playing dominoes, checkers, and pool, nothing that innocent. However, beyond the bead curtains of a doorway he could hear faint music. The houseman scarcely gave them a glance as they walked through the curtains.

In here the change was abrupt: dice and cards at the tables. The music, growing stronger, issued from still another rearward room.

At that moment a broken-faced man, nearly the size of Sublette, advanced and stood between them and the tables. His eyes, under yellow lashed ledges, were the hard gray of flint, and they asked the silent question, "What will it be?"

"Where can we get a drink?" Sam asked.

"Anything else?"

"What else you got?" Sam drawled and winked at him.

"Back there. No rough stuff."

Just then the rear door opened, releasing a gush of piano music, and a man reeled out.

Sublette, rubbing his hands in mock anticipation, barged ahead of Sam and through the doorway and over to a table. This was it, Sam saw: girls, bar, plus a tired little man laboring over the keyboard of the out-of-tune piano.

The girl who came to their table looked maybe sixteen at the oldest and somewhat unsure of herself. A very short, red dress girded her slim body. She teetered on high heels. Oversized smears of rouge failed to cover the pinched paleness of her small-boned face. She was chewing gum and puffing furiously on a cigarette.

When Sublette greeted her with, "Two beers, sis," she jerked into a nervous giggle. "On your way to church or somethin'?" With an exaggerated air of worldliness, she fumbled the cigarette from her over-painted lips and held it awkwardly between thumb and forefinger while the smoke curled up her nostrils. She choked suddenly; her eyes watered.

Sublette favored her his broad, even-toothed smile, and his black eyes, dancing roguishly, rested on her with understanding. "If I was, I'd take you with me."

That rattled her. "Aw, you can have beer. I just make more on the hard stuff by the drink."

"We'll take care of that. Just bring us the beer, sis."

When she served them, Sublette paid, and as she picked up the silver, he pressed a bill in her hand. She looked at it and blinked. "What's your name, sis?"

"It ain't sis."

"Come on, now. What is it?"

"It's Lottie."

Sublette's smile widened. "That your stage name or your given name?"

She looked startled, then flattered. "If I'se goin' on the stage or gonna be in the movies, I sure wouldn't pick no country name like Lottie," she retorted, striking a pose, right hand on hip. "Be somethin' grand like"—she blinked—"like Clementine or Millicent."

"I like Lottie much better. Can we count on you to keep an eye on our table?"

"Maybe," she said, striving for subtlety.

"One more little thing. Is my old pal Kirk around?" Her face clouded, became wary.

"I mean Kirk Singer," he said.

Without speaking, she lifted the point of one thin shoulder and took her post by the bar.

"I scared her off," Sublette mumbled. "Too sudden. She thinks she's being loyal. Better if we'd asked about Sunny."

"Not yet."

While they sipped beer, the shape of Gene Poole grew before Sam, Gene telling his stories in this room, listeners gathered around him, Gene buying drinks, talking to the girl Sunny. He shook off the thought.

Sublette ordered again, and after adding another generous greenback, asked, "Where you from, Lottie?"

"Tulsa," she said, not without hesitating.

"Bet a hundred she's fresh off some little farm," he observed, after she had teetered back to the bar. "I've got a daughter about her age. Durned if I wouldn't pay Lottie's way home if she'd go."

"She wouldn't. She'd remember how dull life was back on the farm. How exciting this is."

Sublette paid him a searching look.

"I know, I'm mighty low," Sam admitted. "But I don't intend to stay that way."

As the afternoon wore on toward evening, the place

began to fill rapidly. Another musician, just as tired-looking, took over at the piano. Two men worked behind the bar now. From time to time couples went up the stairs. There was still no girl who fitted the blond Sunny's description, and still no Singer. Gaslights cast a bluish glow.

Sublette rose, saying, "I'll take a gander up front for our man," and left. He returned shortly and shook his head and sat down and signaled Lottie.

When she served, Sam paid and more. "I don't see Sunny around. Where is she?"

"You know her?" The wariness again.

"Now, would you know if I did? How long you been here?"

"Coupla weeks."

"I just wondered about her."

"Upstairs. She ain't been feelin' good all day."

"Sorry to hear that. Same room?"

She glared, superior in her knowledge. "Thought you knew so much? Mr. Singer's apartment—that's where!" She flounced off, high heels clicking.

"Blue, I'm going up those stairs before long."

"You can't do any worse than get shot. She's Singer's girlfriend, remember?"

"But where is he?"

"Maybe with her."

"Good way to find out."

Standing, Sam drifted in behind a couple heading for the stairway. There, he delayed until the pair reached the top and he heard their steps going off. At the head of the stairs he opened the door and found himself looking down a murky hallway that ran the length of the building, curtained at the far end. Voices droned on both sides. A woman laughed shrilly. Something crashed.

Onward, he saw that each door bore a number. He hesitated before the curtains, questioning them, then stepped through and came to a door without a number. Across its face was painted: PRIVATE Hearing no voices within, he rapped on the door. No one answered. He rapped again, softly, insistently.

"Who is it?" A woman's tired voice. "A friend of Gene Poole's."

A wait, and the tired voice answered, this time on a rising, angry note. "What do you mean? He's dead."

"That's why I'm here."

"Go away. Leave me alone."

"I must talk to you, Sunny."

"I said go away." But there was less anger in her voice. "I need your help, Sunny."

He heard the creak of bedsprings, and slow steps, and the lock turning in the door. It opened a crack, then a little more. Wide, violet eyes met his. Loose, honey-colored hair framed a distraught face. There were pouches under the big eyes, her makeup was streaked, as if she had been crying, and her hair looked slept on. Her bow-shaped mouth was slack. A buxom, good-looking woman on the off side of her early thirties; now beginning to fade.

"Who the hell are you?" she challenged, "and why'd you come here?"

He held his hat. "I'm Sam Colter from around Red Mound. I knew Gene in Texas."

"Never heard of you. Never heard Gene mention you."

"Likely not. I can't talk to you out here."

She wasn't afraid, she wasn't afraid of anything much. He saw that as she swung open the door and closed it behind him in the gaslit room. She tightened the belt of her rose-colored robe and waited for him to speak.

He said, "I just heard about it in Red Mound."

"Why come to me?"

"Last few times I talked to Gene at Vail's he kept mentioning you."

A sliver of feeling quivered in her face. "You came here just to tell me that?"

"I knew you and Gene were friends. I want to know how it happened, and I want to do something about it."

Response rose to her throat. She stifled it. The bow-shaped mouth twisted. "The usual . . . hijacked, I guess. Blackjack has its man a day, mister, one way or another. Sometimes two or three. And what makes you think you can do something about Gene?"

"I can't unless you help me."

She turned to the window overlooking the street, gazing vacantly at the oily darkness. The rhythmic pounding from the wells, distinct through the thin walls, seemed to acquire a drumlike resonance with the coming of night, he thought, keeping time for the frenzy. She kept twisting her fingers. "How can I help you when all I know is he's dead and I'll never see him again?" She faced around and placed a hand at her throat. "I don't know who shot him or why. If I knew I'd tell you. No—that's wrong. If I knew, I'd shoot the son-of-a-bitch myself!"

"You liked Gene, didn't you?"

"Why not? He was a very nice man. He knew how to treat a woman. He was gentle. We used to talk a lot." The harshness left her voice. "I thought he liked me. Just a little means a good deal when you're trapped and that's all there is."

"When was the last time you saw Gene?"

“Sunday evening. He came in . . . had a drink . . . visited awhile. Didn’t stay long. Said he had to go meet a man. Didn’t say where. Just before he left he said to me, “Sunny, why don’t you go back home? You’re still young. Some fella would grab you. That’s what he said! Somehow it got to me. *He cared what happened to me*. I know he did . . . That was the last time I saw him. He was found late Monday south of town in a tool shack. I called his landlady in Burbank just as soon as I heard. That was late this morning.”

“Gene have any trouble here?”

“Him? Everybody liked Gene Poole. You’d talk to him a minute, and before you knew it you’d be telling him your life’s history, even the bad. Everybody liked him.”

“Even Kirk Singer?”

“Where does he come into this?” He saw that she was being very careful.

“I want to talk to him.”

“Leave me out of it.”

“Where is he tonight?”

Sam saw a caution akin to Lottie’s. He saw further her tight-lipped refusal forming and yet, in another moment, she was saying, “You tell me. I haven’t seen him since yesterday afternoon. He drove somewhere. Said he’d be back this morning.” She caught herself. “I don’t know why I’m telling you all this.”

“You are because you want to help. Did Singer say where he was going?”

“Think he’d tell me?”

“Why, yes.”

“Well, he didn’t, and I don’t see . . .” Her voice trailed off. She looked inquiringly at him.

“He was here yesterday afternoon. He should know

what happened. Kirk Singer's been around the oil fields a long time, hasn't he?"

She had no reply, and he realized that he was circling, getting nowhere much, when the question leaped unforeseen to his tongue:

"By the way, was he ever a nitro shooter?"

She went to the door and stood. "I can't help because I don't know anything. Now I just want to be left alone." She opened the door. "You might watch for Duffy when you go out. Nobody's supposed to be up here when Kirk's gone."

"Who's Duffy?"'

"He big guy with the busted face."

"Thanks, Sunny."

"Don't come back here again," she said.

Walking down the hall, he thought of the lonely woman back there whom Gene Poole also had touched, and it firmed in his mind that she had told the truth. She didn't know Gene's killer, and she didn't know Singer's whereabouts. That much was true, anyway.

Feet came pounding up the stairs. The door crashed open, and the broken-faced man bulked there, blocking Sam's way. Lottie, rushing up behind, pointed at Sam and yelled, "That's him, Duffy! He's the one!"

When Duffy's arm hinged back to launch a blow, Sam charged into him. It was like slamming into a side of beef. Duffy merely grunted and bear-hugged Sam and they wrestled. Lottie screamed, scrambling free. The man's strength was not to be believed. He lifted Sam higher and higher, to smash Sam's head against the doorjamb. Sam struggled sideways, punching Duffy's ample middle, and felt his shoulder crash the doorjamb. Pain numbed him. Unable to break the hold, he stomped Duffy's shoes, raising Duffy's startled howl, and rammed his right foot behind the big man's leg and heaved.

They toppled backward, rolling and bumping down the steep wooden stairs to the landing. Sam felt his breath *whoosh.* He was underneath Duffy. He drove a knee to Duffy's groin and rolled away. Duffy threw a punch that skidded off Sam's head. Sam's hat flew. In that instant Sam's legs were free. He kicked with both feet. His boots took Duffy below the ribs. Duffy fell back with a grunted *ahhh,* his heavy-lidded eyes squinching pain.

Sam bolted up and made for the open door, hearing shouts and girls screaming and seeing a three-man tangle. He saw Sublette, wrenching savagely, break loose and knock a man against the bar. Glass crashed as it overturned. Snatching up a chair, Sublette brought it down across the head of the second man. The chair broke like kindling, and the man slumped. Sublette cut a look at Sam and jerked his thumb toward the back door.

They ran out and turned the corner of the building and sprinted along the street to Sublette's sedan and got in. He started the motor and reversed out of the ditch, but instead of heading into the thick of the street's traffic, he drove away from it. When he came to the first rutted road, be whipped into it. Glancing back, Sam saw figures running from the building.

They were on the dusty road south of Blackjack when Sam, looking behind them again, picked up the lights of a speeding car. He tapped Sublette's shoulder. "They're coming."

"They can tail us right on into Red Mound," Sublette said, figuring ahead. "'That won't do. I'll take the Ponca road. This thing can run. What do you say?"

"Make tracks!"

Sublette took the westward turn toward Ponca City with hardly a slowing of the sedan. Sam, watching the rear, saw the car lights pierce the blooming dust like yellow moths, saw the long rays bob and turn and come on. When he tapped Sublette again, Sublette called out, "Just hope there's no loose cattle on the road," and fed the Lincoln more gas. A high-pitched whine rose. They shot ahead.

For a while the pursuing lights neither gained nor lost. Then something struck the sedan, a metallic *thunk,* again, again.

"They're shooting at us!" Sublette roared and floorboarded the gas pedal.

Although the shooting ceased as the other car fell back, its lights still hung on grimly, like animal eyes determined to follow them on and on through the night. Nothing changed for several minutes.

Without warning, the sedan's headlights bared a whiteface cow standing in the middle of the road. Sublette hit the brakes and honked the horn. The whiteface, displaying bovine indifference, lowered its homed head and stared into the blinding lights. Sublette veered right. So did the cow. Sublette cut left. So did the cow.

Sam ducked down, smelling burned rubber, aware of Sublette's cutting right and suddenly left, and they were sliding past the walleyed cow and bumping and bouncing along a grassy ditch. Sublette battled the wheel, won control, and brought them back on the road. The gears clashed as he shifted down for more speed to climb the long hill just ahead.

Sam looked back. Meantime, the car had gained. He saw its lights find the cow, back in the middle of the road. He saw the frantic slowing down, the swerving.

All at once the lights went out.

"What happened?" Sublette called, picking up speed.

"Some rancher just lost a fat whiteface. You can slow down now." Miles on, they crossed the Arkansas River bridge and drove into Ponca City, and took a southward road. Sublette eased up again. "Don't know what I'll tell my Osage friend when he sees these bullet holes in his new car."

Much later, after traveling east, they passed through ranks of wooded hills and down into the town of Pawnee and pulled in at an all-night cafe. Over steak, potatoes, biscuits, and coffee, Sam shook his head. "We're still gonna have to question Singer."

And, making north and east, they drove through the dead-still streets of Ralston on the west bank of the Arkansas River, crossed the high, rickety bridge, and were back in Osage County, miles south of Blackjack.

Well past midnight, they reached Hinton's house. He was still dressed and had coffee on the stove. "Was beginning to wonder about you fellows."

"Had to make a little circle," Sam explained, and filled him in.

"All that huckletybuck for nothing," Sublette said, heading for the coffee. "You know, Singer could be at Vail's."

"Singer's out of it, permanently," Hinton announced, an explosiveness behind his voice. "Took two loads of buckshot from a twenty-gauge shotgun Monday night when he tried to heist a country store in the eastern part of the county. Wasn't identified till last night." Sam started and looked at Sublette. "They didn't know it yet at Blackjack."

"Remember, we left kinda early."

"I heard it about nine o'clock when I dropped by the

Sportsman's Billiards for a cigar. How this Osage County grapevine works! Want you fellows to grab some sleep and get over there. It's called the Crossroads Store. Southeast of Okesa. You can get directions there. Imagine that! Trying to knock off a little country store:'

"Maybe it wasn't so little," Sam said.

Hinton's voice flattened. "Got the autopsy report. I remember Gene said the Tug Lay job was the mark of a professional. Well, Gene was shot identical to the way Lay was-four times. It was a .45, too . . . You fellows better get going."

CHAPTER 17

EVERY FEW MILES SAM WOULD SEE THESE BROAD signs beside the dirt road, standing like flags demanding the attention: stop and gas with worth grundy—crossroads store, or you get your money's worth at worth grundy's crossroads store, or swap and talk with worth grundy crossroads store.

At last, there it was, low-slung, built-on, cluttered, sagging, a mound of boxes and crates behind it, stretched out at the junction like a hound dog soaking up midday sun. A single gasoline pump, its glass bowl empty. Painted across the front of the store, banner-size, this: CROSSWORDS STORE-WORTH GRUNDY, PROP. An audience of idlers crowded the long porch, all eyes on a keg-shaped man obviously enjoying the stage while he talked and gestured.

When Sublette drew up at the gas pump, the speaker waved and, still talking, backed off the porch and down the steps before he turned and waved again. He seemed to carry himself a mite higher than he might usually, on the brink of a strut, but not quite, as he came out to wait on the trade.

He was about fifty or so or less, and his brown eyes, squinting against the sun, were as bright and keen as a traveling horse trader's, set amid rounded features that imparted the impression of seldom being out of sorts, ready for any change in the public wind. His thin brown hair was parted precisely in the middle and plastered down, and he wore a white shirt and green bow tie and neat trousers, and his shoes were shined—in all, the appearance of one dressed up for some special occasion.

"Might as well fill 'er up," Sublette said, sounding generous.

"Be right with you. No time to keep my gas pumped up, way folks been congregatin' here today."

"Understand you had a little commotion out here Monday night?"

"Well, now," the man began and paused, as if propriety required that he present an unpretentious face this day. "I reckon you could call it that." But suddenly his eyes quickened, and anticipation came through. "You some more newspaper boys?"

Sublette smiled impressively, mysteriously. "Guess you're Mr. Grundy?"

"You're talkin' right at him. Worth Grundy. W-o-r-t-h-Worth." He rummaged for a humoring grin. "Some folks seem to get it mixed up with worst." He shook hands eagerly when Sublette gave his name, and with Sam. "Mighty pleased to meet you boys."

"Mind telling us all about it?" Sublette asked.

Again the hesitation, more brief than the first. "Reckon I got the time. Kinda busy. Let me take care this gas, then you boys come right in." He began working the pump handle back and forth. Afterward, with a processional air, be walked ahead of them to the porch, past the gawking idlers, and showed them inside, into a pleasing aroma of spices, cured meat, leather, and tobacco; past shelves of canned goods, stacks of flour and cornmeal, tables of denim pants and shirts and cotton work-gloves, stands of shovels, hoes, axes, ax handles, coils of rope, kegs of nails, buckets, kerosene lamps, and glassware.

"Man has to keep nigh everything on hand," Grundy said as Sublette paid for the gas. "Lady come in here the other day all the way from Bartlesville. On the lookout for a certain cut-glass sugar bowl like her granny had back in Tennessee. Shucks, all I had to do was turn around, reach up one shelf, and fetch it down . . . Got a right smart trade here. Folks come from all over. Some as far away as Red Mound," and he winked, "to get away from them Indian prices . . . Back here is where it happened," he said, showing them to the storeroom, which also served as his sleeping quarters. A broken window gaped at them from the rear wall.

Grundy picked up a shotgun, and in the rehearsed tone of one commencing an oft-told story, he began. "Reckon it was a little past two. Come to think of it, it was exactly twenty-one past, 'cause I had just lit me a match to look at my watch . . . if you want to take that down?"

Nodding, Sublette reached for his pocket memorandum pad and pencil.

"By the way, did you boys happen to bring along a camera? The Tulsa World boys, they took me a-standin' here like this." Grundy assumed an on-guard stance, the shotgun pointing toward the window, his face grimly fixed.

"No, we didn't, Mr. Grundy. Our little Red Mound

paper is just a weekly. Now tell us everything that happened."

Grundy, disappointed, cleared his throat. "I hear this big car pass the store and ease off down the south road. Purty soon I hear it come back real easy like." Face tense, eyes a-glitter, he adopted a determined watchfulness. "Kind of Cadillacing along, it was. Then I don't hear it a-tall. Everything's stone-still, and I think to myself, 'Grundy, he ain't comin' tonight.'"

"You mean you knew he was coming?" Sam asked, frowning at him.

"I'll get to that in just a minute," Grundy replied, glowering at the interruption. A craftiness was spreading over his face. "Well, sir, in about ten minutes or so, although I didn't look at my watch, I hear steps easin' along the back side of the store." To demonstrate, he tiptoed stealthily toward Sublette. "Real light. But I hear 'em just the same. I'm purty alert for my age, if I do say so. So I grab up of Trusty here," patting the shotgun's stock, "and get ready to greet that gentleman. I am standing about where you are, Mr. Sublette, and it's eyeball range, and I say to myself, 'Keep a steady nerve, Grundy.' "

"Mind pointing that shotgun the other way?" Sublette said uncomfortably, moving aside.

Unruffled, Grundy turned the shotgun toward the wall, and his face repossessed the crafty look. "Next thing I hear sounds like somebody settin' a box under the window there . . . Aim to board that up tomorrow. Left it like that for ever'body to see . . . Well, sir, in a bit I hear the window slide up. I get ready, and I don't mind admittin' that of Trusty is wobblin' just a little in Grundy's hands." He stiffened dramatically and aimed the shotgun at the window. "Now I see a man's head and shoulders. He's comin' through! That's when I let him have it-both barrels—BLOOM, BLOOM!" He paused, waiting.

"What happened then?" Sublette asked, taking the cue.

Well, ol' Trusty knocked him clean out the window. I run out there. He's on the ground, all moans and twitches. I run back in, light the lantern, and run back and shine it on his face. I remember him! He's here week or so ago. Bought some gas. Looked around. Well, he's a goner. I see that."

"What then?" Sublette kept on.

"I ring up the Pawhuska operator first thing. Next morning Deputy Alf Scholl, he comes over with the undertaker, who took the body back to Pawhuska. Alf called me back next day late. That was on Tuesday, now. Alf said it was a rough customer name of Kirk Singer from over at Blackjack. Ever hear of him?"

"We have," Sam said, "and it was a good thing you were on the alert. But I wonder why he picked on your store?"

Grundy smiled, amused. "I always keep a sizable amount of money on hand. Have to. Way out here."

"Did he have a gun?"

"*Did he have a gun?* It fell inside. Right over there. A .38. I gave it to Alf."

"Let's go back a little, Mr. Grundy. How did you know somebody might try to rob you?"

"Puzzles me, too. Some days back I got a letter to be on the lookout for such."

"A letter? Who sent it?"

"That's the puzzle."

"May we see it?"

From his shirt pocket Grundy took a folded sheet of

paper that showed the smudging and creasing of repeated looking. Sublette crowded in to look with Sam. Typewritten, it read:

Dear Friend,

Some night within the week or soon thereafter an attempt will be made to rob your store. Be prepared to defend yourself. This man is a killer.

A friend

"Sure would like to know who sent that, so I could thank him," Grundy lamented. "Man needs to know who his friends are. You boys be sure and send me a copy of the paper, now."

They were on the way back, the wooded hills drifting by like floating islands, rising as the dusty road dropped downgrade, dipping as it climbed. Sam sat slumped, chin resting in his hand, feeling a discouraged weariness.

"What do you think, Sam?"

"In a way, I almost wish Grundy hadn't blasted Singer, just wounded him. So we could work on him. And that .38 of Singer's? Tug Lay and Gene were shot with a .45."

"Singer could've had two handguns. Sure. Certain guns for certain jobs. This was intended as a robbery, not an execution."

"One thing does match up, though, Blue. Scotty said Billy Gault got an unsigned letter offering him a bribe to leave Red Mound. Scotty figured Rusty Dunlap got one, too. Same way. It all hooks up with Grundy's letter. Same man sent all three."

"But how did Singer know about the store? It's far off his range."

"I'd say Singer was set up. And, oh, how he was set up."

"Another dead man, Sam. Another dead end. Now we have to start over again."

CHAPTER 18

LATE SEPTEMBER COOLNESS EMBRACED THE PATIENT hills each morning, fled during the burning afternoons, and returned in the evening, hinting of early fall, and the woods, weary of summer's dog days, began to don festive robes of scarlet and gold. Federal agent Gene Poole rested beneath the evergreen shade of a live oak in the Texas hill country, and the Osage investigation had reached a standstill.

With one civil exception, Scotty Hinton said he had never known Red Mound to be so quiet; even the Sportsman's Billiards was without reports of violence done or rumored in the making. That exception was Maggie Bear Claw Burk's divorce action, now ready for filing in state district court at Pawhuska. Further, her attorney confided to civic leader Hinton, if Tate Burk contested the matter, there existed overwbelming evidence of the defendant's adulterous conduct, which assured the plaintiff's victory.

At the moment the Burks were living apart—Maggie and the children occupying her ranch house west of Red Mound, while husband Tate lived quietly in Maggie's Red Mound home, an imposing, two-story brick structure on the south edge of town. Would Burk contest Maggie's suit? If so, no Red Mound attorney had his case. Experienced observers were predicting that, admitting certain defeat in court, Burk would look for another full-blood wife, though he would have to search at length to find one as wealthy as Maggie.

"By now," Hinton told Sublette and Sam, "with her family's wealth concentrated in her hands, she has five headrights, besides all the land allotted in severalty to each member of the family."

Hinton brought a man to Fargo's whom he introduced as Poole's successor: Web Newman, another Texan, a sturdy, straw-haired man of neat appearance, about thirty-five.

"Web will make his headquarters in Red Mound," Hinton said. "Supposed to be looking for lease land. Be staying at the Osage Hotel. We're closing the circle, Sam. Red Mound is the hub of this dirty business. I'm going to move Blue over here, too. This way we can work closer together, back each other up. We'll all be around the day of the big race. You can bet on that."

To Sam's surprise, the match race with the unbeaten Tomahawk was agreed on with a minimum of sparring. Vail had driven to Fargo's one afternoon, and there the match was made: 440 yards for 300 dollars, to be run the first Sunday in October. Fargo Young the starter and Jimmy the Greek the finish judge.

"I'm always suspicious when a man who always drives a hard bargain becomes so agreeable," Fargo warned Sam. "Makes me think he's got something up his sleeve he'll pull out at the very last. Vail's run Tomahawk twice against Plunger and daylighted him both times. I understand Vail slipped off to the Flint Hills last week . . . took that fast little stud Bullet by half a length at two furlongs. So Tomahawk is ready."

"I know he's a top horse," Sam agreed. "But we'd daylighted Plunger too except for that flat-footed start." Sam hadn't told Fargo about young Oden's intention to use the bat that day, and he would not.

"How's Dee doing?" Fargo asked hopefully.

"Fine. Better all the time on the break. Got off like a shot at Pawhuska when we beat Alf Scholl's horse. A perfect ride."

"How'd you ever get Vail to agree on me?" Fargo puzzled.

"I flat told him I wouldn't run my horse if Mitch Kell was the starter. He didn't seem to mind."

"Hell," Fargo spluttered, "he knows he'll get a fair start. He's not givin' away anythin'. He knows that. Just the same, it's not like Hank Vail."

Before Gene Poole's death, Sam would have reveled in such a race, preparing for it with equal trepidation and enthusiasm. Now it seemed unimportant, empty of meaning, when weighed against the issues of life and death. He set about methodically, schooling young Oden, cautioning him not to override, careful of his horse, gradually lengthening Slip Along's readiness. Although the gelding could go seven furlongs, he had seldom run a full quarter the past two seasons.

As news of the forthcoming race spread, visitors drove to Vail's and Fargo's to view the horses. Sam discerned an additional reason behind their interest. People in and around Red Mound were seeking an escape from the depressive aura of murder. A horse race was welcome release, something you could talk about openly and ask opinions and get answers as well as voice your own.

"There is much betting," Jimmy the Greek told Sam, speaking in his formal, Old World manner. "After the race, half the town will be broke, half will be rich."

And from as far as Skiatook and Avant, Pawhuska and Hominy, Kaw City and Ponca City, came the horse-loving Osages, driving their long cars. Among them John Cloud-Walker and his Indian bodyguard. Maggie Bear Claw Burk and her two eager children. Sam always took time to visit with her, waiting, waiting. *(Who murdered Elsie? Who blew up the home of Grace and Ben Jordan? Who shot Antwine?)* Waiting for the one fateful break. Just a few words from her, backed up by her signed statement and presented to the U. S. Attorney for the Western District, followed by complaints filed with the U. S. Commissioner at Guthrie, and a warrant or warrants would go out. Just one might be the wedge needed to break open the investigation. *(Just* a *few words, Maggie. Just one lead. Just one name. One person you suspect and why. One name will lead to the others, because there must be others.)*

Friday afternoon before Sunday's race she drove out again, alone this time. She looked at the horse, chatting with Sam about the race, shyly revealing that she had bet on Slip Along again. Indians were like that. They would bet on your horse simply because you were a friend. Briefly, and she returned to her car and sat down, a heavy woman, trouble like a dark veil across her fleshy features, features meant to be pleasant. It cut into him how alone she looked, almost brooding.

"Something wrong, Maggie?" he asked bluntly, resting one hand on the car door.

Her lips opened and closed, full and maternal. She pulled at her bright shawl. She attempted a smile. "Guess it's these hot afternoons. Be glad when fall comes."

He nodded to that, waiting.

"Why you ask me that, Sam?" An unexpected reply from her. Other times she would have let his question go unheeded.

"You look unhappy. Sometimes it's good to have a shoulder to lean on. Somebody to talk to. Somebody you can trust."

Their eyes met and held. Her dark-brown stare, combining trust and liking for him, yet offset by an emotion he could not define, unless it was fear, struck him as so unreserved and aware that, for an instant, he suspected she must know about him. So. much the better, then! And yet, even as that insight came to him, he saw her take her gaze away, and saw her gradual withdrawal, as once again she settled into her self-imposed isolation.

Forcing a smile, she said, "You are good friend, Sam. Hope your horse wins," and started the car and drove out of the yard.

He followed her with his eyes, thinking, When? When?, conscious of a powerless frustration. Would he ever break through that wall of Indian silence, that damned passiveness of hers, as if she must accept whatever came?

Before dark Saturday, on the eve of the race, he saddled up and rode out to the far side of the pasture and back, and unsaddled and stabled his horse for the night. For the past week he had followed the precaution of sleeping on a cot in the stall next to Slip Along's. Not that he expected someone to harm his horse, but he felt easier being nearby. A gentle gelding like this one was far more vulnerable than a high-strung stud, spooking at the slightest strange noise. Matt Colter used to tell of persons, identities seldom known, like dog poisoners, sneaking into the favorite's stall the night before the race and beating a hammer against the cannon bones (just a few hard licks could render a horse unfit to run his best tomorrow, hurting him every hard-driving stride) or gouging a knife blade into the front leg and shoulder muscles.

Sam loosened his shirt and pulled off his boots and lay down, fully clothed, listening to the creaks and groans of the barn, the stamping of his horse, the chorus from the woods, and the voice of the sobbing night wind. He slept.

A roaring flung him awake and sitting up. A car driving into the yard. He pulled on his boots, stepped outside, and saw headlights. And there, luminous in the moonlight, motor still running, was a white roadster. Fay's roadster. She honked the horn.

He stayed within the corral, of a mind not to go out. However, his touring car was parked in the yard, and she knew that he would be here this night, close to his horse. He drew the .45 from his belt, reached back and laid it on the cot, and went to the corral gate.

Her attention was on the house when he spoke a "Good evening." She started violently, then turned off the motor and lights. "Where'd you come from?" she asked, relieved.

"The barn."

"Afraid somebody will steal your horse?" Her amused voice sounded slurred.

"Not that. But as much money as I hear is being bet, somebody might slip in and do something to him before the race."

"You're saying Hank might?"

"Hey! I'm not saying any such thing. I mean somebody with a heap of money on Tomahawk might. It's just an old precaution many horse owners take the night before a race. My father always did."

"Oh, I'm teasin' you, Sam. I know. Hank's got a

man at the barn tonight, too. All you racehorse guys are crazy. You think more of your of horses than you do your women."

His laugh was light. "I didn't say that either." "Thought maybe you'd like to go for a little ride?"

"I can't leave my horse."

She turned away from him, a pouting gesture. "If you won't go for a ride, least you could do is invite me in for a little dreenk."

"Come in," he said, opening the door for her.

"You're bein' vereee formal, Sam." She fumbled on the seat for something, came up waggling her purse; turning to step out, she swayed against him. "That 'us a slip," she slurred. "Slips don' count."

"All I can offer you is coffee."

"No dreenk? Not one little dreenk?"

In lieu of an answer, he took her by the arm, and as they started for the house, she swayed against him again. Suddenly she jerked still and looked up at the sky. "Be-you-ti-ful night, isn' it, Sam?"

"Always is out here."

In the kitchen he lighted the kerosene lamp, pulled out a chair for her at the table, poured a cup of leftover coffee, and set it before her, expecting her to refuse it.

Pushing her beaded purse aside, she stared at the cup without protest for several moments, and then, as if to please him, she sipped the coffee. "Not a bad dreenk."

That was when he noticed the blue mark on her left cheekbone, like an old bruise slowly fading. It angered him. "How'd you get that bruise?" he asked her.

"We were down at the barns, looking at Tomahawk, when he made a sudden move and threw me against the stall. That devil! He's so high-strung." She touched the place as a child would, tenderly, remembering the hurt

He didn't quite believe her. "When was that?"

"Several weeks ago. I've kind of been staying in."

She shrugged it off, and they talked about the race for a time. When that topic lagged, he said, "Maggie was out here yesterday. Has anything happened to her lately?"

"I don't know. Why?"

"She looked like the end of the world had come."

"Well, she is finally divorcing Tate."

"That should be cause for celebration, not dejection." He decided that Fay wasn't as tight as she had sounded at the car. Her eyes were clear, her hand steady when she lifted the cup. "She's afraid, Fay. Very much afraid."

"Of Tate?"

"She wouldn't say."

"Wouldn't you be after all that's happened to her family?"

"You're damned right I would. Who's behind all this?"

"You always seem to bring that up." She gave a little movement of irritation.

"Why not? I hear it everywhere I go: `Who's behind the Osage killings?' " He leaned across and took her hand. "Fay, you've lived around here all your life. Don't you have some suspects in mind besides Rex Enright and Billy Gault? Those fellows are just too obvious."

Little by little, she withdrew her hand to take up the cup. "I'd like some more, please."

He filled the cup and sat down, giving her face a close search. "You didn't answer me."

"I can't because I don't know any suspects," she said, dismissing it. "And I don't want to know any." She studied the cup, her eyes lingering there; when she looked up at him, he recognized the intensity in her eyes. "I guess you're wondering why I came out here tonight. Well, I did because I wanted to see you."

"Do you always get what you want?"

"Even more," she said, letting the question go by, "I came because I still need you, Sam."

"You don't."

"And because I was so wrong that time in what I did."

He made a pushing-away motion with his hands and stood. "Stop it, Fay." But before he knew it he was making excuses for her again. "You got lonely. Hank Vail was close. A big rancher. Famous rodeo star. You changed your mind. It's as simple as that. Like I said before, it just happened . . . and you were pretty young," which instantly he wished to call back, because instead of that quelling her, she rose and came straight to him and slid her arms around him and laid her face against his chest, murmuring, "I'm so tired, Sam. So tired."

"Why don't you go away, like I said?"

"There are some things you can't run away from."

"Like what?" No word, just silence, and he said, "You can get in your car and leave tonight. Get out of Oklahoma."

"So could you—with me."

"You're kidding. I've got a race coming up tomorrow."

He could feel her trembling, but when he put his arms around her, she grew still. She lifted her face for him, looking up in that needful way she had, which she had always had, and which could mean so many things, and instinctively he kissed her. Her lips, at first warm and giving, turned subtly hesitant, almost cool.

She drew back, reading his face. "Sam, why are you really here? Why did you come back?"

An insight jarred him: So that's it. That's what all this making up is about. He dropped his arms. "You're forgetting about the races my horse has won."

"I only wonder because you ask so many questions."

"The questions I ask are heard every day on the streets of Red Mound."

She moved in again, the length of her body against him. "I worry about you sometimes, Sam. Like when that man was found shot to death down the road. It might have been you, close as it was here. Safer for you if you left the Osage."

"Why?"

"Just a feeling I have, I guess. Just a feeling."

"I didn't know the man."

"Who would shoot him? He was a stranger, wasn't he?"

"Alf Scholl, the deputy, said he was. Just another unanswered question. Like who shot Elsie and Antwine, and who blew up the house? And who shot Tug Lay and who set up Kirk Singer?"

She remained against him, but he did not embrace her this time. She seemed to stay there for a wishful moment. When nothing happened, she went slowly to the table and turned, on her face one of those inexplicable moods, half accusing, half appealing. "I'd hoped there was something left for me, Sam. Just a little trust."

"Works both ways, Fay."

Color pinked her cheeks. She jerked at the catch of her purse, apparently fumbling for a pack of cigarettes. As she did so, something fell out and clattered solidly on the table. A stubby .38 revolver.

She stiffened, gray-green eyes widening on the handgun, and, watching that expression, Sam was at loss to tell what it meant.

He heard his voice, flat and hard. "What are you afraid of?"

"Does it matter now?"

Deliberately calm, she retrieved the .38 and dropped it in the purse, a finality to her motions, a slackness, an acceptance.

The last tag end between them had ended here tonight. In a rush, he sensed that in her and within himself, and felt a lift of relief. But, in no more than a breath, he wished to recall what had gone, for she looked so damned vulnerable and needful. An impulse to protect her overcame him.

"Fay! I'll help you if I can. But you'll have to tell me what it is. All of it."

"I believe it's getting late," she said, and walked past him to the open door. There, as he foresaw she would, knowing her, she looked back at him, projecting the questioning look of a hurt child, and said:

"You really didn't listen, Sam."

CHAPTER 19

AT FOUR-THIRTY, UNABLE TO SLEEP, SAM LEFT THE cot and made a wood fire in the iron cookstove and filled the coffee pot. At five o'clock he paced back to the barn and fed Slip Along a short ration of grain, thinking: Better to have him a little hungry and light at race time.

After breakfast, Sam draped the worn cooling

blanket on his horse and led him around a short while, and when the sun came up he peeled off the blanket and tied him in the corral. There wasn't a cloud in the sky, which as far as he could see was an infinite blue. The afternoon promised to be hot, but not humid hot like August. Didn't matter either way, he figured, for a horse reared in South Texas.

Come eight o'clock, Sam led his horse to his stall and tied him. Walking to the house, Sam sat on the porch. From now until race time he would be close by his horse, in the grip of race-day jitters.

He retraced last night. That little run of tenderness—it had seemed true, because he had felt it so until she started asking questions, until then giving rise to wild hopes that, when the investigation was over, he could take her away, while sensing that could not be. She baffled him as much as Maggie Burk, though in a different way. Fay was a complex woman, Maggie was not. Yet each was afraid of something, each seemed trapped somehow, each had come to him in nameless appeal, still unspoken when they left. Had he failed them? Why couldn't he reach them?

He stirred, unhappy with himself, and walking to the corral again, thinking of the race, a sudden flurry of fears crowded in upon him: blowing a tire and the trailer flopping over, his horse thrown out; some drunk running into him on the way to Vail's, crippling his horse. *Stop it, Sam!*

Willing himself duties, he started the touring car and backed it up to the horse trailer; examining the hitch, he spent half an hour locating a new bolt and going over the trailer's sideboards and tailgate. Moreover, the trailer's left tire was low. He jacked up the axle and removed the tire, found the guilty nail, cold-patched tube and tire, put them back on, tightened the nuts, let the jack down, pumped up the tire, and the trailer was ready.

About ten o'clock Dee Oden rattled up in his flivver. "Anything you want me to do?" he asked, coming over to the porch. He looked moody and taut, and kept fidgeting with his belt buckle and looking off. Sam read the signs as a jockey's usual race-day strain.

"Just be on hand in plenty of time. I'll go out about noon. Understand there'll be a couple of races before ours. Well run about three o'clock. There's no rodeo."

Oden nodded. He left abruptly, slamming out of the yard, gunning the derelict for all it could take.

Now, I wonder what's in his craw besides the race? Sam asked himself, getting up and leaving the porch's shade.

He busied himself packing the touring car: water can and pail, sack of oats and *morral,* tack, cooling blanket, and the box of assorted liniments, which smelled strongest of turpentine. He tightened Slip Along's shoes a little, though they needed it not; he cleaned Slip Along's feet with a brush, and rubbed liniment on the cannons, working it in. Still fussing over his horse, he took the currycomb to mane and forelock, then brushed him gently.

Finally, it was time to go. Cars had been passing from east to west on the road for several hours, raising a dusty pall that alternately boiled and settled. Sam moved faster, glad the waiting was over. After loading his horse, he made one last inspecting circle of car and trailer, and took off.

Turning north out of Red Mound, he had to hold up as the traffic increased. A driver honked and passed, and the passengers waved and called out to the horse.

"They know who you are!" Sam yelled over his shoulder. "Give 'em a big smile!" He didn't know when he had felt so excited over a horse race.

Thereafter, he was forced to crawl along at twenty miles an hour while he ate dust to the turnoff to Vail's; and when, at last, he drove to the brow of the hill overlooking the Forked Lightning Ranch, he saw a sea of cars and people overflowing the track and the wooden stands, already filled, and on to the horse barns. Some enterprising soul had set up a refreshment stand between the rodeo arena and track and was doing boom-town business.

Sam wound his way down through the gawking, chattering pack to the blackjacks south of the track and parked. Backing his horse out of the trailer, he haltered Slip Along in the shade and gave him a few sips of water, his last before race time.

Time dragged. Sam, fretting for his horse, trod out a path from the touring car to where Slip Along stood quietly, tail-switching flies. Slip Along dropped his head. Like always just before a race, he seemed to be dreaming. *Good, pardner. Good.*

At one o'clock three men converged singly on the patch of blackjacks. First, Scotty Hinton, Blue Sublette a few steps behind him, and on Sublette's heels came Web Newman, the new agent. They strolled to the horse and looked him over, chatted about the race and the betting, and strolled back around the car and trailer.

"Look at that crowd," Hinton said. "Gives me an odd feeling to know that somewhere out there today are the people involved in the Osage murders. All of Red Mound's here and half the county, looks like."

Hinton's voice vented an unusual discouragement, even bitterness, Sam thought.

"Be a good time to rob the bank," Newman said.

Sublette dug an elbow into Newman's ribs. "Don't start givin' me any ideas. I've led a fairly honest life up till now."

There was a wrongness here. Sam sensed it. Newman and Blue trying to joke, and something weighing on Scotty's mind. Sam could tell by the way the older man paced back and forth, pausing to kick at the grass now and then, a giant scowl furrowing his normally placid face. It was coming to a head this very moment, Sam saw, as Hinton quit his tramping and drove his eyes straight at him.

"Sam," Hinton said, "I got news last night I didn't like one little bit. The Bureau's taking you off the case."

Sam, too shaken to answer at once, lifted an objecting hand. He let it fall. "Why . . . Scotty?"

"Because they're afraid you're a marked man."

"You mean they think another Trigger Riggs will come in?" "Something like that."

"Wouldn't he have popped up before now?"

"Who knows? It comes down to this: The Bureau thinks your usefulness in the case is over. They figure your cover is gone." Hinton bowed his neck. "I argued hard. I said I needed you, and I said you wanted to stay. I lost . . . Sorry, Sam. More sorry than I can say."

"When am I out?"

"Effective immediately."

"Guess that means now."

"It does."

Sam had the sensation of a hot wind burning his face all at once. "Well, I intend to run this race."

"Sure, Sam. Sure. Go ahead. I want you to."

The wind seemed to whirl about him, faster and hotter. "What if I refuse to leave? What if I resign and work on my own?"

Hinton's face knotted, a conflict of refusal and understanding. He said softly, "We'll talk about it after the race," and gave Sam a pat on the shoulder. "We'll be around close, Sam. Come on, boys."

Sam slumped on the touring car's running board and ran a hand through his hair, his thoughts churning. What the Bureau and perhaps even Scotty didn't understand was the personal obligation he felt. This was home! And his home had been violated and a buddy murdered. Leaving now would be like running out on your friends just when they needed you most.

He hadn't moved when he heard someone walking through the grass. He looked up and saw Dee Oden, who asked, "Everything O.K.?"

"Fine," Sam said, masking his feelings.

Oden went to the horse and stroked the long face and soft nose, and smoothed Slip Along's forelock, and patted his neck and spoke to him, and the old campaigner nibbled playfully at his jockey's shirt sleeve.

Sam watched in silent approval. By now Dee knew the horse, and the horse knew him. Each had a liking for the other. That could mean a great deal in a close race when you called on your horse to give all he had. It could mean the difference between winning and losing.

But when Dee turned back, Sam saw that his mood of the morning hadn't changed. He made Sam think of a man down on the world, and, worst of all, down on himself.

"I'll be back in plenty of time," Oden said. "I want to watch the first race."

"Fine," Sam said, and was going to say no more when, quite suddenly, he yielded to the impulse to erase what he saw on the slim, young face. "You know, Dee, you win today and you'll be the hottest jock in these parts, bar none. You'll get offers to ride big races from here to Illinois and down to Louisiana."

"That'll be the day," Oden scoffed, his shoulders sinking. He left without meeting Sam's eyes.

Sam glanced at his watch. It was one-thirty. The first race would be starting before long. He came to his feet and resumed his pacing. At one forty-five he saw the elongated figure of Fargo Young hurrying across from the track. Fargo would take a step or two, then quicken his stride. His flying coattails and his ungainly legs and arms turned him into the likeness of a hastening turkey cock.

"Boy, howdy," Fargo panted, exuding mothballs as he pulled at the coat of his dark suit, "are they comin' in! Biggest crowd ever out here. They say Red Mound's a ghost town. Bettin' is somethin' fierce. Some boys are down to their BVDs." He mopped with a red bandanna. He bit off a hunk of plug tobacco and wallowed it around for thought. His face darkened perceptibly.

"What is it, Fargo?"

The old man looked carefully about before he spoke. "Hate to tell you this, Sam. I sure do. But I just saw Dee and Hank Vail in a big powwow behind the stands." Sam saw the struggle going on inside him, and the hurt and the letdown.

A cold sickening invaded Sam. He said, "Go on. Guess I better hear the rest."

"I saw Vail pass some money to Dee, and I saw Dee take it. Hate to say this, since I recommended Dee to you."

They faced each other in silence. After a long pause, Sam said, "Not your fault, Fargo. Maybe we both tried too hard to help Dee, when the truth is a man's got to want to make it on his own. I see now why Dee's been so moody today. Why Vail didn't kick when I insisted that you be the starter. Hell, he had the race fixed even that far back."

"Also explains why Vail has bet so much. There's plenty money on your horse, too. What you aim to do, Sam?"

Sam rubbed a hand across his forehead, trying to reason what Matt Colter would have done, remembering the brush-track ruses his father used to tell and laugh about. Something pricked his memory. It sprang alive and formed. He remembered now. It had worked once for his father, in a strange town, a crooked jockey in the irons; but that didn't mean it would here.

"You could ride that horse," Fargo suggested. "You did when you beat Miss Whizzbang."

"At one furlong I'd take the chance. But I'm thirty or thirty-five pounds heavier than Dee. Too big a handicap for my horse at twice that distance against a goer like Tomahawk."

"So?"

"I'll put it this way. If somebody else tells me he saw what you saw, I'll tell him to keep right on bettin' on my horse."

"You mean Dee will ride?"

"Yes."

"I don't savvy you." Shaking his head, Fargo moved

off. "It's your horse and your money and a lot of other folks' money, too. Just remember, I told you."

"Thanks, Fargo."

Sam closed his eyes in angry hurt. He could confront Dee with what he knew, try to shame him out of it . . . No—that wouldn't do. Dee would have some excuse. There'd be a wrangle. Vail must have paid him plenty! Meanwhile, this other thing had to be done before Dee came back.

At low ebb, Sam turned to the car and removed the bridle's throatlatch and hid it under the seat. Next, he bridled and saddled his horse and cinched up, worrying that Dee might wonder about the early saddling and discover the missing throatlatch.

When Sam returned to the car, the first race was just starting. He watched the two horses rushing between the lines of spectators packing the flanks of the track. He heard the shouting. That looked like Miss Whizzbang taking the lead, running well. If so, the filly had won handily, and Art Cook would be snapping his galluses.

Fretting, Sam eased the cinch and lingered by his horse. *Pardner, it's all up to you now.*

Once more he stood by the car. The waiting seemed endless until the next two horses, led by their owners, materialized and pranced past the stands and on to the starting line. Fargo had them approach twice before he set them off together, as evenly as a team in harness.

As he watched the break, Sam had the total detachment of a spectator. Seeing the sun on rippling horseflesh. The cloudless sky dripping bronze. The horses like beautiful wild creatures suddenly freed, manes flying, skimming the prairie earth, only their bobbing heads and the crablike forms of their jockeys showing as they dashed between the wings of the crowd, which appeared to open for them like a parting wave.

Now the race was over and the last moments began to slip past. Dee Oden was coming. He was late. Good! In his haste, he might be less observant. Young Dee. Slim. His head down. Sam's anger struck twofold. Not only because of what Dee was doing to his friends and the horse, but also because of what Dee was bringing on himself.

Oden sat on the running board and took off his shoes, pulled on his riding boots, and stood. His eyes found the horse, then Sam. "Already saddled?"

"Already because you're late," Sam said bluntly. "Let's get over there."

He gave Oden a leg up and, taking the reins, led away for the stands. Not seeing Tomahawk, Sam took a roundabout course; by the time he had circled to the track, there was still no Tomahawk. His suspicion flared. Was Vail trying to sweat him, withholding his horse from sight until the very final minute?

Alongside the track and in the stands, the restless crowd stirred, shrill and impatient, constantly shifting. When Sam started by, applause burst forth. It mounted and swelled and held. Sam led on, warmed. His old horse had his following today. Slip Along threw up his head in recognition, turned curious. An Osage man stood up and whooped—John Cloud-Walker. Sam waved to him.

Two horses were coming from the barns. Sam saw Vail mounted, leading the handsome chestnut sorrel Tomahawk. Yards down the track, when the opposing horses passed, Vail waved an expansive hand.

Sam did not return the greeting. Presently, while he continued on, he heard clapping and shouting for Tomahawk.

In no time at all, it seemed, Vail was jogging up

behind, and the horses were nearing the starting line where Fargo waited and was calling instructions. "I'll drop my hand and holler *'Go!'* " And, in moments, when Sam walked his horse on a way and turned for the approach to the line, still holding the reins, Fargo's steady voice reached him again. "You aim to lead your horse right up to the line?"

Sam nodded and drew Oden's surprise, but he did not look at Oden until he gave him the split reins.

And Fargo said, "You'll have to walk on the outside. I can't have you between the horses," and Sam nodded again, already on the right side of his horse.

Pace McKee, aboard Tomahawk, had turned the chestnut sorrel as well, and now the horses, knowing the break was near, stepped nervously toward the watching Fargo.

The line was but a few yards away now. Sam, holding the bridle's cheekstrap, kept watching Fargo. He saw Fargo lift his hand slowly, higher, yet higher, and pause as the walking horses drew almost even.

It happened in a split second. As Sam saw Fargo's hand drop and heard his shouted *"Go!"* Sam stripped the bridle off Slip Along and then tore the reins from Oden's hands. That, and Sam jerked clear and slapped his horse across the rump and the race was on.

Slip Along lunged, but he broke half a jump behind. It couldn't be helped. Sam saw that as he glimpsed young Oden's startled face.

Dirt flew . . .

When the horses were gone, Sam put hands on hips and stood at the starting line, motionless, mouth tight, worried, gripping the bridle and reins.

Dust rose . . . His horse trailed, but he was running true, running lower, leveling out, running on instinct and heart. Oden crouched forward, helpless to do otherwise . . . The horses looked very close now, lapped. No veering by McKee this time. Their charging shapes growing smaller and smaller, nearly invisible in the film of dust, almost spectral. Head to head, they seemed. The crowd was roaring.

Sam knotted his fist. He punched the air. *Come on, pardner! Come on!*

In breaths the race was over. The crowd was spilling out on the track, and Sam couldn't tell whether his horse had won or lost. But, by God, he was proud of him, no matter—for Slip Along, knowing what to do, had run his honest best and as free as the wind.

Sam flinched as Vail tore past him on his horse.

Sam hurried. He was trotting. Now be was running. He lost sight of Vail, swallowed up in the swarming crowd. Far down the track, he saw Slip Along frisking this way and that, still keyed high. A cowboy ran up and put a rope around Slip Along's neck. After that, Sam saw his horse no more. Late, he realized that he didn't see Dee.

Sam's chest burned. He was hacking for wind when he reached the stands. A short, powerfully built man made a path to Sam. Jimmy the Greek, the finish judge. A huge grin split his broad face.

Sam had to yell at him to be heard. "My horse won?"

And Jimmy the Greek held up his hands and gapped them about the length of a horse's head.

Sam yelled and threw up his arms, aware of a whirlpool of people around him and the confusion of voices and hands seeking his. He heard a screeching whoop. A shape loomed before him, and its copper plate of a face belonged to John Cloud-Walker, who pumped Sam's hand formally. Someone was pounding Sam's back. Sam turned and met Hinton's eyes, on either side of him Sublette and Newman.

The crowd parted, shrill again, making way for the cowboy leading in the winner. Sam hurried over there and slipped on the bridle and took off the rope and handed it to the cowboy; and while Cloud-Walker ceremoniously draped a red Indian blanket over Slip Along's withers, and while the throng closed around, Sam caught sight of Dee and Fay at the crowd's edge.

A man hurried up to her and spoke rapidly. Her face changed, troubled, as she listened. Sam saw her questioning attention seek him. At once she pressed through to him.

"Maggie's on the phone at the house," she shrilled at him. "She wants you, Sam. It's urgent!" Her eyes, in that moment, seemed to mirror many things.

A moment, a long moment. Sam had a sense of light streaking and breaking through a dark cloud. Maggie's cloud. "I'm coming right now," he told her, and handed the reins to Cloud-Walker. "Take my horse, John." Fay was already going, he saw, as he looked for Hinton and found him at his elbow. "You heard what she said, Scotty. Maybe this is it. Wait for me at the house."

He caught up with Fay. It seemed like such a long way to the house and up the long steps and inside, Fay keeping pace every hastening stride. "Here," she panted, leading him to the phone in the hallway.

He picked up the receiver. "This is Sam," and heard no voice. He spoke again, louder.

A voice came on, dim, fearful, plaintive. A woman's voice. "Something's wrong with Tate. He's takin' me to our house in town. Can you come there quick, Sam? Please. . ."

"I'll be there." The receiver clicked before he could get out another word.

"What is it?" Fay's tremulous voice betrayed her agitation. Her large eyes looked enormous, and her face paled.

"She's scared to death—it's Tate. He's taking her to their house in town. Can we go in your car? It's gotta be fast."

"Why do you even have to ask?"

He ran down the hall with her and outside, down the stone steps to the white Marmon. Not far away he saw two cars, motors idling. Hinton in one. Sublette and Newman in the other. And, to Sam's surprise, Oden's flivver was rattling uphill from the rodeo stands.

As Fay jerked open the car door, Sam waved for the agents to follow. "Who's that?" she snapped at him when he got in.

"Friends. just friends."

She darted him an obscure look, started the Marmon, backed out, and tore for the road.

CHAPTER 20

FAY DROVE SKILLFULLY, SWINGING THE AGILE roadster around car after car departing the races, shifting into second gear to regain lost speed. Once she turned in on the road to Red Mound, the traffic thinned and she gave the Marmon its head.

Sam worried whether Scotty and the others could keep up. The question of distances occurred to him. He called above the rushing of the wind:

"How far is Maggie's ranch from town?"

"About five miles. Hank's place is seven."

"They could get there before we do." Even under these circumstances he thought it odd that she should say "Hank's place" instead of "our place." He brushed the perception away. "Step on it, Fay."

She floorboarded the roadster so abruptly that Sam was thrown against the seat. The hills flicked by. In minutes he saw Red Mound's disarray on the flat. Entering town, she reduced speed and turned to him.

"What does it mean, Sam?"

"It's a cry for help. Keep going!"

She held the horn down and cut around a startled driver. Her voice hardened. "Sam, who are those men back there?"

"I told you—friends. Believe me, they are friends!" He hitched around. Scotty was making dust at the outskirts of town, closer than Sam had thought possible. Sublette's sedan followed.

Alternately honking and braking, Fay raced down Main Street. There was little traffic, thanks to the races. The side streets were empty, awakening in Sam the image of the town drowsing in unconcern while murder threatened another Osage's life.

Fay hit the brakes and whipped the car into a squealing turn west.

Sam smelled burning rubber. Three blocks on, she cut south and drove rapidly.

In the town's last block, like a red-brick guardian over the scattering of bungalows, stood Maggie's two-story house. It faced east, symbolic somehow to Sam of an Osage's wish to meet the rising sun each day. Here also the town dozed, seemingly indifferent.

But then, as the street dipped and Fay took them

nearer, Sam spotted two figures struggling in front of the big house. Down the street a man waited behind the wheel of a dark sedan headed north. "Sam!" Fay burst out. "I just hope you'll try to understand!"

Understand what? He tore his eyes from the figures to stare at her, astonished at her pleading tone. He shouted at her, "Stop here-stay in the car."

Out and running before she stopped, Sam saw Tate Burk drag Maggie screaming from the yard to the curb. She fought savagely, desperately. Some fifty yards on, the sedan was in menacing motion, approaching deliberately.

That car—that car. Everything seemed to telescope as Sam ran still faster. But he couldn't fire at it because Maggie and Burk struggled between him and the car.

Burk stopped. He slapped Maggie, he knocked her down. When she lurched up at once, he hit her again, and as she reeled backward, he grabbed her and pushed her toward the center of the street. There she collapsed, an inert bundle in a purple dress.

Sam sprinted. And for one hanging fraction, as if carved in relief, he saw Maggie's agonized face turned resigned to the sky and the sedan rushing toward her and Burk waiting.

Sam crouched and groped, clutched an arm, and yanked backward with all his strength, the roar of the sedan hammering his ears. But he heard no thump. By then the sedan was past, and he was whirling on Burk, the .45 leaping, without thought, to his hand.

Burk's hands shot up. He stood open-mouthed, in stunned disbelief, in utter astonishment.

Shots blasted north along the street, so rapidly they seemed to run together. Sam jerked to look. Sublette and Newman, beside their car, were firing at the sedan. It sped by Hinton's coupe and suddenly lost momentum, banged into a tree, bounced back, and stopped dead. Sublette ran to the driver's side, wrenched the door open, and a man tumbled limply out.

The next Sam knew, Hinton ran up. "We're federal officers," he informed Burk. "You're under arrest for the attempted murder of your wife. We're all witnesses."

Maggie Bear Claw Burk, forgotten these last moments, swayed to her feet and stepped toward her husband, her established taciturnity falling from her face like a discarded mask. A terrible clarity stood out in her accusing dark eyes. Trembling, she raged at him:

"Now I know why you wanted the kids and me to stay at Grace's house that night it was blown up. Why you didn't seem glad later when I told you we came home early because Richard got sick . . . You wanted us dead—your own family! . . . Now I know why Mama died when you were alone with her in the house. Her so old, so helpless . . . an old full-blood who never harmed anyone, who was always generous. And now I know what was meant when I overheard you talking to Hank Vail, and he said, Tug *Lay will do the job—he'll do anything for money*—just before poor Elsie was murdered . . . You wanted us all dead, didn't you, Tate? So you'd get everything: Mama's headright—Papa's, which had gone to Mama—Elsie's—Grace's—mine. Everything!"

Her face contorting, her teeth bared, she screamed and lunged at him and struck his face—again, again, again. Burk took the blows numbly, not lifting a hand.

Again, again, again, until Sam drew her back.

"Maggie," Hinton said most gently, most gravely, "will you sign a statement to that effect, and whatever else you know about the murders of your family?"

She nodded, unable to speak, each of her old sorrows living and tearing again across her weeping face. In the somber hush that followed, Sam glanced around and saw Fay, and surprisingly there was young Oden. They also had heard.

"Burk," Hinton said as Sublette and Newman arrived with the handcuffed, wounded driver, "we want the whole story. What set this off?"

A sort of relief overspread the smooth face. His voice dropped to a monotone:

"Maggie was goin' to divorce me. I'd been left without a cent."

"Too bad! Go back. Start at the beginning when the plot was hatched. I want names. There are more besides you."

"Hank Vail hired Tug Lay and Kirk Singer for me . . . ."

At mention of Vail's name, Sam saw Fay pale and draw back and become still as Burk continued:

"In turn, Hank was to get one of Maggie's ranches and income from two of the Bear Claw headrights. Lay killed Elsie, and he also killed Antwine Cloud-Walker. He wanted Antwine's diamonds—that was on his own."

"Was Billy Gault involved in any way with Antwine's murder?"

"No."

Hinton was relentless. "How much did Lay get for Elsie's murder?"

"A thousand."

There was an audible gasp from poor Maggie. Sam slid an arm around her.

"Did Lay gun down Rusty Dunlap, the cowboy on the Ives ranch?"

"He did," Burk said, and balked.

"Speak up! Why?"

"Because Dunlap mouthed around town he saw Lay and Antwine in the pasture the day Antwine was murdered. Said he rode up on a ridge, looked down, and saw 'em on the runnin' board of Antwine's car, havin' a drink."

"Who wrote the letters to Gault and Dunlap, offering them bribes to leave the country?"

"Hank Vail."

"What about Singer? What part did he play in all this?"

Burk averted his eyes from Maggie's decimating stare. "He blew up the Jordan house with nitro for five thousand cash. Hank and I split the fee."

Maggie gave a lurch and closed her eyes. Oden edged forward, his face like pitted rock. Hinton went on:

"Did Rex Enright have a hand in blowing up the house?"

"That rodeo showoff? Naw."

Hinton's voice fairly crackled. "Who murdered Gene Poole?"

"Singer."

"Did Singer suspect Poole was a federal agent?"

"Naw . . . it was just that Poole was snooping around, asking a lot of questions. Main thing, Singer figured his girlfriend Sunny was in love with Poole."

"Who hired Trigger Riggs to come after Sam Colter?"

"Hank Vail did—after Lay said he recognized Colter as a lawman in Texas. Hank didn't want to take any chances. After Riggs got rubbed out, Hank was sure

Colter was a fed. Idea was to string Colter along, dangle that big horse race in front of him, until Hank could bring in another killer from back East."

"Who killed Tug Lay?"

"Singer—at Hank's order. Singer went with Lay in Lay's car. Hank followed . . . picked up Singer. Lay got to where he wasn't reliable. Drank and talked too much." Burk was talking faster, as if eager to tell his story and be left alone. "Singer made a mistake. He hounded Hank for more money for takin' care of Lay. So Hank set him up. Told him that storekeeper kept a big wad of cash around."

"Then," Hinton supplied crisply, "Vail warned the storekeeper by letter, had him waiting for Singer?"

Burk dipped his head affirmatively. He was tiring.

"One more question, then we take you to Pawhuska. Did you kill Maggie's mother? Maggie says you did."

Burk looked down at the tips of his expensive cowboy boots. By habit, he reached into his vest pocket, found his gold toothpick, and stuck it between his slack lips.

"Answer me!"

Burk jogged his head up and down.

"How?"

"I smothered her with a pillow."

Maggie sobbed hysterically and would have fallen had not Sam held her up.

Hinton extended an apologetic hand to her. "Sorry, Maggie. But everything has to come out. We have to know the truth so you won't live in fear again, ever. The plan, starting with your mother, was to eliminate all members of your family and concentrate the headrights and ranch holdings in your name. You know the rest."

The roar of a powerful motor smashed the lull.

Sam spun and looked. Fay was whipping the Marmon around, taking off north, the roadster's tires screeching and gears clashing. Hinton's coupe was the nearest of the agents' cars. Sam ran to it. He stepped on the starter and shifted into low and was turning to follow Fay when Oden slammed into the seat beside him.

"Get out!" Sam yelled. "You tried to throw that race!"

"I did. I was working for Vail all along, hoping I could find out who killed Holly. Even took Vail's money to make it look good." He was rushing his words, pleading. "I hated myself. I didn't want to. I wanted Slip Along to win. I love that horse. You've got to believe me, Sam! I did it for my Holly!"

Sam read truth in the slim, young face.

He gunned the coupe into second gear and held it there, and saw Fay, three blocks ahead, go into a skidding turn and recover quickly and shoot eastward for Main. When Sam rushed to the turn, he braked hard, lost speed, shifted gears, and with the motor lugging, accelerated to Main. Scotty's coupe was hardly a sprint horse.

Sliding into the turn, Sam saw Fay already in flight at the north end of Main. Behind her a wake of townsmen gaped after the fleeing white roadster.

Sam floorboarded the sluggish coupe, ignoring the arm-wavings while he sped past the stores. He came to the street's end. Ahead, as far as he could see into the humpbacked hills, dust was a roiling snake over the road from cars leaving the races.

A minute later be got his first sighting of white. Oncoming cars were forcing Fay to slow down. Even so, Sam couldn't catch her. Once he saw her swerve to a ditch, the roadster rocking from side to side.

Moments, and she whipped back on the road and disappeared into the thick haze. He pressed on, slowing when he had to, forcing the laggard coupe to its utmost. Dust gritted between his teeth. Oden gripped the door, staring straight ahead.

Sam caught sight of her again. By this time she was nearing the turnoff to Vail's. He saw her pull up suddenly, forced to wait while two cars leaving Vail's bumped over the cattle guard. She kept glancing back.

She gunned through, the Marmon bucking high as it rolled over the crossing's unyielding floor of oil field pipe.

Another departing driver was approaching the cattle guard. Sam refused to wait. Holding the horn down, the coupe whining high-pitched in second gear, he bulled for the crossing. The oncoming car slid to a stop. Sam bumped through and away, in time to glimpse the white blur of Fay's roadster disappearing over the crest of the hill above the ranch.

When Sam made the hill, Fay was racing alongside the horse barns toward the great house. Sam hit second gear again, headlong. Down, down, the wind whistling through the coupe's open windows, the radiator beginning to steam. Hank Vail's Forked Lightning Ranch slumbered beneath the sinking afternoon sun, as placid and restful as a pastoral scene on a bank calendar, for the crowd had gone.

The barns flashed by.

Sam saw Fay scramble from the roadster and start running up the long flight of steps. He roared up below the house and flipped off the ignition, and was out of the coupe before it stopped rolling. Oden materialized strides ahead of him, running insanely, charging up the hill.

Sam yelled him back. Oden seemed not to hear, seemed possessed as he took the steps three at a time, running like a deer, hatless, hair flying.

Fay, running on, was calling Hank's name over and over.

Vail appeared suddenly at the door. One look and he stepped back inside and reappeared gripping a rifle. Fay, not pausing, shouted, "They're federal agents! They're coming for you! Tate's spilled everything!"

Sam winced, sickened, the .45 filling his hand.

Vail started to run. Fay clung to him. He drove the butt of the rifle into her shoulder. The blow knocked her loose and down.

In that twinkling, Vail was open. But Sam couldn't fire. Oden was there. He charged Vail, screaming, "You had Holly murdered! *YOU* MURDERED HER!"

Vail flipped the rifle level. It slammed. The bullet knocked Oden backward, spun him. He broke down, arms flailing, straining for Vail, still spitting the hating words.

Sam's rage burst at the sight. A dangerous emotion, for he caught Vail's shift toward him, and as Sam hurled himself flat, away from the steps, the rifle cracked. The bullet struck stone and ricocheted with a whine.

Sam braced the .45 in both hands, only to curse under his breath. Again he couldn't fire. Fay was on her feet and clinging to Vail.

"You've newer loved me, Hank. But you need me now. I know everything."

"You know too much," Vail yelled.

There were two blasts. Sam saw Fay crumple and fall clear of Vail, twisting as she fell. There was the oddest expression on her face, the eyes so wide, the lips parted, as if she couldn't believe Vail had shot her.

Belly flat in the grass, Sam heard the .45 roar and felt the solid kick jar his hands. Vail staggered, but did not go down. He struggled to swing the rifle around to bear on Sam, who let go again. Vail lurched backward and struck and sprawled there.

Sam jumped up and ran over. Vail was down to stay. Sam pitched the rifle downhill and knelt by Fay. He slid his arms under her, reading her shock, feeling his face wrench. Funny, how he should notice her dress. The one she'd worn the happy day she'd bought the Marmon and they'd gone riding, the day. . . Tiny blue flowers gracing a white dress. A very pretty dress, he remembered, which had clung to her. Now it was bloody and dirty. He was terrified to think that she was going to die, and she was, he knew; for he had seen too much not to know.

He must do something. When he tightened his arms around her to rise, her eyelids fluttered and opened. Something in her eyes, deep and true, stayed him. Her lips moved. He had to bend closer to catch her words. "We could've made it, Sam."

"Don't talk. I'm taking you to the hospital."

"I feel so cold, Sam. Hold me."

He held her and could almost feel her slipping away. He felt for a pulse and found none. A greenish mist got into his eyes, blurring her face. In the distance a sound became audible that he sensed had existed some moments before it registered upon him. It was a car slamming fast down the hill and speeding toward the house. Then footsteps running. Voices. More footsteps. Now shuffiings. These sounds seemed dull, still far away.

Someone stood beside him and looked down. A man. Sam felt a hand on his shoulder. He heard Scotty Hinton say, "I'm afraid she's gone, Sam. I'm terribly sorry."

Sam swore softly, thinking what could have been and yet could not be, and gently released her and took off his hat and placed it over her face. All at once he felt unbearably weary; he slumped and spoke without turning his head. "She tried to stop Vail from escaping, Scotty. She tried to. Vail shot her. Shot her twice. I saw it." He wanted to leave her something. Let it go into the official report. Let it be in the newspapers. "Did you hear what I said, Scotty? *She tried to stop him.* She tried."

"Sure, Sam. I heard you."

"And she drove me to Maggie's, remember? Oh, how she drove." Let that go into the record, too. Let all the people in the Osage know. Let them know about Fay Marcum, Red Mound's prettiest girl. Fay Marcum, who loved life, yet never knew herself. But he was dreaming again, and there was no place for dreams.

An intolerable feeling drove him to his feet, and suddenly remembering young Dee, he hurried to him, and when he found Dee lying on his side and looking up at him in shock, the young faces came before Sam's eyes momentarily. But this one, he thought, this one is going to make it.

CHAPTER 21

BENEATH THE COPPER SHIELD OF THE OSAGE Sun's midmorning rays, Red Mound appeared not yet to have risen for the day. Only a scattering of people stirred on the streets. Here and there a slow-moving car. An eddy of wind playfully gathered up some Main

Street dust and released it, twirling and spinning like a dancer's light-brown skirt, dissolving, vanishing.

Sam Colter, driving slowly, glared back at the town. Bitterness made lines along his mouth. Well, it was over, indeed it was over, no thanks to Red Mound's smug citizens, hiding inside their shell of indifference. God, how he despised the place!

He parked the Chandler touring car and the loaded horse trailer in the center of the street and got out. When he headed for Scotty Hinton's office over the bank, idlers lounging around the Sportsman's Billiards drifted out to the trailer.

Sam turned to look.

In the coming years they would remember Slip Along—a son of Old Baldy, out of the slighted Louisiana speed mare, Wendy, a grandson of the great Peter McCue—the droop-eared gelding born of the wind, now departing as quietly as he had come, yet not unheralded.

But that was the way with legends, Sam thought. They could be among you so briefly, and their purpose soon done, you didn't realize their greatness until they had gone on and you never saw them again. But you remembered, and with each telling the legend would grow:

"I saw Slip Along beat Tomahawk. They say he ran the quarter mile in twenty-two seconds that day. On a brush track, too, at Hank Vail's Forked Lightning Ranch. Did it all on his own. No bridle on. Knew exactly what to do. Knew where the finish line was, you bet. I tell you, that old horse was flyin'! . . . Hank Vail? They say he was the mastermind behind the Osage murders. Tomahawk was his top horse. I tell you . . ."

Hinton was clearing out his office. He stopped at once and waved Sam to a chair. "So you're headed for Texas?"

"I'll be back when Dee is fit to travel. He's lost a lot of blood, but he's doing fine. There's a job waiting for him in Texas. My mother still lives on the old place. We have some young horses coming up. We need a good hand. Dee wants to come. He can start over down there. He's young. What about you?"

"Moving camp to Oklahoma City for a spell. Of course, well all have to testify at Tate Burk's trial. I kind of hate to leave Red Mound." A wry smile cracked his face. "Kind of busts up my insurance business."

"I don't mind leaving. I hold Red Mound responsible to a great extent. I blame the people for letting things go on and on."

Hinton favored him an unruffled look and continued his chatting. "I don't know how many Red Mound residents have come around to express their appreciation. Sam, these people have been concerned for years. They've been afraid, too. They asked the county for help, and they even went to the governor. Officers were sent in, but they couldn't get anywhere."

"I know I'm bitter," Sam admitted. "I can't help it."

"It's far easier for outsiders to take a bold course, such as we did, than it is for local people."

"It went on one helluva long time," Sam said, unforgiving. "Innocent people died, and others were hurt. Too much has happened. I'm not sure I'll ever come back here except to pick up Dee and be at the trial if I'm needed."

Hinton flopped a file on the desk and rested both hands there, looking down at Sam. Hinton's eyes were understanding and wise. Not only those of a tough-minded man, but also those of an older man who had experienced much of life: knowledgeable, compassionate. "My father endured a great many hard jolts in his time. A cotton farmer, he scrabbled all his life supporting a large family. He died scrabbling, but he never lost faith. He said you should never make a major decision right after you've lost somebody or there's been a big upset. He believed you should let the dust settle, so to speak, before you could see clearly. Before you regained your judgment."

"You trying to tell me something, Scotty?" A vague resentment raked Sam.

"Guess I am, in a way. If there's one consistent thing in our lives, Sam, it's change. We all resist it. You came back here hoping the Osage would be pretty much as it was when you were a boy. Well, it changed while you were away. It changed for the worse. Ruthless men took over. They exploited and murdered the Osages, and they buffaloed the white citizens. Well, the Osage has changed again. It's open and free and nobody's afraid. The 'fraid lights will be just a bad memory. You helped make that change possible in a big way, Sam. I'm proud of you and Blue and Web—and Gene."

"Gene gave his life."

"And you almost did yours. What I'm trying to say, Sam, is don't stay down on these people. They're not trained investigators. They didn't know how to go about righting things on their own. We were in the dark ourselves until Maggie broke it open when she called you. We were on the defensive till then."

"You remind me of my father," Sam said, smiling a little for the first time.

Scotty Hinton wasn't finished. "I paid Tate Burk a

visit yesterday in the county jail at Pawhuska. He's singing like a canary. Everything he knows. He's doomed. He knows that."

Sam shrugged. He set his jaw.

"Burk cleared up some puzzles I've wondered about. I learned that Vail dominated Burk—dominated him completely. As the old saying goes, he played Burk like a piano. Burk was also the weak link that brought Vail down. Had Vail survived the gunfight, Burk would be the prosecution's chief witness. At best, in that event, Burk would hope for life. As it is, he'll get the chair."

Sam, silent, wondered what Hinton was leading up to next.

"Burk told me more. Fay knew all about Vail's big still and was active in his lucrative bootlegging operations. She made some of the decisions. They even sold whiskey as far as Wichita, Tulsa, Oklahoma City, and Dallas. Hauled it by the truckload. Tug Lay handled distribution to the oil fields and other county outlets. Fay took part in everything, all right, and kept the books."

"That's not hard to figure," Sam said. "I saw her at Ma's. What bothers me is did she know Lay killed Elsie and Antwine? Did she know Singer blew up the house?"

"I asked Burk that. He answered it this way: Fay was deathly afraid of Vail. He'd threatened to kill her if she ever went to the authorities. So we don't know how much she knew. We'll never know." Hinton moved to the far end of the desk, paused in thought, came back, and fixed Sam a deliberate look. "Burk was in the office one day at Vail's soon after Trigger Riggs was found, when Fay asked Vail who Riggs was. Vail got mad. He lost his temper and threatened her again. Fay stood her ground. She said she wanted to know if Riggs was brought in to get you . . . Vail knocked her down. She got up and left the room. Burk said he never heard her mention Riggs again."

There was silence, a longer silence. Sam could only nod, reminded of the night at Fargo's on the eve of the race. Everything tied in now: the bruise on her face that she had touched so like a child; her urging him to leave; the .38 in her purse; her fear; her contradictions. He sensed again the elusive quality of her. Had he really listened?

"There are exceptions, Sam, and we've known some, like mad-dog killers running amuck. But few people are all bad or all good. There are shades of gray in between."

A burden seemed to lift from Sam's shoulders, akin to the passing of a troubled dream, yet he would not forget that dream. He stood and held out his hand. "Thanks, Scotty."

The idlers still lingered around the trailer, commenting and looking at the old horse, when Sam crossed the street. He smiled inwardly, thinking of The Legend of Slip Along. He nodded to them, opened the door, started the cranky motor, and drove out of town and across the broad flat, traveling slowly, feeling a reluctance, an unfulfillment.

Rattling and bumping up the lookout ridge, he pulled off on the crest and stopped, letting the motor idle, and gazed back at the Osage hills. For long moments he looked. Perhaps it was only his imagination, perhaps only an illusion with roots deep in his past. But he would swear they moved just a little.

Sam Colter waved and drove on.

We hope that you enjoyed reading this
Sagebrush Large Print Western.
If you would like to read more Sagebrush titles,
ask your librarian or contact the Publishers:

United States and Canada

Thomas T. Beeler, *Publisher*
Post Office Box 659
Hampton Falls, New Hampshire 03844-0659
(800) 818-7574

United Kingdom, Eire, and the Republic of South Africa

Isis Publishing Ltd
7 Centremead
Osney Mead
Oxford OX2 0ES England
(01865) 250333

Australia and New Zealand

Bolinda Publishing Pty. Ltd.
17 Mohr Street
Tullamarine, 3043, Victoria, Australia
(016103) 9338 0666